LAMBTON COUNTY LIBRARY, WYOMING, ONTARIO

THE SURVIVORS BOOK FOUR
THE ANCIENTS

BY

NATHAN HYSTAD

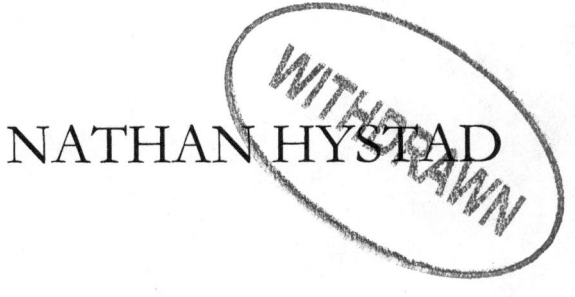

Copyright © 2018 Nathan Hystad

All rights reserved.

No part of this publication may be reproduced, distributed, or transmitted in any form or by any means, including photocopying, recording, or other electronic or mechanical methods, without the prior written permission of the publisher, except in the case of brief quotations embodied in critical reviews and certain other non-commercial uses permitted by copyright law.

This is a work of fiction. All of the characters, names, incidents, organizations, and dialogue in this novel are either products of the author's imagination or are used fictitiously.

Cover art: Tom Edwards Design

Edited by: Scarlett R Algee

Proofed and Formatted by: BZ Hercules

ISBN-13: 978-1724910103

ISBN-10: 1724910108

Also By Nathan Hystad

The Survivors Series

The Event

New Threat

New World

The Ancients

The Theos

Red Creek

ONE

I emerged from the tunnel as a gust of wind buffeted me with enough force to push me down. I slid on the icy sloped surface, shouting a warning to Slate, who was still safe in the confines of the cavern. We'd been expecting frozen mountains, so my suit had small built-in ice picks that I now extruded, swinging my arm to lock into the surface. I lay there flat on my back. The only thing keeping me from descending the angled hill into the unknown was the pick on my suit's sleeve, embedded into the frosty cliffside.

"Need some help, boss?" I heard Slate ask through my earpiece.

Drafts of cold air poured over me as I lifted my head up to see how far I'd gone. At least twenty feet, which was more than I'd thought. "Toss me a rope."

Seconds later, I heard something hit the ice beside me, and I grasped out with my free hand, clutching the strong, thin cord. When I had it wrapped around my arm, it started to tug at me, and I braced myself. Slate pulled me up in smooth strokes, and I slid on my back at an incline to the hole I'd exited. Slate's head poked out of it, his face determined through his EVA mask.

He dragged me into the opening with him, and I sat down, breathing hard.

"If you guys are done playing, we have a job to do," Mary said, finally coming up the tunnel that led from this world's portal. She was recording everything, taking her time behind us, and hadn't seemed to notice my misadventure.

"Sure. We're done goofing around," I said, still trying to catch my breath. I'd been careless to move forward without scouting ahead first.

"What do we know about the outside?" she asked.

Slate took this one. "We know it's as cold as Christmas at the Campbell house, and the wind's pushing fifty miles an hour. We're halfway down a mountainside, with nothing but ice and gloom surrounding us at all angles."

He'd concluded this from sticking his head out for ten seconds while throwing a rope to me.

"This could be the planet we've been waiting for. With all of this ice, we have enough water to feed ten thirsty worlds." I stopped leaning against the wall, my heartrate finally back to normal.

"We'll take samples and talk to the others. I have a good feeling here," Mary said, activating the cleats in her boots. The one-inch metal blades jabbed out, giving her firm footing as she climbed toward the exit. Why hadn't I remembered them?

I peered down, seeing Slate's cleats already out, and I tapped my arm console, feeling them protrude out of my boots before sinking into the icy surface.

"We'll head for the surface. Let's see if we can climb; otherwise, we use the packs." I took my thruster and slung it over my shoulders, wearing it like a backpack. The belt clasped around my waist, I made for the opening to the cold world.

"We'll find a suitable planet for our terms with the Bhlat." This from my wife.

My wife. I couldn't believe we'd been married for almost a year already. "I'm heading out. Clamp on."

Once we were tethered to each other, I took the lead, guiding us up and outside. This time, I was ready for the onslaught of pressure and leaned into it. With a glance behind me, I saw the others do the same, and we moved as a unit in a straight line, snow crossing sideways at us.

I took a second to get my bearings, which wasn't easy in the storm. Everything was white as far as the eye could see. Peaks and valleys littered the landscape, and the small amount of information we had on this world told us conditions would be similar across the small planet.

My suit kept me warm, and my arm console's readout told me the outside temperature was minus forty-five Celsius. Not something you wanted to stay in too long. The ground was hard, ice packed down God knows how deep. The wind kept the snow from sticking to the surface, and the pure ice was so clear, I could see at least a few feet down through it.

My boots dug in with each step, softly sending shards and slivers flying as we pounded our suits down the decline of the mountainside.

"Hold on a minute. I'm going to take a sample." Mary

stopped at the rear of our line and knelt, pulling a core drill from her pack. It was compact, and she had it set up in a few minutes. I took the time to scan the horizon, looking for signs of reprieve from the whiteout conditions. I couldn't see any. For all I knew, this planet had storms like this nonstop.

The sounds of the core driller carried through my helmet, and soon Mary was taking the ice cylinder and adding it to a freezer box in Slate's pack before she stowed her supplies away.

We were about a half mile from the ground. I looked forward to getting the samples there and moving on. We already had our air readouts, and I doubted there was much life on this planet. I wanted to hand over a lifeless rock to the Bhlat, if possible, and it appeared this just might be the right one. It was light outside, the system's star a great distance away. It was enough to provide brightness when the weather conditions were more ideal, but not enough to give the world much warmth.

We made the trip down without any issues, though it took longer than we wanted. A few times, I nearly turned on the thrust pack, but we eventually made it down the short cliffs without needing to. It had a limited fuel source when used in atmosphere. Out in space, the smallest amount of drive kept it going for long distances, as long as you weren't worried about time.

I approached the bottom of the first leg of our trip, and was met with a wall about five feet high. It was pure ice, slick as a cube in one of Magnus' scotches. I couldn't see around it.

"What do you think? Head over it?" I asked, turning to Slate, who shook his head.

"Blast it." The ever-ready soldier slipped his pulse rifle from its spot on his back, and I stepped away, my tether to him pulling tight.

Mary stood beside me. Slate was right in front of us, and he pulled the trigger, red beam cutting into the ice block. He held it there, and soon a hole the size of a small door was open through it.

Mary moved forward and pushed her head into the space. "The surface is just a little way down. There's a small cliff. I say we get through, then use your pack to carry us the rest of the way. We'll have enough juice to fly back up after." She started to wiggle through the four-foot-deep opening, crawling so we could only see the sharp bottoms of her boots.

"Be careful," I said, but I was too late. I caught her swear in my earpiece, and her feet disappeared from view. "Mary!" I yelled, bracing myself for the inevitable tug once the tether took hold, but it didn't. Slate was jerked lightly, then he fell backward, looking down to see the carabiner empty of her rope. The clasp was broken.

"Mary!" I yelled again, sliding my body into the hole and feeling Slate grab my feet. I could see Mary down the steep ice slide, and she wasn't moving. "Mary, come in." No response came.

Without thinking, I started the thrust pack, soft blue light pushing out and down from behind me. I used the controls and lifted up, dragging Slate with me. He hung below, without so much as a cry or complaint, and we rose into the air, over the wall of ice. I descended to the spot where I'd seen Mary's unmoving body.

"There," Slate said, pointing down, and I lowered almost too quickly, the pack threatening to spin us out of control. With a twist of the controls, I recovered, and we landed ten feet from Mary. The ground was even here; I unlatched myself from Slate and ran to her side, tripping on my cleats as I did so.

I didn't care. Only Mary mattered. "Mary," I whispered, seeing her lying there lifelessly. She was facedown, but nothing looked unnaturally bent. I turned her over to see her eyes closed, and I grabbed her arm, checking her vitals on her console's readout. I saw her pulse rate at the same time her eyes fluttered, then opened.

"Dean?" she asked groggily.

My heart nearly broke with relief. "Mary, can you move your fingers?" She did. "Toes?" I saw her boots adjust ever-so-slightly. She nodded. I saw blood freezing around a cut on her forehead, but other than that, she seemed okay.

"I hit my head. We'll keep an eye on it." She pushed herself up into a sitting position and I held her arm, propping her up on the freezing ground. She looked around, and I joined her, getting a new vantage point on the land. We were in a valley that ran for a few miles between opposing mountains. "We still have a job to do."

"You can take a break. You could have killed yourself back there," I said, but she was already taking the core driller out.

Slate trudged back toward us. I'd seen him leave after

he saw Mary was okay. "The wind calms a hundred yards that way." He pointed down the valley. "We can send our probes out there."

Mary grabbed her ice sample, lifting it to look through it into the cloudy sky. She tossed it to Slate, who deftly caught it before stowing it away into his pack.

"Help me up?" Mary asked, extending her arm. Once on her feet, she was a little wobbly, and I kept my hand around her as we followed Slate. The wind pierced us, making each step more difficult than it should have been.

The ground leveled out, and the wind lessened as we went. Slate stopped, lifting his hand up to tell us to do the same. "The wind slows around here. We can take a break and watch the probes." He unslung his pack and pulled out a small bundle. With the tug of a ripcord, a tiny shelter opened up. It wasn't much, but it would keep us covered, and all three of us could fit inside the cramped space.

We'd used one on a previous trip, and the memory of us all sweating inside the tent, hiding from mosquitos the size of bats, wasn't one I'd soon forget. We'd considered taking two shelters this time, but pack real estate was valuable, and with a team of three, we'd had to prioritize.

I dropped my thrust pack, happy to have the strain off my back, and dug out the probes attached to it.

We had three drones, each with a hundred probes inside them. We'd fly them, dropping the sensors as needed. They also recorded the landscape, giving us more information than the Gatekeepers had of this world.

"Link up," I said, and we connected each arm console

to one of the flying devices.

"Done," Mary said, her drone lights turning green.

"Done." Slate's turned yellow.

"Done." Mine emanated a soft purple glow as it powered up, ready to be controlled.

Leaving most of our supplies outside, we made our way into the tent, happy to be out of the snow and wind. I was once again thankful the EVA suit wasn't bulky like the old NASA ones. Things had come a long way, and with our new network expansion, our technology was improving all the time. Clare was back on New Spero, working with a team on what she called "game-changing" projects. I couldn't wait to see what she came up with.

The tent left us enough room to all sit next to each other. A tablet lay on the ground between us, showing the camera views of our three drones. Right now, we only picked up blurry white images as they lay on the ground outside.

"Calibrated. I'm lifting off," Slate said, and we could see the camera feed on the tablet between us.

Soon two more images streamed in as all three drones were in the air and hovering. The wind jostled them around, but they were made for all conditions and fought their way through. We knew which way to go with each of them, as we kept this aspect consistent on each world we'd visited. I honestly couldn't believe how many planets were vacant of any kind of life. But there was water here, and that likely meant organisms.

Mary nodded toward the tablet. We all looked out the corners of our eyes as we continued to control our own drones. Hers lifted high into the sky, and we could see a break in the storm to the east. She dropped some probes and kept moving.

Mine was heading south, and things were getting worse as it went. The clouds became darker, spewing heavy sheets of snow on the already pristine white landscape. I let out a probe every few minutes, constant information feeding from them to our tablet, storing a backup in our suits' computers at the same time.

"It's getting warmer," Mary said, talking about the temperature at her drone's location.

I glanced at Slate's image, and his looked much like mine. His drone headed northwest, while mine veered southwest. We'd circle back at a slightly different trajectory, trying to capture as much area as we could. The probes would pan out, giving us a good idea of the lay of the land.

Clearly Mary had hit the jackpot here, because while our drones threatened to give us no visuals in the storm, hers was showing vibrant skies and an ice-blue ground.

"It's beautiful," our big counterpart said quietly and cleared his throat, as if suddenly self-conscious he'd said anything.

"It is." Mary lowered and shot another probe out. The temperature readout showed minus twenty Celsius, a vast difference from the minus forty-eight Slate's displayed.

We kept powering through the storm, recording everything we could, but it was Mary's images that piqued our interest. Ice hills rose and danced along an otherwise flat area; the mountains Slate and I still played in were long gone in the east. Sunlight glimmered off the icy surface, and I thought how much "younger Dean" would have liked to strap on a pair of skates and go for an adventure down the slippery countryside.

"My drone's getting beat up out here. I think it's time to turn around and head home," I said.

Slate nodded. "Mine too."

We went through the motions and set them on autopilot, back to our location.

"What's that?" I asked, now giving my full attention to the clear picture from Mary's drone. I saw light reflect back at the camera for a moment.

"Just light off the ice, I think," she said.

"Can you take it in closer?" Slate asked.

"I'm not sure what you guys think you…" Her words were cut off as her jaw dropped.

We all saw it at the same time. It was the first sign of another civilization any of us had seen here, and it stuck out like a sore thumb. There was a piece of metal jutting out of the ice. From the drone's data drop, it was just over ten feet tall and twice that long.

"What is it?" Mary asked, but we remained silent. We didn't know.

"Get as close to it as you can," I said, a nervous tremor tickling my throat.

"Wait!" Slate said as she was lowering.

"What is it?" I blurted out, but he was already moving closer to the tablet. "Pull up and head that way." His large gloved finger pointed to the left side of the screen. Mary didn't argue but followed his instructions.

"Oh my God," we said in the same instant.

"It's a symbol." Mary let out a shrill laugh of excitement. She leaned over and hugged me.

I didn't recognize this one, but it was clearly of the same make as the rest of the portal icons. Was it a sign for whoever found it to follow through the portal?

"There's something else," she said, depositing a probe toward the metal symbol. "Just as I thought. It's warm. There might be something under the surface."

"How did you know?" I asked, genuinely curious.

"See here." She zoomed in. "There are small pools of water where the metal breaches out of the ice."

We kept the drone there for some time while I tried to recall the hidden maps from the portals that Kareem had entrusted solely to me. Sarlun had asked about it when I told him of my promise to the dying Deltra. I had seen frustration across Sarlun's face as his proboscis twitched, but he didn't press me.

"It might be one of the locked-away worlds. I just can't recall them all." These two knew of their existence, but we hadn't visited any of those planets yet, and I planned on staying away from them if possible.

"Look around the symbol." Slate ran a finger in a circle over the metal in the image, and I squinted to see what he was seeing. Once I did, I couldn't unsee it. "The ground sinks in a concave ring in a perimeter around the mark. I think there's something under it."

"We won't be able to tell from here. How far is it?" I asked. Mary checked the readout and answered quickly.

"Eleven miles as the crow flies." Her voice held an energy she hadn't expressed since we'd been shown the first sign of the Theos by Sarlun. I knew she felt like we were about to be thrust into a mystery she could solve.

"Then one of us better go back and retrieve the rover." Mary and I both turned to look at Slate.

TWO

*T*he rover moved along at a far better speed than we'd be able to make on foot. We had to take it around the peak and down a valley cutting through the first range, but once clear of that, it would be smooth sailing for the last nine miles.

"What can it be?" I asked, open to any speculation. We'd been in our suits for hours now. I was getting the itch to tear my helmet off and take a deep breath, but the results on this world wouldn't be good.

"Could be nothing, but someone was here and left a message. That warrants a visit to the site," Mary said from beside me. The rover had a single seat in front for the driver, with a bench behind it. Our supplies were loaded in the rear cab.

The tires were large and studded for just such a trip, but the wheels still spun on occasion as Slate took us over a steep hill. Twice we slid back down, and he had to go around. Still, the trip was over before we knew it, and we arrived just as the planet's sun set behind the horizon. I checked the temperature, and it was dropping quickly.

I exited the rover first and spotted the drone we'd

left. It had been easier to leave it for a physical pickup than to fly it back and wait. I'd bent down to grab it and load it in the rover when Slate made an incomprehensible noise. He was running up to the protrusion from the ice.

"Boss, look!" He was already there, and I saw the symbol was much taller than I'd initially thought from the drone's viewpoint. It had to be sticking twenty feet in the air.

I left the drone on the ground and ran to join him. He was skimming a gloved hand on the matte black material. There were symbols etched in the sides, grooves running a quarter of an inch deep. When I'd looked at them from a distance, I could hardly make them out, but this close, there were at least five symbols repeated over and over. Goosebumps rose on my arms, and the hair on my neck reiterated my uneasy feeling.

"The Theos," Mary said, even though we had no proof of anything.

"We don't know that," I whispered.

Slate was capturing images with his arm console so we could study them later. "Whatever left this was making it obvious."

"Yeah, but if you didn't know about the portals, it wouldn't make any sense at all. They were either commonplace when this was left or it's a message to the Gatekeepers," I said.

For the first time since we'd arrived, I remembered why we drove here in the first place. I looked down. The ice-covered ground was crystal-clear, and water slushed against the symbol's edges. I knelt, peering deep into the

The Ancients

transparent surface, and I saw an object below.

"There's something down there!" I yelled loudly, hurting even my own ears. The other two didn't seem to notice. They were right beside me in seconds, and Slate was laughing.

"I'll be, boss. Looks like we have some digging to do." I could hear the excitement in his voice.

"With what?" I asked, hoping he wasn't going to pick out the utility shovel from the tool crib in the rover.

"How about this?" He raised his rifle again. It had worked earlier to cut through the ice, so why not now?

I nodded, stepping back. Mary and I went past the perimeter, and I saw her wobble slightly. "How's the head?"

"It's as good as I can expect," she answered. "I feel a little off, but I wouldn't miss this for the world. I've been hoping for us to cross paths with a hint to their location all year, and here we finally have one."

Slate started to fire his rifle at low power, getting the result he wanted. He first cut a line, then made three more, creating a small box. From there, he made lines about half a foot apart, criss-crossing until there was nothing but small squares within the opening.

"How deep did that cut?" I asked through my mic.

He shrugged and bent down, using two hands to lift one of the ice squares. It pulled free in a three-foot length. "About that deep."

We moved to join him, prying out the squares until we could see a shape below. "I can see it more clearly." Mary aimed her high-powered light down, and I made out a dark solid object.

This time, we each grabbed a rifle and took a section, Slate jumping into his accessed hole and going deeper. After repeating the process three times, Slate called us over to show us his discovery. He'd cut through ten feet of ice and was standing on a metallic surface.

"How wide do you think it is?" I asked, trying to see in the dim night. The rover headlights were now directed at our excavation site, allowing us to see, but creating more glare than was ideal.

"I can't say. Let's keep going." Slate was already moving on, hitting the next section. We continued this way for an hour; soon we'd uncovered an area, starting ten feet to the left of the symbol in the ice, that was thirty feet wide by another twenty.

"This could be a roof," Mary said, kneeling on the black alloy. "If it is, we either try to find a way in, or we dig around it."

Slate slumped down. "If you haven't noticed, we've been out here for hours, and I think my suit may need an empty."

I cringed as I realized mine could too. There was no good way to go to the bathroom on an angry ice world.

Mary wouldn't be discouraged, and as Slate and I leaned against the cut-out ice wall we'd created to make this opening, she crawled around, looking for something...anything.

"Guys." Her voice had a shake in it, and I was worried about her having a head injury.

"Mary, what is it?" I got up quickly, nearly falling over

as my ice cleats slid on the metal surface. I retracted them and rushed to her.

She turned her head, her face split in half with a massive grin. "I found it!"

I ducked down, trying to see, and when she moved her hand, I understood. There was a clean fracture in the otherwise smooth surface. I followed it, and the line went in a small rectangle. "Slate, grab a pry bar!" I called to him, and he was back in a minute with one.

I pointed to the lip, and he jammed the flat face of the bar into it, using his body weight to push on the tool's fulcrum. It lifted, to our surprise. The far side was hinged, and the metal hatch slammed down after Slate pushed it with great effort.

"You first," I said to the big guy, but he didn't even smile. He stared into the blackness of the opening with a frown.

Mary leaned forward, shining her light inside. The space appeared empty, the floor only ten or so feet down. She was about to go in for a better look, and I grabbed her shoulder. "You remember what happened last time you stuck your head into something? It was today, and you could have killed yourself. Let me do it." She waved her hand as if to say, "Be my guest," and I got to my knees. "Slate, would you mind holding on?"

He grabbed my legs as I lay flat on the surface, sliding forward with my hands and sticking my head into the three-foot opening. I felt Slate's firm grip on my ankles and knew I'd be safe with him watching my back.

Mary passed me her flashlight. I stuck my left arm inside, moving the light slowly. There was nothing to see. It was empty. The inside looked just like the outside: black and smooth.

"There's nothing down here. Why the hell would there be an empty alien box on a lifeless planet?" I asked, ready to get back up. I felt a vibration in my stomach, and before I could react, the whole box was shaking like we were in the middle of an earthquake. "Slate, don't let go!" I called, but it was too late.

With a bang, the large alien box shook wildly, knocking Slate over and sending me flying down the hole. I tried to duck and roll as best as I could and saved myself from landing straight on my head. My shoulders took the brunt as I rolled over and slammed into the inside of the box's wall.

The shaking stopped as I lay there, trying to stay still. "Dean!" Mary called from above, and I groaned, letting them know I was fine. Getting to a sitting position, I scanned the room with my flashlight. It was empty, and digging it up had been a complete waste of our time.

"There's nothing here. Can you lower one of our tethers and lift me out?" I got to my feet and moved along the perimeter of the room. The exact same symbols above me appeared to be on the surrounding walls. I made sure my helmet cam was up and running, and continued on, running a glove over the otherwise smooth surface. What did the symbols mean? I couldn't wait to compare them to the portal guide or to the hidden portal worlds. These must be relevant. Could they have anything to do with the Theos Mary seemed so intent on finding?

The Ancients

The tether lowered down, and just as I started to cross the room to grab it, I spotted something from the corner of my eye. The room was wide open, with no interior walls. About fifteen feet from the opening, just right of where I fell in, sat a small object.

"I found something," I whispered, getting a flurry of comments from my friends above. I ignored them and walked right up to it, crouching to see what it was before touching it. A small square stone sat there, about six inches on all sides. The green stone looked familiar, and I thought of the necklace Janine had given me, the one I still wore to this day.

"What is it?" Mary asked through my earpiece.

I rotated it in my hand and saw the symbol from the ice above carved on one side. The other five symbols were on each of the other faces, but smaller than the first one. Otherwise, it seemed like a simple rock. Familiar, but different from the artifact Sarlun had claimed to be a Theos relic. They'd found it a year ago and had been racking their brains trying to determine just what it did.

"I'm coming up," I said, shoving the stone into the small pack still on my suit. I did one last sweep through the room to make sure I hadn't missed anything, and was confident the cube was all it was housing.

As I clipped the tether to my belt, a cracking sound echoed around me. It was like the ice around the buried room was moving, threatening to squash the foreign object. "Get me out!" I shouted, feeling claustrophobic as the noises increased in volume.

My belt was tugged hard, and I gripped the rope, letting Slate do the heavy lifting. Soon I was exiting the cube, the sounds getting louder around us.

"The ice is cracking; we need to move!" Slate called as I undid the belt clip and ran for the rover behind the other two. We hopped in, throwing what supplies we had lingering around into the back first.

The ground shook as Slate gunned it, skidding forward on the smooth surface. He raced away, and I looked back, seeing one of our night lanterns still sitting at the site. It illuminated the side of the symbol. Moments later, a screeching noise carried to us, and the symbol fell down, everything in the area sinking into the ground.

Slate spun the rover around when we were a half mile away, and from there, we could see no sign of the symbol or the hole we'd been digging. The planet had swallowed it whole.

"What was that?" Mary asked.

With a shaking hand, I reached into my pack and pulled out the green cube, which was glowing lightly now. "I think it has something to do with this."

THREE

"Why couldn't we go straight to Shimmal?" Mary asked, still frustrated with me. She paced around our living room like a caged bear, and I didn't want to answer her. I already had three times.

Maggie chased her around, barking at her heels. She wasn't the only one put off by Mary's behavior.

Mary stopped walking, and I could feel her stare boring a hole in the back of my head. "Fine, we'll go first thing in the morning. We have a meeting with the Keepers in two days. I thought it could wait."

"But…"

"Let's just save the fight and agree that this is important. I was tired, and I wanted you to get your head checked out." My real reason sneaked out of my lips, and I heard Mary sigh from behind me. Her hands rested on my shoulders and gave me a light squeeze.

"Why didn't you just say that in the first place?" she asked softly.

"Because you're bullheaded, and you would've just told me you were fine."

"Maybe you're right." She kissed the top of my head,

and I set my right hand on her left, still resting on my shoulder.

"Of course I am," I jested. "Why are you suddenly so excited by all of this?"

"By *this*?" Her voice rose in pitch. "We're talking about finding a long-lost ancient alien race. Maybe gods, according to the theology we've been hearing."

"You don't believe that, do you? The gods part?"

She was tinkering in the kitchen, the smell of lemon tea carrying into the living room. She came into view, setting a steaming cup down on the coffee table in front of me. I mouthed *thank you* to her; she sat in the chair opposite me, her legs folded to the side, hands wrapped around the hot mug. Her hair hung down in her face as she gazed into her tea. When she peeked up at me, I felt like a young man in love for the first time.

"I don't know what to believe. Are you telling me you don't think what we just saw was a clue left for a deserving Keeper to find?"

I grabbed the mug, blowing on the tea lightly before taking a sip. Maggie had migrated onto my lap, and I was careful to not spill any on her as I drank it. "You might be onto something there. A symbol with a buried green stone nearby. What were the chances anyone would find either of them on a remote ice world?"

"Exactly. When you picked up the artifact, the place self-destructed."

"It nearly took me with it, so I'm not sure I like their tactics," I said.

"That's just it. Only the worthy would have escaped

with the artifact intact. We have an object that's the clue to the Theos' location. I know it." She drank some tea, and I found myself being drawn into her excitement.

What if we could find them? Then what? Ask them why they built the portals? Ask them why they ran away, abandoning the universe? For all the talk I'd heard about them over the last year, no one had anything more than hearsay and speculation. We had no idea what they looked like, or where they were last seen.

"We still have that agreement I made with the Bhlat. Do you think the Gatekeepers will agree to let us give them that ice world now that we have this discovery?" I asked, curious as to Mary's opinion.

"I'm not sure. Do you think there could be more artifacts?" she asked.

"I really don't know, but my gut tells me that was it."

"I think it fits with the piece Sarlun has." She finally said it. I'd been waiting to see if she'd thought so too, but didn't want to put it in her head first.

"Same." My pulse quickened at the implications. If we set the cube into the object Sarlun had in his possession, what would it do? It could be a weapon, for all we knew. Maybe the Theos had created these back-door portals into worlds so they could take over and infiltrate them all whenever they wanted. "It's hard to trust anyone after the Event, and then the Bhlat invasion."

"You trust Sarlun and Suma. Now we're part of a group of beings we couldn't even comprehend a few years ago," Mary said, reminding me of our first Gatekeeper meeting. There had been ten worlds represented, each very different from the next. I wished Sarlun had warned me one of them was made of a gas. I'd walked right through it, breaking several protocols.

"Yes, I do, but they've earned our trust, and we earned theirs. The Theos, on the other hand, haven't done anything one way or the other. Actually, if they were behind the old 'hidden green cube in a box' trick, then they did try to kill me, so strike one."

Mary smirked at this and took another drink. Her eyes were closing a little more, a clear-cut sign she was wearing out. I was too, and the warm tea, mixed with the soft snores of a cocker spaniel, were lulling me into a daze.

"We'll learn more tomorrow. Let's go to bed," Mary said.

"I'll be right there."

I started to move, and Maggie sat upright, hopping down and running to the front door. Her left paw touched it ever so slightly, her sign to tell me to let her out.

It was late, the sky dark and ominous. Through the clouds, a few stars shone down, and I wondered if they were still there casting light, or if they were millions of years gone. Maybe that was what we were seeing from the Theos: signs of them long after they'd vanished, like a dead star shining in the distance.

Maggie did her business and walked inside, light-footed, straight for the bedroom. Soon all three of us were in bed, my mind still racing with unanswered questions.

The Ancients

———————

"Where's everyone else?" I asked Sarlun as we were led to his office on Shimmal.

The slender alien twitched his snout and locked gazes with me, his eyes dark and wide. "It's only us today."

"Shouldn't the others hear what we have to say?" Mary asked.

Sarlun tweeted a response, and when it didn't translate, he tapped the device on his desk. "Did that work?" he squawked, his English words coming through now. "They couldn't make it on such short notice."

I wanted to call him out on that, but if he needed a private audience with us, it was likely for a good reason.

"You have something to report about the ice world?" he asked, leaning forward, showing his interest level was high.

"Yes," Mary started, "we found a symbol among the ice." I passed him a datastick, one he'd provided me for bringing him planet details for his portal world project.

He plugged it in, and images reflected on the side wall of the room, an art piece disappearing from the screen to be replaced by shots from our aerial drones. We'd left out Slate's and mine, which showed nothing but ice, snow, and wind.

We'd edited Mary's to skip forward, and when he saw the foreign metal stuck in the ground, he leaned toward the screen. We had a shot of the drone flying over it, getting the symbol in full view.

"Amazing," his quick tweet translated. "I do not recognize this one. Is it from…" He left the question unanswered. He knew I had access to the hidden side of the portal guide, the one Kareem and others had worked hard to cover forever. Sarlun had never asked me for the details, and I knew it was eating him up inside.

I shook my head. "Never seen it before."

"I think it's their world. It has to be," Mary said.

"The Theos, you mean? Not necessarily, but perhaps," was all Sarlun said.

The screen began to show the images Slate had taken up close of the black metallic symbol. All along it, every few feet, were the curves and slashes identifying five other portal worlds. I recognized three from the Gatekeeper portals but hadn't been given a chance to check the ones the Theos Collective had blocked. If they'd worked so hard to close a section of planets off, they must have done so for a reason. Not being able to access the Bhlat homeworld would have been a good thing, under normal circumstances.

Sarlun's nose lifted up and down in excitement, and he started to swipe through a tablet. "The icon on the left" – he paused the screen, pointing to the four rectangles sitting in front of a small circle – "is none other than Atrron. I've been there before…once. I remember how impressive a place it was. Of course, it would be linked to the Theos." His language fluttered out in a series of tweets, the translator doing its job well.

We discussed the other two worlds Sarlun knew of. Having never visited them himself, he couldn't say more than was on file from the other Gatekeepers.

We got to the footage from the rover, and Sarlun stood up as the hole we'd dug caved in on itself. "What did you find down there?" he asked.

"What makes you think we found anything?" Mary asked, a twinkle in her eye.

"Because the only reason for them to have the symbol get swallowed up by the ice would be if someone had passed their first test." Sarlun started to sit back down but moved to the screen, staring at the paused image.

"Why have a test in the first place? What do they want?" I asked.

"The Theos were the most intelligent race ever to exist, but they also had an insatiable appetite for puzzles and challenges."

"Centuries after anyone's seen them, and now we find a clue to follow. To what end?" Mary fidgeted with her hands. Her wedding ring spun around her finger as she contemplated the problem.

"If I were to speculate, I'd say they want to be found," Sarlun said.

"Why?"

"That, I can't tell you."

I dug into my bag and wrapped my hand around the cube. "Maybe this will teach us something."

His black eyes widened. His narrow mouth opened and closed a few times before he said anything. "That's the missing piece."

"I'm not sure, but it seems likely," I said.

"Come with me. I don't want prying eyes." Sarlun

opened his door, and we followed him out of his white pristine office into a similarly-designed hallway. Every so often, we walked past a Shimmalian, and we smiled and made pleasantries with a couple. They seemed to have a hard shell, but once they got to know us, they softened and treated us like equals.

"Where are you taking us?" Mary asked as the lights became dimmer, and the walls seemed to lose their sheen.

Sarlun didn't reply. He just motioned for us to keep following, and soon we were at a gray steel door. There was a keypad with strange cyphers on it, and he quickly tapped a pattern, the door sliding open.

"What you're about to see doesn't leave this room. Agreed?" His choice of words caught me off-guard, but I played along. The translator still impressed the hell out of me.

"Agreed." I said it first, followed by Mary. She waggled her eyebrows up and down at me when Sarlun wasn't looking.

Sarlun shut the entrance as we passed through, and a bright white light came on in the center of the ceiling. "Welcome to my collection."

It took a second for my eyes to adjust, but when they did, I saw rows upon rows of shelving, each filled with strange-looking items. I whistled a long note, unsure of just what it was we were seeing, but impressed nonetheless.

Mary stepped forward, but Sarlun stayed put, watching us as we investigated the room. It was a large space, probably close to two thousand square feet, with fifteen-foot ceilings. There were at least three yards between each shelf, which were each around twelve feet long and eight high. I followed Mary to the first row and spotted dozens of stone objects. Some looked like crude tools, bowls, hammers, cups; much like a section you'd see at a museum of natural history.

"Where are these from?" I asked, reaching for a long spoon-like tool. A blue force shield activated, stopping my fingers from going forward. It left a slight tingle in my hand.

"Those were from my very first world. I was a young Shimmali man of thirty cycles," Sarlun said. I had no idea what age that put him at, compared to an Earth year. "Tranlok Four. The planet had gone through an extinction event. We weren't sure what happened to them, but the most advanced creatures were using these tools when I arrived. They were in that stage for what we think were centuries, never adapting or evolving. Quite the unique story." Sarlun gazed at the shelves wistfully for a moment.

I smiled at how similar the rudimentary utensils were to those of our own Neanderthals.

"What about these?" Mary asked from a row over. I crossed over to see what she was looking at. She pointed to an intricate helmet, asymmetrical but beautiful.

"That is from the Loorg world. They rule over all the creatures there, taking pity on none. Their leader Lord Plo's troops fought battle after battle with each region, and with every defeat, he took a portion of the defending general's bones. This helmet is made from pieces of all forty-seven of them." Sarlun seemed pleased with himself.

"How did you get it?" I asked.

"One of us witnessed the revolt against Plo. He was beheaded on the battlefield, and amidst the chaos, we took it." The Shimmalians were proving more interesting to me by the minute.

"When will we be ready to visit an occupied planet?" Mary asked Sarlun. So far, he'd only sent us to worlds with no intelligent life.

"When the rest of the Keepers say you're ready," he said, and Mary shot me a glance, rolling her eyes.

"And you? Do you think we are?" I asked.

He appraised me for a while. No part of him moved. "I do."

Relief flooded me, with a side of anxiety. Until we went to alien worlds teeming with life, cultures, and politics, we were essentially just going for hikes on distant planets. I didn't mind that. We could go home afterward and feel good about what we'd done, without wondering if we'd negatively affected or altered another race.

I'd already been to at least a dozen planets, each a far cry from the last. What would the next one bring?

Sarlun walked past me, moving with purpose to the far end of the room. Here the shelving full of ancient artifacts ended. He tapped a control panel on the last shelf row, and a blue light flickered, then shut off. He touched his fingertip to a black box and it separated in half, exposing an object the same color as the one in my pack. I'd only seen images of it, but now I could tell it belonged with the cube.

It was slightly wider than the one I had and looked like a platform for it. Four teeth erupted from its edges, making a smooth table for the cube to sit on. I smacked my lips, everything suddenly turning dry. I looked around for water but didn't see any.

Mary was beside me now, both of us staring closely at the artifact exposed to us. Sarlun smiled his thin-lipped grin, reaching his hand out to me. With only the smallest hesitation, I grabbed the cube from my pack, setting it in his thick palm.

As he touched both pieces, the gemstones began to illuminate with green light. I felt the stone against my chest start to heat up, like it had on the night of the Event. I pulled it out and let it sit against my shirt, the green stone burning brightly.

Mary looked around, like we were about to be lifted into the sky. Some fears never dissipated. I saw her check to see if she had Bob's ring on the chain she kept around her neck. She hadn't worn it in a few years now.

"We're fine," I assured her.

"Interesting," Sarlun squawked.

"You're telling me. The same stones used in the Kraskis' elaborate plan were one and the same as these you seem to think are from clues left by the Theos. What if all of this was a backup plan by our old friends? Maybe the Kraski aren't actually gone. Has anyone checked their homeworld?" Sweat beaded on my forehead as I wondered just what the real story was.

Sarlun didn't answer, and I took his silence as confirmation. He appeared to be puzzling it out for himself.

"We haven't. I didn't see the need. Especially with your world now gone."

"Earth's gone, but New Spero is thriving." I closed my eyes, imagining angry black vessels lowering onto our new world. I wouldn't let that happen.

"Regardless, the Bhlat took their world. That's why they were running away," Mary said.

"Do we really know that? Or were we trusting the words of a traitorous hybrid?" I spoke the words more venomously than I intended.

"We'll look into it. For now, let's see what we have here." Sarlun turned and set the original artifact down on a table. They were still glowing, though the moment he let go of one, they dimmed. He glanced at me, then placed the newly acquired cube on the stand.

FOUR

*N*othing happened.

"Not quite what I had in mind." The expression on Mary's face said she was clearly disappointed.

"A cube has six sides," I said, lifting it up. I moved it so the largest symbol faced upwards, toward the heavens, and put it back down.

The room illuminated with green light, so much that I feared we'd blown ourselves up. We were now in another place, where we could only see green for all eternity.

"Dean!" Sarlun screeched, his translator saying my name. I let go, and the light level lowered; once again, I could see the shapes of Sarlun and Mary in front of me.

The brightness continued to decrease, and the two artifacts rattled on the tabletop. No one spoke for a minute, all of our attention fully focused on the table.

A shadow in the shape of the symbol emerged from the top of the cube. It matched the one from the ice world and the top of the cube. It hovered there, four feet across, and we moved away from it, unsure what it was made of.

"Sarlun, have you ever seen anything like it?" Mary

asked the Shimmali Gatekeeper.

He tweeted an airy noise, but the translator didn't pick up what he'd said. It was either too quiet or not an actual word.

When he was about to reply, the shadow began to move again, this time growing into the shape of a man. It floated there, its feet linked to the cube by wispy blackness. The shadow didn't solidify; it stretched out even further until we saw thin legs, a long torso, and arms that went well below the knees. A head turned back and forth, as if assessing us.

Goosebumps rose on my arms. It was like something out of a horror movie, and it had poured out of a cube I'd been carrying around for two days. It had been in my house.

"Hello," I said to it, unable to hide the tremor in my voice. Its head, a smoky black visage, rotated and paused. I wished it had eyes, so I could tell if it was looking at me.

Sarlun hit a button on his translator and said a string of words in his language. He must have turned it off, because no words came out in English. "What are you doing?" I asked, wondering just how much we knew about Sarlun and the Shimmali people.

Sarlun didn't reply but went to one knee before the shadow. He kept repeating a phrase that sounded like a beautiful bird's song.

The shadow had been still but responded after Sarlun stopped tweeting his song.

Sarlun turned his translator back on just in time for the shadow to speak. It did so in pure Shimmal, and the device turned it into English for us. "Who goes there?"

"It can speak?" Mary whispered the question. The shadow was still moving slightly, its head turning a little.

The movements were familiar. I noticed a pattern repeating. "It's on a loop," I said. "It's not really here, is it?"

Sarlun shook his head. "No. It is ancient."

"Who goes there?" the voice asked again.

Sarlun stood up straight, back proud and voice strong. "Sarlun Shim, Head Gatekeeper of the Theos Portals."

He motioned for us to speak. Mary nodded to me to go first, and I cleared my throat. "Dean Parker, CPA and Gatekeeper, hailing originally from Earth and most recently New Spero." I hoped my accounting title impressed the long-dead shadow creature.

"Mary Lafon – Mary Parker," Mary corrected herself. I'd told her there was no pressure to change her name, but she'd admitted she wanted to. "Captain in the US Air Force and Gatekeeper, from Earth and now New Spero as well."

I winked at her, glad she'd used her old title too.

We didn't have to wait long for it to speak. "Which of you summoned me here?"

"Technically, we all did. Sarlun had one piece and we brought the cube." Mary's words translated through into Shimmal chirps and tweets.

"Which of you summoned me here?" it asked again.

"Dean Parker did," Sarlun said, and the hair on the back of my neck rose.

"Very well," it said, and we stood motionless, waiting for more.

"That was anticlimactic," I said, turning to Mary. Then the shadow moved quickly, rushing toward me. Before I had a chance to duck or run, it entered my soul.

I stood on a cliff, thousands of feet above a deep blue ocean. Even from this height, I could hear massive waves roar and crash against the rocky outcropping below. A yellow star hung in the sky, too close to be our old sun, too pale to be in Proxima.

I tried to recall how I'd arrived but couldn't. Was I alone? I turned slowly, seeing no one else. The water surrounded me. The chunk of land I stood on was hardly a hundred feet long, and I crossed it, seeing an extremely high cliff face once again. Shouldn't I be afraid?

Under normal circumstances, I'd be terrified at being at this altitude with nothing but an angry body of water threatening to crush me at all fronts, but that was the rational part of my brain. It was now telling me that I didn't need to fear anything. Was I dead, then?

I pinched my forearm and felt a sharp pain. I looked down and saw I was wearing a white Gatekeeper outfit, tailored to my human body. When had I changed into this?

"Dean Parker," a voice said from behind me. When I spun around, no one was there.

"Dean Parker. You've earned the right to search." The English was solid, but spoken the way a computer program might inflect words.

This time, I turned and saw the shadowed figure. It was walking of its own volition, not linked to the cube. It all flooded back to me: the ice world; placing the artifacts together to have a strange mist emerge from them.

"I don't understand. Search for whom?" I asked, certain I knew the answer but wanting to hear it from the creature.

"The Theos."

"Why did you disappear?"

It took a second, and I thought its head was facing away from me, staring into the endless moving sea. It was a very human-like image. "This is for you to find out."

"And at the end of the clues, will I find you?"

Another pause. I was still under the impression that this was an intelligent recording I was conversing with. "Yes."

"Why the games? Why not just tell me where you are?" I asked.

"Only the worthy may seek us. Only the True may find us."

I cleared my throat, watching the misty man wisp in front of me. "How many True have found you before?"

"Through the ages, few have sought us. Never have we met the True."

His phrasing set alarms off in my mind. I thought back to Kareem's words about me being different. *Change the universe.* His dying words stuck to me like glue now.

I waited for it to speak again, but it was obviously programmed to wait for a verbal prompt before it responded.

"How do I find you?" I asked.

"You must follow the path."

"What path?"

"You have the tools now. Use the map."

"The map?" I wondered what that meant. Maybe it was referring to the symbols on the artifact. "What order do we follow?"

"The order is set. All pieces will fit."

The answers were obscure, yet clear. I understood and pressed my luck. "Is there a wise place to begin?"

"You would benefit from beginning at the bottom."

"What's there?" I asked, guessing I'd get some obscure doublespeak back.

"The Forest of Knowledge."

"What can you tell me about it?" I replied.

"The Forest of Knowledge."

I probed it a few more times, hoping to get a different answer, but it kept saying the same response. It felt like my spell with it was coming to an end. "Am I the True?" I asked, nervous sweat beading down my back even in this weird world.

"That will be revealed in time."

I started to ask it another question, but it cut me off. "The Theos await you. Only then will we stop the Unwinding."

"What's the Unwinding?" The shadow form started to dissipate, changing from a wispy cloud in a thin humanoid shape to the symbol for the Theos. It was a vertical line, with three horizontal lines cutting across it. With a gush, it rushed toward me, entering me, and when I looked up, I was back in the room with Mary and Sarlun.

"Dean. Dean!" Mary was shaking my arm, a look of panic in her beautiful eyes.

"I'm fine," I coughed. "But I really need some water."

Sarlun rushed to the doorway and opened a cabinet in the wall, bringing three bottles of crystal-blue liquid with him. I didn't wait for him to come back; I met him halfway, grabbing a bottle and guzzling back the contents. What I actually tasted was smooth and slightly sweet on my tongue.

When I was done with the entire bottle, I set it down on the table beside the artifacts, which were no longer glowing. They were as still as a stone.

"What the hell just happened?" Mary asked, her no-nonsense tone thick.

"What did it look like?" I asked, genuinely curious if my body had left, or just my mind.

"You were standing there like a possessed zombie. The thing just shot into you, and you wouldn't respond." Mary's words rushed out of her like a waterfall. Water...why was I so thirsty all of a sudden? Maybe it had something to do with a thousand-year-old ghost of a god invading my personal bubble.

"How long was I gone?"

Sarlun took a sip of his drink, his proboscis protruding into the opening and sucking the cool beverage back. "Not long, but long enough to worry Mary." He looked me in the eyes. "To worry *us*."

I was really beginning to like this guy.

"Dean, get with it. What happened?" This from Mary.

"I was somewhere else. At first, I didn't remember where I was even supposed to be. I was on an island the size of this room, only thousands of feet above sea level, a soft yellow star shining down on me. I wasn't worried or confused, just present. It arrived shortly after."

"It?" Sarlun asked.

"The figure from the cube. It didn't take another form, just the lanky shadow. I don't think it was ever really here. I believe it was a recording, an imprint from a long-dead race."

Sarlun chirped at that. "The Ancients survive. They are hiding. They're not dead."

"You say tomato, and I say dead. Semantics." He didn't understand the reference; before he could inquire, I kept going. "Anyway, here's what I know: I've been given permission to search for the Theos."

Mary clapped her hands together, smiling widely. "Yes!"

"This is good news," Sarlun said, his thin lips parting for a smile of his own.

"The Gatekeepers will be happy?" I asked.

His smile vanished in an instant. "They must not know."

This caught me off-guard. "Why? Aren't we a team? A union? Or a guild, or whatever?"

"There are things I wouldn't even trust to each of them. Something like details of the Theos would be worth more than you could imagine. Worth more than your lives...more than whole worlds. If word got out that we had these" – he motioned to the two green stone pieces – "we might already be dead."

"I didn't know how serious all of this was. You sure you're still excited about the search?" I asked Mary, who now wore a frown instead of a grin.

"You think some of the Keepers would hurt one of their own?" she asked Sarlun.

"I don't know, but lips are loose at times, especially in the confines of a home, or among friends and loved ones. I can't risk it," Sarlun answered.

"What else did it say, Dean?" Mary asked.

"To follow the path and to use the map."

"What map?" she asked.

I grabbed the stone cube, feeling its weight in my palm. I'd sealed my fate once again in something bigger than myself. My gut felt the same twist as it had when I was racing down to Peru a few years ago.

I traced my fingertip across the largest shape, the same one the shadow had transformed into only minutes ago in my mental journey. "We've already established each of these is a world; some of the symbols match the icons on the portal tables. I'll research the others, but I have a clue."

They were both leaning toward me, eager to hear what it was.

I flipped the cube upside down and pointed at the underside. "We start at the bottom."

FIVE

"You guys are really going through with it?" Magnus puffed on a cigar while his son Dean ran in their back yard, kicking a ball around. A little boy and girl played with him; they were all shouting and laughing in the sunny afternoon. It was refreshing to hear sounds of children playing all the way out here in New Spero. Life had a way of prevailing against the odds.

"Hell yeah, we are," Slate said, sipping on a pint of beer. The aroma of grilling beef carried through the air and into my nose, causing my stomach to grumble in hunger. Magnus and Natalia were hosting a baby shower; all the women were on the back deck, cooing and trying to appease the ready-to-burst Russian woman. Mary had volunteered to have it at our place, but they didn't care about the old custom this time. Nat didn't seem happy with all the attention.

"Mag, I can't believe you're about to have another baby. You guys ready for it?" I asked, glancing to the deck, where I spotted Mary. She was wearing a floral green maxi dress; the wind caught it, sending ripples through the length of cloth, her hair cascading along with it. I wanted to go take her hand and lead her away from the party, to spend some time alone before we ventured to Atrron.

She saw me watching from the BBQ and firepit area, and waved a low and secret flick of her hand toward me. I think she had the same idea as I did.

"No, but I wasn't ready to save the world from an evil race of aliens, so I think I can handle little Mary," he said.

I spit out the beer I'd just drunk, spraying it in a comical fashion. "Mary? You can't be serious. Naming your kids Dean and Mary? It's not just weird, it's demented! They're brother and sister." The words rattled off in rapid fire, and Magnus and Slate started laughing hysterically.

"You're too easy." Magnus was still chuckling, and Slate clapped him on the back. "We don't even know if it's a boy or girl yet." He flipped some burgers, placing a few on a plate when he was satisfied they were ready. "Back to your secret mission. These Theos: do you really think you'll find them?"

My finger rushed to my lips, telling him to be quiet about it. "I told you what Sarlun said. Don't even say their name until it's all over."

"Who's going to do anything about it? Billy, the Terran One podiatrist?" Magnus pointed to a man throwing a Frisbee with a friend. "Or maybe Tricia, the local hairdresser?" He nodded to the deck, where the ladies were still handing out gifts.

It seemed so normal, but in my gut, seeing a tradition from Earth like a baby shower felt out of place on New Spero. "Regardless of who you deem dangerous, gossip can be our worst enemy. Just keep it on the down-low. You should have seen Sarlun's face when he said entire planets would be collateral if they got in the way of something as small as the artifacts he's hiding. The last thing I want is for Suma and her planet to be in danger."

Magnus nodded. "Sorry for being a jerk. Maybe I'm just a little jealous this pup's going, and not me." He gave Slate a light punch on the arm. As if on cue, the three dogs ran over, the younger ones in front of Carey, who was slowing down in his advancing age. It felt like yesterday that I'd scooped him up to take him on the journey of a lifetime, and now here he was, an old man.

I knelt down and scratched his head, then stroked his fuzzy back a few times. He rolled over and asked for a stomach rub; I, of course, obliged.

"You sure you don't mind keeping Maggie for a few days? Hopefully less," I said, not sure how long the trip would take, or if I'd be back to New Spero before we hit the second location on the cube map.

"We're happy to. She's probably missed being around these other chuckleheads anyway. Dinner is served." With that, Magnus and Slate carried plates stacked high with meat. Everything from a tofu dog, to spicy chicken, to good old homemade burgers. I was drooling as much as Carey was, and we followed along – Carey probably hoped something would fall from a dish, and I wasn't far off.

We ended up by the deck, where three picnic tables were butted up against each other. Pitchers of sangria and buckets with ice and beer sat in the middle of the tables,

The Ancients

where Magnus and Slate set their dishes down. I made a few trips inside to grab the food in the fridge: potato and Caesar salads. And what barbecue would be complete without Jell-O loaded with fruit inside?

The ladies were finishing up and came to join us as we sat down.

"Come on, kids! Time to eat!" Magnus called across the yard, reciprocated with cheers from the little ones. Little Dean ran up, his knees covered in grass stains. "Go wash up. Your mom will kill me if she sees you eating with those grubby hands." I heard him whisper this to his son, and the boy saluted him, running for the house.

"A salute? That's a good kid," Slate said.

"He sees people at the base do it to me and wants to be like them. They wear uniforms, and to a four-year-old, what's cooler than that?" Magnus poured Nat a glass of water, tossing in some ice cubes from one of the buckets.

"Thanks, husband," Natalia said, giving him a weary smile.

"Nat, you look beautiful," I said as Mary sat down beside me.

"I don't feel so pretty, and I'm always exhausted," she said.

"Nat, I wish I looked as good as you, and I'm not pregnant," Mary said, complimenting her friend as she threw her arms around her.

"But you should be. Why don't you leave all this planet-hopping around to someone else and have a baby? We could spend the afternoons together while the little ones had a nap." Nat smiled at Mary, who poured a glass of sangria and tapped a fingernail on the wooden table.

"We'll consider that. Maybe when this adventure is done, we'll seriously talk about it." Now Mary was looking directly at me, her sunglasses reflecting my image back, so I was unable to tell if she was being serious or just appeasing Natalia.

Magnus smiled at Mary's comment, nudging me with his elbow. I shrugged. "She's the boss."

Slate was across from us, and a young woman came and stood beside him. She gave the big man a shy smile and waved lightly at Mary and Natalia. "Thanks again for inviting me. It's been so nice to do something like this."

"*Da*, have a seat, Denise." Nat pointed at the bench to the right of Slate.

"You don't mind?" she asked Slate, and he glanced up at her, taking a longer look than was necessary.

"No, ma'am. Please do," he said, getting a small laugh from Magnus.

"Shhhh," I whispered at Magnus. I recalled Slate telling me his fear of dying before he met someone and had a family; how his short life had been filled with revenge and regret. I loved the guy like a little brother and only wanted happiness for him.

Slate and Denise didn't seem to notice anyone else as they started to make small talk.

"Who's got the ketchup?" Mary asked, and we carried on, having a wonderful evening with friends. The whole time, the shadow of a Theos was lingering on my mind. *The Theos await you. Only then will we stop the Unwinding.*

The Ancients

"You have everything you need?" Magnus asked us for the third time. He was wearing aviator sunglasses indoors, and I knew he'd partaken in a few too many libations the night before. Most of us had, though Mary and I'd cut out early, leaving Slate and Denise enthusiastically talking by the solar lights on the deck.

"If we take anymore, we're going to need a mule," Mary said, folding another rope into her pack.

"Sarlun doesn't know the Forest of Knowledge, but he's heard of a religious sect living in a heavily wooded area, about an hour by scooter. We're trying there first," I said. The planet held many life forms, but we knew little about them. Sarlun's information was sparse at best, but we had enough to get us started. He'd supplied the translator plug-in for that region's dialect.

We were at the base at Terran Five, and Magnus had sent our hover scooters over to the portal caves already. I wished I'd been given a chance to stop in and see James and my sister Isabelle, but I promised myself I'd do it as soon as we were back.

Magnus led us to the landing pad. A transport vessel lowered to the ground, a blonde woman rushing out, followed by another familiar face. Nick was growing a beard, and it was filling out nicely. I ran a hand over my own chin, wondering if I could pull it off.

"I'm glad I found you," Clare said, her voice dripping with excitement.

The red sun was rising in the morning sky; it would be a hot day on New Spero. It was the kind of day where you'd rather sit on your porch and play with your dog than head out into the unknown.

"Good to see you two. Sorry you couldn't make it last night," Mary said to them.

"She wouldn't let us leave until she was done. I could have used a night of fun," Nick said with a wink.

"Next time," I assured him.

"What do you have for us?" Slate asked, intrigued. He loved gadgets, and with all the alien technology we kept receiving, Clare was creating some amazing devices to help us out.

She reached into a bag and pulled out a silver object. "The cloaking suits have value, but they're bulky and not a hundred percent reliable. Set this on the ground, and… It's better if I just show you."

Clare pressed a button on it and set the small rectangular device down by her feet. A beam of light shot up, and when it vanished, she was gone. We could see the lander behind her and Nick to her left.

We were all silent as we watched, the only noise from a nearby bird chirping. We'd brought an assortment of animals along with us to New Spero, a futuristic Noah's Ark before Earth was destroyed for good.

"How'd you do that?" Mary asked, going around the beam to see if Clare was there. I followed, but she wasn't visible, no matter what angle we looked from.

"Pretty cool, hey?" Clare's voice asked.

I stuck my hand through and felt it hit something solid. "Whoa, watch where you're grabbing!" With that, the illusion disappeared, and Clare was standing before us again.

"That could come in handy," Mary said, picking up the device.

"I used some Shimmali interfaces and the idea behind our ship's cloaking. It just reflects the image from behind your vantage point. Of course, as Dean just proved, you still hold your mass and can be touched," Clare said, before showing Mary how to work it.

She spent the next few minutes revealing a few other inventions, each one getting tucked into our bags.

We hugged them goodbye and loaded the transport. I wished I wasn't wearing a hoodie, as the heat made me sweat while we worked.

Slate got in first, taking the back bench. Mary took the pilot's seat, and I plunked down beside her. The trip to the caves was a quick one and didn't leave me a lot of time to worry as we lifted off, heading for the range a couple of miles away. The air conditioning helped ease my temperature as we moved toward the portal.

I looked at Terran Five out of the viewscreen. The city was twice the size it had been, with our new influx of people from Earth. New Spero wasn't the same place it had been when we'd arrived a year and a half ago, but it was thriving.

The cities now had an energy to them, a positive flow that was easy to get caught up in. Some of the people here weren't just getting a second chance; they were getting a third, and not many took that for granted. There were times we walked downtown Terran One and I forgot we were in a colony. The first step to healing was being comfortable, and we'd taken huge strides to do just that as a people.

Almost as soon as we took off, we landed, the terrain not yet covered in snow for the season. We had cameras set up, and motion lights to keep the lizard creatures away from the portals. The guards at Terran Five hadn't seen any sign of them here for a long time.

We moved efficiently, carrying our supplies into the cave entrance. For good measure, Slate sounded an air horn, just in case one of the animals had slipped past the video feeds.

We took the familiar route and ended at the portal room, from where we'd traveled many times. The hover scooters were sitting where Magnus had said they'd be, and we attached our bags to them.

The EVA suits were safely stowed in a package adjacent to the scooters. Sarlun had told us the air mixture and, though it was breathable, a lot could have changed in the thirty years since any of the Gatekeepers had set foot on Atrron.

"Can you help me with this?" Slate asked, and Mary clicked the latch on his helmet. He returned the favor, and we were as ready as we'd ever be.

The hieroglyphs on the walls were activated, and I stared at them, emblazing each of their unique patterns in my mind. Each one was special. Mary was already at the center table, scrolling through the screen of icons. "Found it," she said.

The Ancients

I took a deep breath, still looking at the cave wall. What were we about to find, and what was the point of this wild goose chase for a long-gone race of beings? I briefly considered calling it off. Slate stood beside me, aware I was feeling trepidation.

"We have to," he said, his soft words echoing in my earpiece.

"Come on, Dean. It's time," Mary said.

"Let's go find us some gods," I said, and Mary tapped the icon.

SIX

"Sarlun really needs to give better directions," Mary said, trying to recalculate her GPS while riding. We slowed down, the wind pressure decreasing in turn.

The landscape was the most unique terrain I'd ever seen. Long purple grass covered rolling hills; tall yellow trees stretched out into the heavens. I'd never witnessed such majestic plants, and I'd walked redwood parks in California. Gravity was less on Attron than on Earth or New Spero. Our readouts put it close to that of Mars.

"Over there," Slate said, pointing as we flew toward the thick treeline.

If I thought the yellow trees we were seeing were large, I now spotted ones twice as high jutting through the canopy, at least a dozen of them. Their immense branches were covered in orange leaves that gave the illusion of a sun hanging in the sky above. It was amazing.

"I think we found the Forest of Knowledge," I said, still open-mouthed.

Soon we were heading into the treeline, the dark purple grass becoming lighter and sparser as we went. "I can't see them anymore," I said, referring to the tall orange-leaved trees that were now hidden beneath the outer forest canopy.

"There," Mary said, pointing to an opening in the branches above us. I saw the tip of the tree-sun and knew we were on the right path.

I tried to not speculate on what we'd find when we got there. Instead, I took a deep breath of my EVA suit's oxygen and began to enjoy racing across the distant world. Sarlun had zoomed out a 3D map of the universe, showing us just how far we were from our system. Even with our current ship drives, it would take centuries to make it here.

Every time we set foot on one of these portal worlds, we were the first humans to do so. I wondered if this was how Neil Armstrong had felt, treading on the bland dust of the moon.

A large bird-like creature perched high in an upcoming yellow tree, its wings smaller than one would expect. I assumed they didn't need as much wingspan on this low-gravity planet. While the landscape was colorful and vibrant, the bird was dark gray, making it stick out like a sore thumb as it sat there watching us.

Now that I'd seen one bird, I picked out dozens of them in the trees as we hovered by. Their thin necks turned to follow us as we passed.

"Life," Mary said, saying nothing else about them.

Life was a good sign.

Sarlun had told us there were city-like developments on Atrron, but they were far away and still preindustrial in advancement. There were days I longed for the simplicity of that kind of life, but then I remembered the average lifespan, and how a simple thing like a toothache could end in death. Given the options, I'd take our current predicament.

A few other creatures ran along beside us, quickly falling behind our hover scooters. I didn't get a good look at them; they were just blurs of darkness.

Mary was in the lead, and she slowed after ten minutes.

"It looks like a dwelling," Slate said.

The building was squat and made from logs, sealed at the seams with a creamy mud. Smoke poured from a crude chimney, letting us know it was occupied.

Following Mary's lead, I got off the scooter and grabbed my pulse rifle. I really didn't want to need it, but we had no idea what we'd be up against. Slate went first, his eyes hard and dark behind his mask. He motioned us forward with a hand signal and we spread out, Mary to the right and me to the left as Slate headed for the front of the small structure.

As we neared it, I saw it wasn't as small as I'd thought. The few hundred-foot-tall trees around it skewed the perspective.

We had the translators on, and I prayed the language Sarlun had programmed in would work properly.

"Greetings," Slate said firmly. I cringed at his unfriendly tone. The language it translated to sounded like a mix of a snoring bear and a braying donkey.

Mary and I flanked the building, ready to back Slate up if needed. A rustling noise passed through the log

The Ancients

walls, like someone was dragging a sack of potatoes across a gravel driveway.

A string of low docile words were spoken from inside the building. "Who there goes?" my earpiece played.

Slate stepped back as a figure emerged from the tall hut. I couldn't see the front of the building, but Slate looked up, his eyes wide.

I moved forward, and my gaze lifted to see what he was taken aback by. The Atrron being in front of him was at least ten feet tall, its arms long and thin, its legs no thicker than the arms. It was dark gray. Heavy patches of hair grew out of its feet and hands, along with its pelvic area, which told me he was male; otherwise, he was hairless. His head was tall and thin too, small purple eyes looking back to me, his oval mouth partially open.

He repeated the phrase. "Who there goes?"

"Uhm..." Slate stuttered.

"Dean Parker of New Spero," I said, the words translating to the local guttural language. The giant alien appraised me as if he was looking at a newborn. His thin hand moved toward my head, three pencil-shaped fingers mere inches from my mask.

One of the gray appendages brushed my helmet before he turned to see Mary coming up behind him. "Who there goes?" he asked again, this time to Mary.

"Mary Parker of New Spero," she said calmly.

He reached for her face. This time, his hand sat on her helmet as he stared her in the eyes. She didn't break his gaze: an intergalactic staring match. He eventually lifted his arm and moved back to Slate. "Who there goes?"

"Zeke Campbell of New Spero." This time, Slate found his voice and stood up straight, still not coming up to the creature's chest.

Seemingly satisfied with hearing our names, he stepped past Slate, away from his hut. Each movement was slow, calculated, like a cautious deer in a meadow with known predators. It made me uneasy.

"I guess we follow him," I said, staying a few yards behind the Atrron local. Bones pushed against taut skin as the gray creature moved. Every step I took felt strange, the low gravity giving me a slight hop as I lifted each foot off.

The tree trunks got thicker as we moved along, and I spotted a few other huts along the way. Each time we neared one, he called out; a war cry or a greeting, I couldn't tell. Our translators didn't pick it up. The first time another alien appeared from inside a hut, I nearly grabbed my rifle.

A half hour later, we were still walking. Twenty or so of the tall hosts were in front of us, each methodically placing one hairy gray foot at a time.

"Think they could move any quicker?" Slate asked quietly, muting his translator.

"In a rush to get somewhere?" Mary asked him. "This is fascinating. Do you see all the birds, or whatever they are?" She pointed to the upper branches of the soaring trees. I did see more of the muted-colored animals than before, their watchful eyes following everything that was transpiring on the forest floor below them.

"There are hundreds of them up there," I said, watch-

The Ancients

ing the giant in front of me peek above him before continuing.

The trees around us changed, then progressed into a bare space a hundred feet across.

"Look," Mary said. Slate and I tilted our heads to see that we were in the center of the immense orange-topped trees we'd seen from far away. The branches didn't start until at least fifty feet up and kept going for what seemed like a mile. Just looking up at the swaying goliaths nearly had me spinning with vertigo.

The ground here was almost all free of the debris you'd expect in the wilderness. The grass was thick and purple, and the urge to walk on it barefoot, like the Atrron were doing, passed over me. I could almost feel the blades of grass on my skin. As a kid, I would race around our property without socks and shoes all the time, getting scolded by my mother because, God forbid, I might step on a broken piece of glass.

The aliens moved to the middle of the forest opening and stood side by side in a semi-circle, facing us.

"I guess they want to talk," Mary said, leading us over to them. I noticed how different they each looked. They were of varying heights, and though all had hair on their feet and other areas, a few of them were shaped a little differently. I wondered if those were the females, or if the first one we'd encountered was instead. It was possible they didn't have sexes as we knew them. I'd leave that to the experts. For now, I wanted to see what they knew about the Theos and our mission.

The one we'd met with first spoke before any of the

others. He'd become the de facto leader as the original one to make contact with us. It was a good system. "Why you here are?" the translation came.

Mary and Slate waited for me to answer. They'd decided that since the Theos had singled me out, it might be necessary for me to do the talking. Maybe the shadow had left an imprint on me somehow.

"We are on a mission to seek out the Theos. We were sent here by them," I said. Before the translation finished, I noted how many of them shifted side to side in either anger or excitement.

"Gods you seek?" he asked.

"Yes. They told us to come here first. That you would have the next clue."

His head tilted to the side, reminding me of Carey for a moment. "Then time it is."

I waited for more, but all I heard were half-murmurs from the rest of the Atrron people.

"Time for what?" Mary asked them.

"Here stayed we have. Thousands upon thousands, cycles of star. Wait, they told us. Wait for those who seek." His eyes shone with emotion as he spoke. "We wait. No come one. Creator no come one back. We wait for seekers. When come no one, we more wait."

My heart went out to them. They looked so sad and tired, not much more than skin and bones, waiting in huts by the edge of the Forest of Knowledge for someone to show up. "They asked you to stay here and wait for the seekers?"

"Yes. So wait we."

The Ancients

I cut my translator and spoke to Mary and Slate through my mic. "These Theos have quite the nerve. Telling the Atrron that they're their creators and then convincing them to stay here for God knows how long. Centuries? Thousands of years?"

"Dean, maybe the Theos did create them," Mary said. I was beginning to worry that her fascination with them was getting a little too deep.

"You don't really believe that, do you?" I asked, trying to not sound accusing. It didn't work.

"What's that supposed to mean? Have you seen what they were capable of? A shadow from thousands of years ago taking your mind to a different plane, to tell you about the quest to find them? What about the Kraski? Didn't they create hybrids? Who's to say that wasn't playing God as well?"

I took a deep breath. "You're right. I'm sorry for jumping to conclusions." I flipped my translator back on.

"We want to end this for you. If we move on, will you be free?" I asked, and they all stood up straighter, energized by the word *free*.

"Free we be will."

"How many have come to seek before us?" I asked.

He tilted his head again, then looked down the line of people to either side of him. "Just you."

This floored me. My pulse raced, and I felt the sweat and anxiety I'd been pushing back rise to the surface again. We were the only ones to ever find the clue? The fact that I might be the True thrilled and worried me equally. The days Mary and I had spent on New Spero, just living our lives and being part of a community, were perfect, but the idea we could find the Theos and understand the universe in a metaphysical sense was just too great of a prize. We needed to find them. *I* needed to find them.

"What do you have for us?"

"In star find you the answer," he said.

"In star? What does that mean?" Slate asked. "If we have to go into space here, we're not prepared. There are two stars in the system, but we have no way to go into a star. Blow it up, maybe?" His words translated, and he got a lot of confused looks from the creatures before us.

"Slate, your mind always goes to blowing things up first, doesn't it?" Mary asked, getting a nod from the big soldier.

"It can be fun to blow things up. Admit it, you like the odd explosion," he said, getting a laugh from her.

"What star were they speaking of?" she asked the giant, getting no response. "A lot of good they are. Okay, a star. Is there a tree in the shape of a star, or a symbol on the ground, maybe carved somewhere?" She started to walk around the perimeter of the forest bed, running a hand along a large tree trunk that was at least forty feet wide.

She looked up, and my gaze followed hers as she lingered on the orange ball of leaves where the treetops connected far above. "A star. Dean, doesn't that look like a sun to you?" Mary asked.

"I thought just that when we first spotted it from a distance," I said.

The Ancients

Mary smiled at us. "I think we found our star."

SEVEN

*T*he creatures all looked up, and their energy changed, like they finally understood the ancient riddle they'd been left with. They had their "aha" moment.

"In star find you the answer," they all repeated at the same time.

"That gave me chills," Mary said.

"Great work, Mary. Now how do we get to the top?" I asked, but Slate was already backing up.

"I'll bring our gear," he said, running the way we'd come.

The Attron watched him go with interest.

"Don't worry, he will return. We're going to solve this little puzzle, and you can get on with your lives," I said. "Do you ever visit the cities?"

"Cities?" Our first guide repeated the word as if he didn't understand it.

"Large towns where your kind live and love," Mary said.

"Understand not we do."

"Mary, I don't think they've been in contact with their own people. The Theos must have seen to it." That they

The Ancients

could force a group of living intelligent beings to stand guard for something so trivial as a game of hide and seek angered me.

"We'll show you when this is all over." This seemed to calm them, and soon the sound of a hover scooter approaching echoed to us.

Slate showed up, parking his scooter outside the opening in the copse. He carried two of the thrust packs. "Should be easy to get up there in this gravity," he said.

"Who goes and who stays?" I asked them.

"Why don't you and Slate go for this one? He'll watch your back, and I'll see what I can learn from them." Mary motioned to the group of twenty Atrron observing us with interest.

Slate handed me a pack that was lighter than normal, and I slung it onto my back, fastening it with the clamps on my suit.

"Be careful," Mary said, and I wished I could give her a kiss before venturing into the sky. I leaned forward, letting my helmet touch hers. It was as intimate a moment as I could share with her.

"I love you. See you soon," I said quietly, and when I looked back, the Atrron were closer, extremely curious about our interaction. "It's okay, she's my wife."

They repeated the translated word as if it meant nothing to them.

Slate didn't wait around; instead, he powered up and activated his thrusters. I did the same as he lifted off the ground, heading slowly upward to the sky-high orange leaves far above us.

My feet left the ground, and I felt the adrenaline of solving the first stop on the map to the Theos. I cranked my thruster, catching up to Slate, and we soared at the same speed, ten feet separating us from each other. Below us, Mary and the Atrron became specks in the distance as we carried on.

The treetops grew closer and closer, and I immersed myself in the thrill of being able to fly around like a superhero for a few seconds. It was cut short when I heard an odd noise coming from all angles around us.

"Slate, buddy, what the hell is that?" I asked as a cacophony of sound surrounded us, vibrating through my earpiece.

"Don't get startled," he said, his voice tense.

"Why?"

"Remember those birds?" he asked.

"Of course."

"They're here, and they brought friends."

I could see them now, thousands of them in thick swarms heading toward us from every direction.

"This can't be good."

"Keep going. Remember the trick I pulled when we first arrived at New Spero?" he asked.

I did. He'd stolen a ship and erratically flown away, getting the base distracted, allowing our escape. "It's too dangerous," I called to him, but it was too late. He changed trajectories, heading sideways rather than upwards.

"I'll be quick," I said and cranked my thrust controls, shooting like a bat out of hell toward the treetops. Orange rushed at me, and now I spotted individual branches. When I looked toward Slate, he was a speck being chased by a thick cloud of bird-creatures. A few were still making their way toward me, so I ducked and weaved past thick undergrowth. I didn't know where to go, so I worked my way into the center of the trees, the apex of the fake sun of leaves.

I slowed, hovering in mid-air, the maddening noise of the horde of flying attackers still carrying over the distance. "What's happening up there?" Mary asked, her voice crystal-clear in my earpiece.

"Just a few thousand birds chasing Slate around. Slate, what's your status?" I asked.

"This is insane! Did you find anything?" His voice was a yell.

"Not yet," I said before seeing a platform of intertwining twigs above me. "Wait, I found something."

I hovered to it and lowered myself onto the woven wood. It took my body weight without so much as a creak.

In the middle of the ten-by-ten platform was an orange crystal box. I bent to pick it up, and a familiar smoke poured out of it. The Theos symbol rose in the air, the same pattern from the gemstone cube. As soon as I wondered if it would take the shadow man shape, it did.

"Greetings, seeker. Are you the True?" it asked. The black mist figure's head turned toward me, then away.

This was a crucial moment. I knew what I had to do. "I am the True. Please allow me passage to the next phase. I will follow the path until I find the ones I seek:

the Theos." My heart pounded harder every few beats.

It floated there, not saying a thing.

"Dean, any chance I can get the hell back to the ground yet?" Slate asked, his voice strained.

Before I could answer him, the shadow spoke again. "Welcome, True. You have completed your first task. In the box is the path. Thank the Atrron for their service. They will be rewarded as promised."

The shape changed, forming the symbol once again before dissipating into the box from whence it came. The orange box was solid, with no lid, but as the mist receded, it began to glow, a line along the top quarter of it. When it went back to its normal state, it clearly had a top that could be opened.

I was about to open it, when I heard Slate call for me. I threw the box into the pocket of the thrust pack and jumped off the platform, turning the power on as I dropped at a slower speed than I'd expected. There he was, falling a few hundred yards away. "Slate!"

"Dean, go get him!" Mary yelled from her spot on the ground.

"The damned things caught up to me, and a few of them flew into my pack. They must have hit the thrusters, because it won't work." His words came fast, and I raced toward his falling form.

The small-winged gray animals were all around me now. I tried to fly between them and hit a few with my helmet. I soared headfirst to get to Slate before he ran into something.

"Stick your arms out!" I called to him as I approached. I took the time to look past him and saw he was about to hit a treetop. "Now!" I yelled, and he did so.

I flew by him, spinning around and jamming the thrust up. He slammed into me, face to face, grabbing my body as we started to move backwards. "Hold on," I said, and he didn't argue as I adjusted our trajectory again, narrowly missing the tree. We were still moving downward, now only forty yards from the forest floor. The birds all stopped, as if there was a forcefield keeping them there.

I was able to get us under control and slowed our speed as the ground rushed to meet us. Slate was hanging on to me, his arms wrapped around my waist, and his long legs hit the grass first. A split second later, it was my turn, and I rolled as I impacted. I spun over myself and ended up on my stomach.

"Slate!" I rolled over and saw the big man on his back.

"Holy crap, boss, you did it!" he said, his chest rising and falling as he laughed hysterically.

"Where are you?" Mary's voice came through.

"Just east of where you are. We're okay," I said and started to laugh with Slate. It was infectious. By the time Mary arrived, with a few lanky towering Atrron behind her, we were in tears, hiding our terror with hilarity. We'd made it down alive, and I had what we'd come looking for in my pocket.

"Did you get it?" Mary asked. After seeing we weren't hurt, she was straight to business.

I reached inside my suit and pulled out the orange stone box. It was around eight inches square and fit into my hand as I showed her and Slate. The Atrron beings caught up to Mary and made a strange noise at seeing the box.

"Done is it. Plant to knowledge obtain," the one we'd first met said.

"What does that mean?" I asked them, getting to my feet.

No one replied. They just turned and walked away, as if expecting us to follow them.

"Plant it?" I opened the box as Mary and Slate stood around me, all of us leaning in curiously.

Inside was a large metal seed.

"Is it encased in an alloy?" Slate asked, tapping it with his suit's gloved hand.

"I'm not sure. What good do you think planting a steel seed will do?" I asked.

"Let's go find out." Mary took one last look at it and began to walk in the direction the Atrron had gone. Their heads were still visible as they slowly made their way. It was only a couple minutes later when we arrived back at the opening between the gargantuan trees I'd just flown to the top of half an hour ago.

The Atrron gathered in their semi-circle formation, and our guide pointed to the ground. It used to be packed firm, but now there was a six-inch-wide hole that went down three feet.

I shrugged, taking one last look at the seed in my hand. It had hard edges, lines cut into a rounded metallic object. I wasn't sure if this would work. It wasn't organic.

I dropped the seed into the pre-dug hole, and when

nothing happened, I looked to the Atrron, who were stepping backward.

"Anyone have some water?" I joked before the ground at my feet began to rumble.

"Dean," Mary said.

"Are the birds back?" I asked, looking to the sky.

"Dean, get down!" Mary yelled as she tackled me away from the hole.

Silver sprouts shot out of the ground with an insane velocity. Mary and I clawed desperately away from the shiny growing plant.

When we were far enough, I could see what shape it was taking: a tree. A looming metal tree, right in the epicenter of the dozen other ancient trees around it. It kept growing until we could no longer see the top, well past the orange leaves I'd just flown to.

"That was… unexpected," Slate said, standing behind us.

The Atrron were on their knees, braying in their harsh language. The translator only picked out a few words, as they were either in elation or anguish. I couldn't tell. I heard the words "god," "bounty," "heavens" mixed among the otherwise indistinguishable phrases.

"It's not done yet." Mary stood up and walked to the trunk, which was at least fifty feet across. "There's a door."

My heart raced as Slate and I joined her at the entrance to the tree. The outline glowed, and I stuck a hand out, expecting to hit a solid surface. Instead, my glove entered the tree.

Without hesitation, Mary stepped forward before I could tell her that it might be dangerous. Slate set his arm in front of me and followed Mary. Moments later, his head popped out through the solid-looking door. "It's clear."

The Atrron were watching us with vested interest, but they didn't move from their kneeling positions. I entered.

EIGHT

Soft lights lined the walls and floor leading to the center of the tree's interior, to a circle of blue gemstones. Mary was enthusiastically staring down at it, seeking answers. I approached behind her, hearing only my own shallow nervous breath in my helmet.

Slate was walking the perimeter of the room, which looked larger inside than outside. Its walls were rounded in the shape of the massive metal tree trunk. "Nothing to see over here," he relayed.

"It has to have something to do with this," Mary said, staring at the stones. She knelt, getting a closer look, and that was when I saw the dim symbols on either side of them.

"Mary, look between the stones, not at them. The light they give off makes it hard to see the ground." I could make out five symbols, the same five from the cube I'd found.

"You're right. The symbols. Here's Atrron," she said, touching the ground. As she did, they all illuminated, and Atrron faded away, leaving no sign the etching was ever on the floor. The floor hissed, and a shadow oozed out.

Mary jumped back from her crouched position and fell back. I reached a hand out to her, not taking my eyes off the Theos shadow.

"You have completed your task."

"Damn right we did," Slate said, without getting a reply.

"Why is this called the Forest of Knowledge? The Atrron don't seem to have advanced technology." I wasn't sure if the ancient Theos ghost would have an answer for me.

"Knowledge is more than technology."

His reply hit me hard. He was right. Did technology teach us how to love? How to exist, to breathe, to smell the flowers?

"What knowledge do the Atrron have?" Mary asked.

"The Atrron don't die."

"What do you mean, they don't die?" Slate walked up beside us, his hand on his left hip.

"The Atrron are the original forms we put here to guard the Forest." The shadow shape moved slightly, turning its head in its illusion to seem responsive.

I'd assumed they'd been trained generation by generation to stay in their huts and wait, but if what the Theos said were true, those Atrron had potentially been waiting for thousands of years. Given the circumstances, I thought they'd held up quite well. "How does one obtain infinite life?"

"You are gifted it." His answer came out matter-of-factly, like it was common knowledge.

I shuddered. The idea of a race of beings giving us infinite life scared the hell out of me. No wonder Sarlun had been so careful to not let anyone know where we were going. It had made sense before, but now it did so on a larger scale.

I wanted to keep asking it questions, but the shadow had its own agenda. "You have completed your task."

"What of the Atrron? What happens to them now?" Mary asked, clearly worried about the eternal race.

A screen appeared on the far wall, showing us Atrron from outer space. I knew the planet from our files, and the distinct yellow continent in the eastern hemisphere. It zoomed in, showing us elaborate cities spread out in beautiful concentric circles, the outer high-rises resembling the twelve trees around us now. In the center stood a larger one, a foretelling of what was to come. It was strikingly eerie.

"They come for their brethren now. They will be reunited as heroes and bask in the glory of the ultimate sacrifice."

Ships hovered low to the ground, caravans of them moving toward the real trees in the distance.

Satisfied the Atrron were going to be okay after duty had stolen so many years, Mary asked the question we'd all been thinking. "What's next?"

A noise whirred from above, and a box lowered of its own volition from somewhere inside the tree. I'd assumed there was a ceiling above us, but now I thought the room might just keep going upward. The gemstone box hit the ground outside the circle, where the Theos still wavered in the dim light.

"I got this, boss," Slate said, lifting the lid. Invisible hinges allowed it to lever back. Inside were three helmets.

"What do we do with these?" I asked it.

"Swim," it said, and before I could answer, the shadow changed forms into the Theos symbol, then disintegrated back into the floor.

"Swim? I'm not much of a swimmer," Slate said, holding one of the helmets in his grip.

"Do we go back to the portal, then, and try the next place on the map?" I suddenly felt very tired. Maybe I could convince them to head back to New Spero for a day or two before continuing on.

We each grabbed a helmet, which were surprisingly light, and Mary spoke as I started to make for the exit. "I want to keep going."

"Boss," Slate said, nudging me. The blue gemstones making up the circle were beginning to glow brighter. A powerful light shot up from the ground all the way to the treetop, beyond our sightlines.

Mary, with her helmet in her right hand, stepped forward. I tried to grab at her, narrowly missing her pack's strap. She entered the light, and in a flash, she rose up. I blinked, and she was gone.

"Mary!" I called after her, but it was too late. "Guess this only leaves one choice." My feet were already moving.

"Boss, we have no idea where it leads!" But I was already gone into the light.

I became weightless, flying much faster than I had with the thrust pack. I looked up and swore I spotted the

The Ancients

soles of Mary's EVA boots before I slammed through a circle of blue light.

When I passed the light, everything changed. I began to fall. I was spinning, the ground coming to me in a rush, and just as I was about to land, I hit the surface like a cannonball and began to sink. It wasn't hard ground at all. It was water.

The helmet ripped from my firm grip as I submerged. I gasped for breath before realizing I was in my EVA, my suit secure and waterproof. It was too heavy, though. I fought to swim to the surface, but my tiring arms and kicking feet just couldn't get enough momentum to bring me up.

I was sinking.

"Dean, come in." It was Mary's voice, coming through my earpiece.

"Babe, are you all right?" I asked.

"I'm fine. I made it to the beach. Where are you?" I heard mild panic in her voice but could tell she was trying to stay calm.

"Beach? I just fell into deep water and haven't seen anything. I can hardly make out up from down."

"I see you on my tracking."

"What a rush," a new voice said in my earpiece. I was dropping fast.

"Slate, I see you. Follow my voice!" she yelled loudly, hoping he could hear her.

"I'm dropping," I said. "The suit's too heavy."

"Take the boots off," Slate said, his voice gruff, and I realized that was what he was likely doing. I listened to him, knowing they were the heaviest part of the suit. They sank as I pulled them free, and I felt a moment of worry as I watched them descend into the dark water. I'd need them later, but if I was dead, it wouldn't matter.

"They're off!" I called and pushed my tired arms to pull me upwards, finally able to fight the current and rise to the surface. I took a deep breath as I breached, even though I always had oxygen in my suit. It was a reflex. I spotted the Theos helmet nearby and made my way to it, grabbing it and clipping it to my suit.

Mary was directing me at this point, and soon I felt the sea floor below my feet. Long green foliage wafted around me, and the memory of the creature wrapping and dragging me underwater rushed into my head. I hurried and found Mary and Slate on a black sand beach. I stumbled over to them, Mary meeting me halfway. She helped me forward and I slumped down, every inch of my body exhausted.

"That was fun. Can we do it again?" I joked, lying back and closing my eyes. "Mary, maybe next time, you can cool your jets before leaping blindly into a Theos rocket beam." I opened my eyes slowly, taking note of everything around me. If I wasn't in a space suit, shot there by a long-dead race, I'd think I was back on Earth, sitting on a beach in Hawaii.

The sky was clear blue, perhaps a lighter shade than we were used to back home. Home. I reminded myself Earth wasn't our home any longer. Small wispy clouds danced in the sky, a deep ochre star burning bright in the distance.

"The air is breathable," Mary said, and I heard the familiar hiss of an EVA helmet being disconnected.

I sat up, seeing Slate following her lead. Mary pulled the elastic off her ponytail and shook her head, long hair blowing in the breeze.

"Since neither of you have keeled over from a silent and undetectable airborne virus, I think I'll join you. I'm getting a little claustrophobic in this thing." I unclasped my own helmet and lifted it off, setting it beside the one left by the Theos. Theirs was smaller, thinner, like a second skin. It was almost translucent. The air smelled a little off, like someone had tried to create the ambiance and scent of an ocean but subtly missed the mark.

"Let's camp here for the night and figure out what we need to do," Mary said, taking charge. I was happy to let her. She looked nowhere near as exhausted as I felt.

"Our supplies…" Slate started but cut himself off. "Looks like we're down a couple thrust packs and hover scooters. Let's evaluate."

We each emptied out our pockets and the packs we'd had on our persons in Atrron. I was kicking myself for not going back to retrieve anything else before stepping into the light. As if she was reading my mind, Mary apologized.

"I'm sorry. I needed to see what it was. They haven't done anything to harm us yet," she said.

"I'd say attempting to bury a box on an ice world with me in it, and then tossing us into an ocean, might constitute as attempted harm." I undid my suit, getting out of it, enjoying the sun and breeze on my sweaty jumpsuit.

"You were fine each time." Mary was quick to side with them. I wasn't going to call her on it. She was a little too intense about this adventure, eager to take each step without thinking.

"Here's what we have," Slate said, his inventory done. "Seven power bars, three pulse rifles, two gallons of water, ten iodine tablets, the Relocator, Clare's new hiding device, and a partridge in a pear tree. Oh, and our knives."

"What about our tent?" Mary asked, and Slate unclasped the outer part of his pack.

"You know, just because I'm the biggest doesn't mean you have to make me the pack mule." He gave me a sideways grin.

"It's not because you're the biggest. It's because you're the youngest. Now stop complaining and put that tent up," I ordered, laughing at him as he shook his head and stood.

Mary and I took a walk inland, looking for something akin to wood to burn.

"You seem upset with me," Mary said after a silent minute of walking.

"I'm just worried about you. This quest seems like a fool's errand. Like manipulation from a dead alien race. What's the point? Do we really want eternal life? Do we need more than a bed, a pup, and an acreage to be happy?" I asked the questions, stressed that she wouldn't say yes. That what we had back home wasn't enough for her any longer.

"No, Dean. But there's a chance we can help stop this

The Ancients

Unwinding you were told about. We helped those Atrron sentries back there. Maybe we have to help others before we're done."

My blood began to boil, thinking of the ego the Theos must have had to arrange this elaborate game. "And if we hadn't come, they'd still be waiting. Waiting for someone else for another thousand years, because the Theos were so arrogant as to force a race to wait at their beck and call." I took a moment to let myself cool down. "For all we know, the Unwinding is a load of misinformation, meant to manipulate us into playing along."

"You don't really believe that, do you, Dean?"

I thought about it, but she was right. "I don't. But I'm just saying, you seem to trust them implicitly, when we've never met them. We don't even know if they'll be there when we finish this quest."

Mary took my hand and leaned in, kissing me fiercely. Her breath smelled stale, recycled, but I kissed her back, craving her touch. "I'll be more careful," she promised.

A while later, we arrived back at camp with arms full of twigs and undergrowth from the area. Not as much as we'd hoped for, but given the circumstances, we weren't about to complain. We'd have a fire, at least.

"About time," Slate said. The tent was up, our meager possessions hidden away inside. He sat facing the water, the black sand only scant yards away from our camp, which was perched on a slightly elevated piece of land just off the beach. It looked like we'd be safe from the tide, as there was no evidence the water made it this high.

"No sign of any animals," I said, setting the load of

brush down.

The sun was lowering in the sky, a distant orb reflecting off the large body of water.

"I really thought we'd go home between these…" Slate searched for the right word. "Challenges."

"So did I. Or at least, I thought we'd have the option of going home." I made a teepee of kindling and broke a few longer pieces of fallen branches. The trees were familiar, but different and alien at the same time. Thin green bark covered them; the leaves were green, but in star-like shapes. Just before the sun went down, the fire was burning, too-fresh kindling crackling and popping as flames licked it.

"What did you want at home? You always seem to be happier when you're off on an adventure with us," Mary said, passing us each a power bar. Slate's stomach growled at the sight of it, and I wished we had our other packs, with real food stuffed in them.

Slate shifted his gaze uncomfortably. "Denise."

"The woman from the barbecue? That's great, buddy." The words sounded condescending even to me, but I didn't mean them to be. I was happy he'd met someone. "I thought you two were hitting it off."

"She's great. We talked all night. I haven't made a connection like that…let's just say, in a long time."

The fire flickered, shadows dancing on his stoic face in the minimal dusk light. "What's her story?" Mary asked. "A story to take our minds off the task might be helpful."

Slate looked uncertain whether he should share her

intimate details, but after looking at us, he shrugged and started to talk. "She grew up in western Canada. The prairies. She was still in high school when the ships came." He took a small sip of water before looking back into the flames. "She was on vessel thirty."

"Weren't they one of the luckier ones?" I asked.

He nodded. "As a whole, but she lost her grandparents and her dad on the vessel. Denise was one of the few who was actually put under stasis, so she never had a chance to say goodbye. She came to on the trip home, like countless others."

"That must have been horrific." Mary was leaning forward from her sitting position on the ground, arms folded across her knees.

"She cried for weeks. She moved to New Spero the moment she was offered the option. Her mom's still alive and lives with her. I guess she's quite the woman."

"What does Denise do?" I interjected. It felt so mundane to ask what someone *did* any longer, as if their profession really determined who they were or what they'd survived. It was still second nature to be curious about their jobs, or it was just a courtesy thing, like asking how the weather was.

"She's a cop. She became a cop after the Event on Earth. Runs a precinct on Terran One. Not sure they call it that any longer, but you know what I mean," Slate said.

"I wouldn't have guessed. She seemed so…" Mary cut herself off.

"What? Cute? Likeable? Sound like anyone else you know who can kick ass and take names when needed?"

Slate asked, and we could see the red rise in her cheeks even by the firelight.

"Okay, busted. And thank you." Mary poked at the coals with a thin stick. "So you like her?"

"What? Is this first grade?" Slate asked before conceding after a short pause, "Yeah, I like her."

Mary and I laughed, and he tossed a small rock at me, narrowly missing my leg.

We stayed up for another couple hours, trying to relax after a stressful day, and discussed our plan for the next morning. The only thing we knew for sure: things rarely worked out like you intended.

NINE

My wrist device buzzed: an alarm letting me know it was time to get up. I nudged Mary beside me, and she groaned.

"I'm awake," she said. "Slate, time to go." After a moment, she jolted up. "Slate's not here!"

A second of panic coursed through me, but the logical part of my brain took over. "He probably just beat us to the punch. Or he's writing his name in the black sand."

The tent opened, and that imposter of a beach smell wafted in. I stretched my back and legs after getting out, scanning the distance for signs of Slate.

"He's not here," I said, the worry creeping back.

"Maybe he's scouting the land?" Mary asked from inside the tent. Moments later, she came out, wearing her jumpsuit, her brown hair pulled back in a tight ponytail.

I shook my head. "Something feels wrong." I moved down the beach, wishing I had my boots with me as rocks dug into my socked feet. I slipped the Relocator into my pocket, not wanting to leave it in an unguarded tent. I tapped it, saving the camp's location into the transportation device.

I saw Slate's boot marks in the black sand, heavy imprints leading down to the water. He'd gone for a stroll. I followed along, Mary in tow, as I jogged along the ground just above the sandy area. Abruptly, the prints ended.

"It stops here," I said, looking for any more signs of him.

"What's this?" It was a red blotch, no more than the size of a dime, on the rocks.

"Blood." The word came out as a whisper.

"Slate!" Mary began to call his name right away, and I joined her. "I'll get the guns," she said, already running back to our small campsite.

I waited for her, feeling useless as I stood there, trying to decipher where he could be.

Tall thin grass sprouted from the crimson dirt a few yards to my left, and I walked over to it, seeing sections of it crushed in a line heading toward the treeline. Once Mary was back, I waved her over, showing her my discovery.

"It looks like someone came and took him. Damn it. Why didn't we keep watch?" I was mad at our slip-up. Even Slate hadn't seemed concerned with the possibility of hostile locals.

"There's nothing we can do about that. Now we just find our friend before it's too late." Mary thrust a pulse rifle toward me, and I grabbed it, stalking after her alongside the footsteps in the grass.

I felt vulnerable out here with no armor or shoes, and hated leaving our gear unguarded and out in the open by the beach. We didn't have a choice, though, and I pumped my legs quickly and efficiently as we ran to find Slate.

The landscape changed into open fields as we passed by a half mile of thickets, my feet increasingly sore as we kept moving.

"Smoke," Mary said, pointing at a thin plume in the distance, rising toward the light blue sky.

"Where there's smoke," I said, letting the rest remain unsaid.

I guessed the fire to be a couple of miles away and dreaded the trek across the fields, but as we went, I found the grass gave my feet a little respite from the rocky beach and hard forest bed. A mile in, we arrived at another stretch of woodlands, and Mary slowed, resting behind one of the larger trees. The ground rose and fell in soft hills between us and the smoke source.

"I see a sentry at six o'clock." I turned, sneaking a peek, and saw a form pacing back and forth in a medium-sized circle. After I spotted one, I noticed at least five more from my vantage point. "They've got us covered."

Mary slipped the scope off her rifle and leaned against my torso, looking past my head toward the guards. "They're beautiful," she said, voice full of awe.

"Any sign of Slate?"

She tapped the side of the scope and moved slightly. "There's a village a little ways in. They had to have brought him there. What's the move? Our options are limited, and I expect no matter which way we try to get into town, they'll have sentries."

We discussed it, but the resulting plan didn't sit well

with either of us. "He'd do anything to save us. Maybe they aren't even hostile." After seeing Slate's blood by the beach, I doubted my own words, but had to sound convincing so Mary would let me play my part in the scheme. I was more than willing to play the goat in the proposal if it meant she'd be safe.

"If anything goes wrong, get back to the camp and finish the mission. There's a portal on this world somewhere too. I just don't know where it is," I said, taking her hands. This was one of the planets not among the regularly accessible portal selections. It had been tucked away by the Theos Collective years ago, blocked off either because it was too dangerous or because something particularly nasty lived here. I hoped we didn't see either of those reasons come to light.

"Nothing's going to go wrong. I'll be right back." She was off, heading back toward camp.

As soon as she was out of sight, I slung my rifle on my back and began walking toward the village, doing my best to seem friendly. I tried to look like a tourist who didn't realize he was walking down a dark and deadly alley.

It only took two minutes of this to get the attention of one of the locals. They approached and stopped at a distance, but close enough to get a good look. This one was female. Her legs were long, covered with tight leggings that looked made from animal skin. She had black markings lining her neck, and a baggy shirt with crude weapons strapped to a belt below it.

Her thin eyes turned down, and even from thirty

yards away, I could see the beauty Mary had mentioned under her breath. Her hair was a thick green, giving it the impression of seaweed rather than hair. She watched me without reaching for one of her knives, and I wondered if that bode well for me.

I was about to talk, in an attempt to convey my friendliness, when something stuck me from behind and it all went black.

"*D*ean, you good?" I heard a voice say in English as my eyes struggled to open. The back of my head throbbed and I rolled over, taking the pressure off the wound.

"Slate?"

"How'd you get caught?" he asked.

"Same way you did. By not expecting it." I chided myself for being so foolish. I'd wanted to be brought to their village, but I was so distracted by the local sentry that I didn't hear or see the other one sneaking up behind me. It was a classic move I should have been prepared for.

"Where's Mary?"

"She should be coming. We had a plan." I sat up, looking for my Relocator. It was gone. "Damn it!"

I looked around the room. We were in a log cabin with a small window on one side. Getting up, I swayed from the head injury and steadied myself against the wall.

"Not much to see," Slate said.

The opening was small, no more than an eight-inch space, two feet wide. Not enough room for anyone to slip out of. I saw village people roaming around, doing what appeared to be daily chores. A male carried a green woven basket with animal furs, followed by two little girls play-fighting with sticks as if they were swords.

"Is this part of the Theos' objective?" I speculated.

Slate sat on the ground, his wide back against the wooden slats, his face grim. He had a small spot under his nose where dried blood had caked above his lip. "I don't think so. It said 'swim' and gave us masks. I think we have to go underwater, and this is definitely not in the ocean."

He was right. This was an unexpected delay, and I had no idea now how we could get out. I had to put my faith in my wife, that she could come and help us out of here. I'd been hoping to get brought in, find Slate, and relocate back to the camp, where we'd find Mary. If that didn't work, she was ready to come in guns blazing.

But I knew that would be her last resort, and I was grateful for it. The people here seemed so normal, so…human. I almost laughed out loud at my thought that being human was the normal thing. I suspected hundreds, if not thousands, of other races around the universe would beg to differ.

"We need to get out and finish our task. Throw on the masks and…" I didn't know what was next. The hints were too insubstantial and vague.

"We'll figure it out, boss. We always do."

The Ancients

The statement calmed my nerves. We did always find a way to solve the puzzles before us. Could that last forever, though? Eventually, even the best had to falter.

I continued to stand, my head still pounding but feeling clearer with every minute that passed. My feet were aching, and I reached down, pulling a large splinter from the center of my left foot. Relief passed through me at the removal.

A group of armed females was approaching from a large building down the dirt path, which was probably a roadway for them, though I didn't see any form of vehicles.

"We have company," I said, and Slate got up, groaning as he did so. "Did they rough you up?"

"Just a bit. I may have hit one of them. It didn't even hurt her."

"Her?"

"You think I won't hit a female alien if she's trying to capture me? Then you don't know me very well. I'm progressive." He said it with a grin that faded quickly. I imagined him remembering how I'd looked at him after he'd shot Mae. You couldn't unsee something like that.

"I don't blame you. I'm just noticing a trend with this race. The females carry the weapons. They're the tough ones."

"Hah, I'd say. The one who clocked me in the nose was less than half my weight but carried a punch Tyson would be jealous of. I think even Natalia would lose that battle."

A lock rattled on the large wooden door before it

opened, letting four green-haired bodies pour in.

We stood, backs against the far wall, only a few yards separating us from them. They had knives out, clutched between white knuckles. This couldn't be it. My heart leapt into my throat at the notion they might cut our throats and wear us like animal skins.

The lead woman crossed the room, her arm jutting out until she gripped my face with her left hand. Three strong fingers squeezed my cheek and turned my head from side to side in a calculated move. She was looking at my neck.

The lines on her neck, which I'd first taken for a tattoo, were actually slits in her throat, each one lifting slightly to show greenish flesh underneath as she breathed. It reminded me of a fish's gills, but I could also see her chest rising and falling beneath the baggy top she wore, so she was breathing with lungs.

She said something in her language, and it was the first time I'd heard one of them talk up close. It was a clean sound, almost sing-songy. Her narrow eyes squinted even further as she moved her face in closer, and she opened her mouth. I saw thin teeth and again was reminded of a salmon.

Every sign indicated they came from the water. If that was the case, why were they on land? Evolution? I thought it must have gone deeper than that, or the gills would be gone by now.

She said something else and moved from me to Slate. Her middle finger ran to his lip, and his teeth bared in a growl.

The Ancients

"Slate, take it easy. We're going to get out of here."

"Whatever you say, boss." He closed his mouth, his eyes intense as they stared daggers at the alien before him.

The other three stayed by the door, and the one near us grabbed us each by the arm and pulled us toward the exit. She wasn't doing it in a painful way, just a confident tug to make sure we followed along.

"Why don't they tie our hands together?" Slate asked me quietly.

"I think they know we're males," I said.

"What the hell does that have to do with it?"

"Don't you see? The women wear the animal pants and kick ass Xena-style. The men are docile here. Mary's going to love this." I almost laughed but cut it short because we were nowhere near out of the woods.

"Great, maybe there's hope yet. We can attack, get one of those knives…"

"Slate, let's just take the passive tactic for a while here. Mary will come for us."

We were outside. A breeze blew against us, giving me relief after sitting in the warm stuffy cabin. The town was quaint; cabins lined the way, and the locals milled around working or gardening behind their homes, but when they spotted the invaders being paraded through town by their sentries, they all took notice and followed along. Children gawked, pointy teeth displaying their excitement.

I nearly tripped as I stepped on a rock, but the one behind me grabbed me under the armpit and thrust me back up. This went on as we passed by the entire town, and hundreds of their people now walked beside and behind the procession until we came to the edge of town, where a fire roared high. That would be the source of the smoke we'd seen earlier.

The clearing was in the shape of a large circle, reminding me of the clearing on Atrron. Short, thick trees created a border, doing more to mirror the other planet's Forest of Knowledge.

"This stinks of *them*," I whispered to Slate, who nodded in agreement. I purposefully didn't say the race of missing deities, because I didn't know how these locals would respond.

The fire was in the center, and heavy smoke poured from it in plumes. We were forced to our knees in front of it. Again, they were firm but not abusive. They wanted to show us something. We faced the fire, away from the townspeople, and I could feel every one of their gazes on the back of my head as I looked into the flames.

The sentry who'd appraised us at the cabin moved between us and the fire, and took a bowl from an old gray-haired woman. The elderly female's back was crooked, but she still had passion in her eyes and wore the knives on her belt. The bowl was shoved in front of my face so quickly, a splash of tepid liquid hit me in the forehead.

"I think she wants you to drink it," Slate said.

"Thanks. How about you go first?" I joked, trying to make light of the situation. If they'd been trying to kill us, they could have done it already, not in a circle with the whole town watching. I hoped.

I reached for it, taking the wooden vessel and pressing it to my lips. I said a silent prayer to anyone listening and felt the fluid hit my tongue, instantly tasting bitter liquid. I didn't keel over, so Slate grabbed it and took his own sip.

Something was wrong. My vision began to blur, my mouth feeling numb. "Sla…t." I tried to say his name, and he looked at me with a dulled panic.

The woman moved behind us, placing a hand on each of our heads before holding our faces forward to stare into the burning wood. The smoke danced heartily, and I forgot about the bitter drink. Instead, I focused on the flickering flames and the face that appeared within them.

TEN

"Dean Parker," its voice said. "You've made it to your second challenge." This face was more like an outline, much like the shadow essence of the Theos we'd seen a couple of times now.

"What do we have to do?" I asked, though my lips no longer moved.

"Take the map and follow it to the village."

"What map? Did you drag these people from underwater to guide us?"

"I do not understand. There are no people on the land. The map is near me." The face moved.

"They have us captive," I started but remembered the thing I was talking to was nothing more than a prerecorded message. I didn't know how it had ended up in their fire. They must have thought of it as their god. I couldn't imagine how a face within smoke and flames would seem like anything else.

The voice spoke again before vanishing. "Follow the path to the village."

My tongue was dry and stuck to the top of my mouth. I shook my head, trying to get the fleeting remnants of the unpleasant drink out of my mind.

"Slate?" I asked and turned my head as the grip on it eased up. He was still looking into the fire.

"I'm here. The goal's in the water," Slate said with thick words.

"Good. I thought I was hallucinating." I looked down into the bottom of the firepit and spotted a glint of green, otherwise covered in dark ash. They had a Theos artifact inside there, giving them the impression of a face in their fire. They probably kept the fire burning as an offering to it. I wanted to tell them they were praising a long-dead piece of technology, but I had no way of communicating at that point. Not until Mary came.

The female came back with a wide smile on her face and what appeared to be real joy. We'd brought the god out of its shell, and they were happy. She helped me to my feet, and others around cheered.

It happened so fast, I didn't have time to stop them. Two of the women were between us and the fire, and one of them held the Relocator in her three-digit hand. She started to tap at it, the other looking curiously over her shoulder. I tried to blurt out a warning, but it was too late. The people were still cheering for their god's appearance, and when her finger came down and tapped the screen, I noticed the two women's arms were touching.

They both disappeared into thin air.

More quickly than I'd have thought possible, Slate and I each had blades at our throats. We threw our hands in the air.

"It wasn't us. We're not wizards!" I called, knowing

they wouldn't understand. I think our captor could comprehend the inflection, because her eyes softened slightly, but the cold metal didn't move. It pricked my neck, sending a line of warm blood down toward my chest.

The ground beside us erupted like a small bomb had gone off. Mary! My eyes darted side to side as far as I could move them while keeping my head still, but I couldn't see my wife anywhere. Another blast, this time to the right of Slate. People were starting to panic.

We heard an alien phrase uttered robotically. Mary was there with her translator on. She was hiding somewhere, though. The women looked around, seeing nothing. One of them walked to the fire to see if it was their god speaking.

The one holding the knife to my throat called back, her musical tone more strained than before. She got a reply from Mary, but I couldn't hear what she'd said in English. The prick of the blade eased away from me, and I breathed a quick sigh of relief. Glancing over at Slate, I noticed his hand was in a tight fist, ready to attack, and I shook my head at him. He looked down, not happy with the order.

The women were moving away from us, toward the other side of the fire, where the voice was originating. We got up off our knees, mine creaking with stiffness as I did so. Mary appeared from nowhere, right at the treeline of the open space. She was wearing her full EVA, holding a pulse rifle up, ready to attack if needed.

The females stopped in their tracks, startled at Mary's sudden appearance. Even from the distance, I thought they recognized Mary's feminine features, and they knew she was a woman. A powerful woman who could speak their language, had a weapon that could blast holes in the dirt, and could teleport. They must have thought she'd been the one to take the two disappearing locals away.

They got on their knees. The rest of the villagers did the same.

Mary picked up the new cloaking device Clare had given us and tucked it into a strap on her leg. It had done the trick. She strode toward us with purpose, her rifle held at ready just in case one of them did something stupid.

She tapped the translator off. "Hello, boys. Need some help?" She was loving this.

"I'd say we were doing fine on our own," Slate said with a wry grin.

"It looks that way," Mary said, running a gloved finger over the small nick on my neck. "Sorry I wasn't here sooner, but I saw the Theos shadow in the fire and didn't want to interrupt."

The villager's leader tentatively came up to us, her dark green hair shimmering in the sunlight. She spoke a phrase, and Mary turned the translator back on.

"Please repeat," Mary said, and the woman did.

"Who are you?"

"We are visitors. What can you tell us about the water?" Mary asked.

"The water?"

"The ocean," Mary said, lowering her rifle.

"The *aquadomum*." I picked up the fact that her translation came through as a variation of Latin and wondered if it was just our device's way of conveying an unknown phrase with the closest meaning.

"Come," the woman said, turning around and walking away. Two of her armed friends followed behind us, but at a respectful distance. We passed by the onlookers. Some were still kneeling, while others just stared, trying to understand who or what we were.

The road led us to one of the cabins, where we entered through the door, and the woman pulled out an object from a desk on the far side of the main room. She beckoned us inside and waved her hand toward the wooden furniture, gesturing for us to sit. The space was small but cozy, the smell of wood sharp but pleasing.

She said something quickly out the door, and soon a tray of nuts and berries was brought in, with wooden glasses full of a colorful liquid.

"Boss, I'm not drinking anything else of theirs. Not after that last *treat* we had," Slate said.

Mary disconnected her helmet but kept her earpiece in. She smiled as she took the offered beverage and passed one to their host, who accepted, and took a drink from it. Mary joined her. "Guys, this is pretty good. Tastes like a flower."

I tried mine and found that was an apt description.

"What is your name?" Mary asked the woman.

"Aquleen," she said proudly.

"I'm Mary, and this is Dean, and the big guy over there is Slate."

"Are they your workers?" she asked, and I nearly

The Ancients

laughed while Slate frowned.

"Well, I do make Dean do a lot of chores around the house, but..." She stopped herself as Aquleen just stared blankly at her. "They are not. They are equals."

"But they are not egg-bearers."

"You're correct. What do you have to show us?" Mary asked, changing the subject.

Aquleen held a clear device in her hand, the size of a cell phone. It looked out of place in this rustic cabin. "This," she spoke solemnly, "is for you, I think. Long ago, my people, the Apop, were driven from our home. My mother's mother's mother recalls the stories of her mothers, and we know we used to live in the *aquadomum*. The Picas came and forced us out. We ended on the beach, learning we could be in air as well as water."

I leaned forward, sipping the refreshing drink.

"We have tried to go back, to vanquish them, but failed every time. They still have our *semrock*. We were to protect it, or so said our writings, but we didn't."

Semrock had to be the seed for this world, the one the Theos had hidden for their game of hide and seek through space and time. It sounded like a different race had come and stolen their home. It looked like we had more to deal with than we had at Attron. As with any game, I suspected each location would get incrementally more difficult.

Mary took the clear device and looked at it from both sides. She tapped the side of it and it lit up, lines forming on the small surface. "Look, guys. That's the beach. There's the cache box the Theos hid for us to find this stuff, which our new friends have already pilfered."

Slate and I loomed over her, seeing the map zoom out and an icon eventually began to pulse. I pointed to the blinking red light on the screen. "That has to be the *semrock*."

"At least we know where we're going," Slate said. "Mary, ask them what the Picas are, and where they came from."

Mary asked, her words translating. Aqueen's jaw clenched and her brow furrowed in anger. "They come from deep in the sea. They are evil creatures, and they have taken so many of those we love. You will perish should you go after the *semrock*."

"What do they look like? Do they have weapons?" Mary asked.

"Weapons? They have their horns and teeth." Aqueen moved across the room and took out a leather-bound book. She flipped through a few pages and passed Mary the volume. Clean drawings were etched on the taupe paper. The subjects were long and fish-like, with two horns stacked on their heads, one above the other. They had large mouths, like sharks.

"We're going to go swimming to get this seed, and those things are under the water guarding it? I don't think so," Slate said. "Our pulse rifles won't work under water. What are we going to do, stab them with a knife?"

I knew he didn't love swimming, but we had no choice. It was our only way out unless we searched the planet for a portal, which would be like finding a needle in a haystack.

The Ancients

"We'll figure it out," Mary said, turning to Aquleen. "Do you have spears? Anything we can use against your foe?"

Aquleen nodded.

"Are you able to breathe underwater?" Mary continued, and the woman nodded again. "Perhaps someone could guide us, then? If we get the *semrock*, will the Picas leave?"

Aquleen stared at Mary, a sheen coming over her eyes. "You will help us get our home back?"

"We'll try," I said. "Will you guide us?"

She said that she would.

There was a commotion from outside, and the two women who'd disappeared using my Relocator were soon inside the cabin, talking over one another.

"Calm." Aquleen held a hand up to silence them.

"It took us to the beach. The gods are with these strangers," the shorter of the two said.

"That may be true. They seek to help us get our *semrock* back."

They each gave us a doubtful look, and I stuck my hand out. The woman hesitantly placed it into my palm. "Is it a god gift?" she asked.

It had come from Kareem, who had been one amazing engineer. "Not a god, no. But from a friend."

"We don't have time to waste, Aquleen. Show us the spears, and let's get your home back," Mary said, taking charge of the situation. Under the circumstances, we knew they would take to following her lead more than Slate or mine.

"Come with me," the green-haired woman said.

ELEVEN

The water was cool at first, but I was quickly acclimating to it. The mask we'd been gifted on the Atrron world fit perfectly, as if it was made for me. I saw Slate put his on, and it molded to his head, making the ideal seal.

We used the earpieces from our EVAs but left our suits in our tent, where Aquleen promised they would be guarded with her people's lives. Otherwise, we had smallclothes from the villagers on. The shorts were tighter than I'd have liked, but I eyed Mary's bathing suit with interest. Mary wore the map strapped to her forearm, and Slate and I held eight-foot-long spears in our hands. Aquleen looked fearless, like a warrior mermaid, as she quickly swam in the ocean, her thin clothing a sheer barrier to the cold.

Slate and I kept our heads above the water as we stood on the sandy bottom of the beach. He gave our guide an appraising look and winked at me.

I killed the mic for a second so our conversation would be private. "Would you focus, Slate? You just met someone, and here you are making googly eyes at a deadly fish-alien."

"She doesn't look like a fish to me. Don't worry, I just hate swimming, and need a distraction to keep my mind from it." Slate ducked under the water, and I marveled at the masks we had on. They didn't need tanks to allow us to breathe. How they worked was beyond me, but these were gifts from a god-like race. After a few panicked breaths, I'd gotten used to it.

"Let's go. We'll check out the Theos box first, see if there's anything left for us," Mary said from a few yards away. She plunged under the water. I took one last look back at our beach and then dropped into the crystal-clear abyss.

Tiny colorful creatures swam around us as we moved deeper. I wasn't the best swimmer in the world, but with light clothing and without my EVA boots on, I found myself having fun as I kicked forward, following the effortless flow of Aquleen in the lead.

Mary turned and looked at me through her mask, her hair loose now, causing it to float freely around her head. She was smiling widely, and I wished we were snorkeling at the Molokai crater in Maui, rather than heading into another dangerous situation together.

The ocean bed got lower and lower as we progressed, and when I looked upwards, I was almost blinded. The sunlight reflected across the clear ocean top, casting wide shadows below us.

"It's just ahead," Mary said through our earpieces, and I checked behind me to make sure Slate was keeping up. His bulky body was only a few yards away, and he gave me a thumbs-up with his free hand. It looked like he

The Ancients

was enjoying it too. I only hoped we could get in and out without facing the deadly Picas.

Aquleen made it sound like they'd been forced out three generations ago, and no one had been back in years. Maybe the Picas had moved on, and we could just go down, get what we came for, and leave, letting her people go back to their underwater world.

We couldn't communicate with her while we were under, but she was using easy-to-understand hand gestures. Pointing down, she swam quickly toward the white sand below, a school of tiny pink fish bursting apart as she passed by.

She'd told us she used to spend time visiting the empty box as a girl, that she felt a connection to it she didn't get anywhere else. She'd sit and listen to stories from her grandmother about what life used to be like in their home underwater and dream of reclaiming it for her people. Before we left, she told Mary that this was her time. Her path had led her to this moment, and she wasn't going to squander it.

Aquleen found the access along the ocean floor with ease and brushed away the sediment from the hatch. With a tug, she opened it, blue light reflecting off her face before she raced through the entrance, leaving Mary to follow. I let Slate ahead of me and stayed behind. When I was sure there was no threat nearby, I entered the small opening.

The area was about the same size as the one from the ice world, and it had blue stones lining the walls. They glowed softly, illuminating the space. We swam around the water-filled cavern, and after a few minutes of searching, we realized there was nothing left inside for us. This would have been where they'd found the box with the Theos, which currently resided in their firepit back in town.

"Nothing here. They've picked it clean. I guess the Theos didn't plan on this happening," I said, swimming for the exit.

The three of us left, and Aquleen stayed behind for just a moment longer. Her green hair floated around her head while she stayed still, looking captivated. It meant something to her, and we gave her a minute with her thoughts.

"I wonder what the Theos had in store for us if they didn't expect the Picas to be at the end game. Or maybe they sent them, destroying this culture's life as they knew it," Mary said.

"I don't know. They seem to be doing okay up there on land," Slate said.

"How would you like to be taken from your home and transported somewhere else, with no way of going back?" I asked, quickly feeling a fool. That was exactly what had happened to us with Earth. New Spero was our home, but we'd never forget Earth for what it was. My heart suddenly felt heavy with loss. "Don't answer that. I'm sorry."

"Nothing changes, boss. We go in, assess the situation, kick ass where needed, return with the seed thing, and move on to the next world. One step closer to being finished." Slate stuck his fist out, and I bumped it.

The Ancients

"I agree with Zeke," Mary said, and Slate gave her a look that said "Really...Zeke?"

Aquleen darted past us, her legs kicking so quickly she could have been an Olympic swimmer fighting for a medal. She waved an arm for us to follow, and we took her advice, moving further into the ocean, away from the shore.

The distance hadn't seemed very far on the map, but an hour later, we were still moving through the water. We always swam at a slight downward angle as the ocean floor descended. I wondered how many miles we'd traveled and cringed at the idea of swimming all the way back. I'd brought the Relocator just in case that was our only option.

Aquleen showed no signs of slowing, and as she kicked her feet, I noticed her toes were webbed. It was obvious she wasn't going at her maximum speed as she waited for us to catch up. She pointed forward, and I could make out what appeared to be a wall of stone underwater.

"I think that's their town," I said.

She changed trajectory, and we cut through the water toward an outcropping of rocks that stood a way from the town barriers.

"She's bringing us to a covered zone so we can scout the situation before swimming into it head-first. She's got a sound head on her shoulders," Mary said to us.

The rocky wall went down for a few hundred yards until it hit the ocean floor and carried on up to the surface, likely breaching the water above. The area was decorated in colorful shells as countless fish moved around the area, dancing like synchronized swimmers. It was beautiful.

We ended behind a peninsula of reef, and I was careful to not step on it and cut myself. My hand rested on the surface to give my body a break, and Slate copied the move.

"I think we need to start an aquacise class back home. This is quite the workout," Slate said, getting a laugh from me.

"You finally have that retirement plan you've always wanted."

His gaze sobered at that, like the word *retirement* was foreign to him. More likely, he'd never expected to live to be that age, so he hadn't really put thought into it. If I kept dragging him into crazy adventures like this, he might not end up an old man on a rocking chair, watching his grandkids play in the yard.

Aquleen turned to us, waving her hand to get our attention. She gestured to an opening in the stone wall fifty yards away. Something was moving inside it.

We tucked ourselves out of sight from the entrance, watching around the corner as one of the Picas roamed outside the waterlogged village. It came out snout first, and I cringed at the power it held; when it emerged fully, I had the urge to grab my team's arms and relocate back

The Ancients

to shore. It was massive. The thing had to be twice the size of a bull shark, its dark blue color an oddity when I'd been expecting the muted gray of Earth's powerful sea creatures.

Aquleen had a look of despair, which transformed quickly into anger. These monsters had killed her ancestors and driven them away from their home. She wanted revenge. I didn't know if a group of four with nothing but spears in their hands could redeem her people.

"We just need the seed. They might leave if it's gone. I guarantee that's what called them here," Mary said, confidence oozing in her words.

"That's the plan," Slate said. His eyes were still wide as he watched the Picas swim around, looking for food. It moved slowly, silently stalking something along the wall. With a strong flick of its tail, the Picas rushed forward, jaws opening around a school of fish. A few lucky ones were pushed aside as the deadly sea monster ate.

We stayed quiet, watching as it did this a few more times. Eventually, it sauntered back inside the opening, and into the confines of the stone-walled underwater village. We waited another few minutes before Aquleen began swimming toward her ancestors' town. She hadn't been there since she was a teenager, and she had gone against her mother's wishes, as any rebellious teen would do. She'd told us she'd never seen inside the walls, but their stories often mentioned where the *semrock* would be. In the center of town, a ring of glowing stones stood on the sand. The seed would sit directly in the middle. Aquleen didn't know more than what her childhood tales had said, but she believed it would still lie there, waiting for them to reclaim it.

"The last time someone tried this, they sent a group of ten warriors, and only one made it back?" I asked.

"That about sums it up. They do it once a generation, hoping the Picas will be gone." This from Mary, who still spoke quietly.

Mary began to swim toward the stone wall as well, and I squeezed the shaft of the spear, wishing I had a stronger weapon. A knife was tucked away in a leather strap on my left leg, but I didn't relish the idea of going head-to-head with one of those creatures. Not only were they huge, but they had the advantage of living in the water. I pictured fighting one of them in a forest, and liked my odds better.

"Come on, boss." Slate pushed away with a few frog kicks, leaving me alone at the reef.

It was only challenge two of five, and I was already second-guessing doing the Theos' bidding. I tried to let the doubt out and moved toward my friends.

"Look," Mary said, peering into a hole in the stone wall. We were roughly twenty yards from the entrance, just around a bend in the barrier.

I positioned myself beside her and took my turn. It was amazing. Their town was spectacular. Columns of polished stone held up walls and roofs across the open space. The far side of their compact village was lined with residences; colorful plants grew in front of many of the unoccupied spaces. I could almost picture Aquleen's people swimming around, lingering at their homes, watching their children play in the town center.

Now it was bleak and bare, the colors muted as I refocused, and I saw the village for what it was. Lifeless, its soul ripped away for generations. Plants overtook much of the area, and few fish swam inside the boundary, for fear of being eaten by the predators that resided there.

I scanned up and saw small amounts of light from the surface reflecting over their circular-walled town. It couldn't have been more than half a mile across, but it was tall, and there was enough housing for hundreds, maybe even thousands of inhabitants.

Her people didn't belong up on land. Aqueen moved beside me, and I saw her eyes go wide. She looked so vibrant and healthy down in the water, I knew we couldn't fail.

"There." Slate pointed down, where one of the Picas roamed below. That was when I saw what I'd been missing: the stones. They glowed softly along the village walls, now giving an ominous look rather than the functional one they were likely intended for. My gaze followed them downward toward the center of the area, but the light was too dim, the floor of the ocean too murky.

We watched, and spotted at least two more of the large enemies before adjusting and finalizing our plan.

TWELVE

"*I* don't think I should be up top. Her people consider women the stronger sex, and it only makes sense for me to be by her side while we grab the *semrock*." Mary spoke quietly, but I could still hear the enthusiasm carry through my earpiece.

"Have you seen the size of those things? If anyone has a chance fighting one, it's Slate," I said, jabbing a thumb back to the man behind me.

"He may have the most training, but this is underwater. I don't know how well it translates."

"You guys do know I'm right here," Slate said. "Boss, let them play that part. I've become good at being a decoy. Come with me, I'll show you how."

I remembered how well he'd done it at Atrron, when he'd almost died after a bird rammed into his thrust pack. I didn't bring it up then. "Fine. Please note my objection." A lot of good that would do if someone ended up dead.

Mary unstrapped the cloaking device from her thigh,

activating it. We'd run tests in the water before leaving, and it held up remarkably well. If only Clare could see it in action now, she'd be squealing in excitement. Mary strapped it back on, and she shimmered and disappeared. We could make out some blurry skin tones as she swam around us, but it was impossible to see her when she stayed still.

"Not perfect, but better than the alternative," Mary said, and Aquleen stared, open-jawed. She was obviously still amazed by our "magic." Mary tapped the device off so we could see her again.

"We've only seen three of the beasts. Slate and I will make for the surface, drawing them as far away as we can. Then we'll climb out onto the rock above the water level, hoping they can't jump out like dolphins and eat us," I said. "Take this." I passed Mary the Relocator, but not before saving its position outside of the walled village. "If things get hairy, get out of there quickly."

"What about you?" Mary asked.

"Don't worry about us. You have the harder task."

"Aquleen and I will get to the *semrock* hidden at the bottom of the town." Mary finished going over our plan.

"Then what?" Slate asked.

"We'll find out. Just stay in communication, and we'll go from here." I tapped my ear, and Aquleen turned from us, knowing enough of what we said from our hand motions to understand she was getting her town back. An intense frown covered her forehead, and Mary set a hand on our guide's shoulder.

"We'll be fine," Mary said, even though her words

didn't translate.

I swam over to Mary and touched her clear mask with my left hand. "Be safe."

"You too," she said back and placed her forehead to mine before turning and swimming into the entrance. She put her left arm through Aquleen's and tapped the cloaking device, and they shimmered away in a blink.

Slate started for the entrance, and I followed him. The three Picas we'd seen were below our current position, so we needed to go fast if we were going to beat the efficient swimmers to the surface.

"Go," I said, taking off as we swam past the village walls. The water felt warmer inside, as if the sun beat down from above and the town held the warmth. I kicked hard, feeling the burn as I pushed myself to the limits. The Theos mask somehow allowed me to breathe as heavily as I needed and still get enough air.

Without focusing on my surroundings, I managed to notice how still and empty it felt there. The water was clearer; different underwater plants stuck to the side walls, stretching toward the sunlight above. My legs protested angrily as I neared the surface.

"They're coming!" Slate called, and I felt his hands brush my feet as I stayed just above him.

"Mary, what's happening down there?" I asked between heavy breaths.

"We're almost at the bottom. Two of them took off after you, but one stayed behind. We're moving slowly to stay hidden." Mary's voice was a quiet as a church mouse, and I barely made out her words.

I glanced behind me and saw the Picas racing toward us. "Damn!" Slate caught up to me as they chased us at a ridiculous speed.

"Hurry up!" he called, swimming past me in a flurry of kicks and paddles. The surface was just ahead, dark stone emerging upwards like a rounded barbican from an ancient castle. The light refracted as it hit the water, and I blinked to keep it from blinding me.

With all my remaining energy, I kept moving, and soon my hands emerged from the water, feeling warm air against them as I grasped at the rock wall. Grunting, I pulled myself up as Slate did the same beside me. My right hand slipped, cutting my palm, and Slate, who stood on a ledge above me, grabbed me by the wrist and pulled me up just as the Picas were at our feet, snapping their huge jaws.

Drops of my blood splashed on the water, and the Picas kept gnashing their teeth. Slate jabbed a spear down toward them, even though they didn't attempt to breach the surface.

"Something's wrong with these things," Slate said, poking at the water from our perch three feet above it.

"Yeah, they're huge and crazy, that's what!" I yelled.

"What happened?" Mary's small voice asked.

"We're up top. Two of them are here, and Slate's trying to poke their eyes out. Do you have it?"

Silence for a moment, then her voice came through almost imperceptibly. "We're close. It's dark down here, the stones are our only light, and they're very dim. A Picas is nearby, but we can't spot it right now." She went silent again.

Another minute went on, and I waited, leaning against the sun-blasted rock wall, trying to catch my breath.

"It looks like the *semrock* is in a clear box at the exact center of town. There's a circular ring of stones, much like the metal tree we grew in Atrron. How do we activate it?" Mary asked.

"Just get the seed, and we'll find out," I said.

"Boss, check this out." Slate was still poking at the water. He stretched his arm, extending the spear down low, and it hit one of the Picas. I expected a quick retaliation and grabbed hold of Slate's shoulders to keep him from being pulled in. Instead, all I saw was a flicker of blue light. It was like the sea creature was a hologram.

"Mary, I don't think they're real!" I said loudly.

"What do you mean?"

"Slate's spear is going right through them. I think they're a program, meant to scare everyone away."

"Then how did Aqleen's people get killed? What drove them off? Didn't we just see one eat fish while we scouted the place?" Mary asked a flurry of whispered questions.

"Good points, but these aren't real. I bled into the water, and it didn't cause them to thrash any more than they already were. Be careful, but I think they're harmless."

"In that case, I'm going in," she said.

Slate brought his spear back up and set the butt of it down on the rock. "Boss, there's something up here." He started to climb, and I decided to join him. There was no

The Ancients

sense in watching the holographic Picas wait for us.

"What is this?" I asked. The round wall stretched into a platform with steps up, like a miniature pyramid. Slate took one side, and I the other, meeting in the middle after climbing the stairs.

At the top sat a hole, much like the one we'd dropped the seed in on Atrron. "I think we found our garden," Slate said, grinning like a schoolboy in the middle of a prank.

"Mary, do you have it?" I asked.

"I'm at the box, I'm opening it. I have it... Dear God. It's here!" she called, and my heart jumped into my throat. The pure panic in her voice sent tremors of fear down my spine.

"Mary!"

She didn't reply, but I could make out muffled breathing. "Aquleen! Look out!" The words were sharp, piercing my ears as the shouts came into my earpiece. Slate looked ready to swim down, but I set a hand on his arm.

"You said they're not real," I told Slate.

"You said they weren't! Maybe one is, and the others are just mirror programs," he said, and my stomach dropped. I had to help.

"Mary, use the Relocator," I urged.

"It has her leg." Mary was close to tears. I could hear it in her voice.

"Free her and get the hell out of there!"

Mary grunted, and I knew she'd likely be stabbing at the sea creature with her spear. "I got it," she called, then said some muffled words.

Everything went silent, and I couldn't wait any longer. I ran down the steps to the edge of the platform and dove toward the water. The waiting Picas opened their jaws as I approached, headfirst into their mouths. I kept my eyes open, passing right through them without feeling anything but water. Thank God we'd been right.

I forced my tired legs to kick with all their strength. In a handful of seconds, I was nearing the entrance we'd taken to get into the walled village.

"Dean," Mary's voice called me.

"Where are you?" I asked, looking around for any sign of them.

"I made it out. We used the Relocator. Aquleen isn't doing so well."

That was when I saw the dark red stains in the water a few yards away. Mary held the warrior, whose leg was twisted and mangled from the left knee down.

"We need to get her up top. You have the seed?" I asked, and Mary showed it to me in her palm. Her spear was gone, probably lodged in the Picas' side. "I'll take Aquleen." Mary hesitantly took my weapon and kept between me and the bottom of the village where she'd left the angry Picas.

"It's still down there. If it catches wind of where we went, it'll be here in a flash," Mary said, her gaze never leaving the emptiness below us.

Aquleen was trying to help her swim, her face twisted in a harsh grimace. I couldn't believe she hadn't passed out. She must have been in so much pain.

The Ancients

"I've got you," I said, knowing she couldn't understand me.

Slate came from above, ready to fight. "Everyone accounted for?" he asked, seeing us all there in relatively one piece. "Boss, let me help," he said, reaching toward the green-haired local. She pointed below us and let out a scream, small air bubbles bursting from her mouth.

The Picas was rapidly swimming toward us, now just a small dot in the distance but growing every few seconds.

"Gogogogogogo!" Mary yelled.

Aquleen grabbed Slate's spear and pushed at me with her other hand, her three digits clawing at me to let go of her. I obliged, and she swam away from us. She looked back, sadness and acceptance in her eyes.

"No!" Mary yelled and started to go after her.

"Don't you see? She's saving us. Let's get out of here." I held Mary's upper arm to keep her from going after Aquleen, and we all started to swim away.

I didn't look back, refusing to acknowledge there was an enemy still on our tails. I blinked, seeing that look in her eyes as she went to stall her people's nemesis. Aquleen would go down a hero, we'd see to it.

Slate was the first to the surface, and he was quick to get out and lower a hand to us. Mary tried to move around the projections that appeared to look like deadly sharks, but gave up after seeing me swim through them. Soon we were up on the ledge, heading toward the platform.

"The honor is all yours," I said, panting once again from the excursion.

Mary stepped up the blocks of the small pyramid and held the avocado-sized *semrock* in her right hand. She reached the apex and stood there for a moment, her chest heaving up and down as water dripped all around her. I saw goosebumps rise on her flesh as a cool breeze blew over us. I loved that woman so much and just wanted to wrap my arms around her, but there would be time for that later. Now, we had a job to do.

"This is for you, Aquleen," she said, and lowered the *semrock* into the hole. A perfect fit.

THIRTEEN

The pyramid began to shake, and Mary hopped down a few steps at a time to where Slate and I waited. A massive light erupted from the platform, covering us, bringing a tingle of alien energy with it. The beam shot upward, blue light barely contrasting against the clear sky.

"Mary, Dean, over here," Slate said, nudging us out of our reverie. He was looking down into the water, which was now basking in the same blue light. "I think the seed grew into the water."

It made a strange sort of sense. The holographic creatures were gone now, and when we jumped into the water, it felt warmer, more inviting. The gemstones built into the walls were bright blue now, and we moved down through the water, my body feeling more rejuvenated the longer I was in the ocean.

"There's power in this," I said. Slate nodded, and Mary took off, racing past the entrance and on toward the bottom of the village.

"It might still be there!" I called after her, warning of the monster we'd left battling Aquleen, but she didn't slow.

Slate and I kicked faster, attempting to catch her, and when we found Mary, she was on the ocean floor, Aquleen's damaged body in her arms.

"She's alive," Mary said.

I watched in the bright glow of the stones as the clear box opened of its own volition, and murky black ink spilled out. The Theos ink-shadow took the form of their symbol before transforming into the lanky figure once again.

It seemed to sense Aquleen's anguish. The stones in the circle around us burned brightly, the water warming as they did so. The shadow bent and flowed with the ocean's movement, never quite looking directly at us, or at the dying woman.

Tendrils of blue light crawled from the stones, sparkling as they touched one another before merging and heading for Aquleen. I now saw more wounds on her, and blood oozed from her mouth as she coughed, her gills leaking the red life-fluid too. The azure light entered her nose first, spreading over and throughout her body.

Slate and I watched from a few yards away, in complete awe, as Aquleen's injuries healed themselves; her damaged, dying body was being repaired. Mary held her until her bleeding stopped; the angry wound on her leg closed up, her skin a fresh soft brown.

Aquleen's eyes sprang open and widened as she saw the light covering her body. She fought to break free but caught Mary's caring face and calmed, seeing she was being helped, not attacked.

Mary let her go slowly, and Aquleen stood on the

The Ancients

floor of the ocean, looking over her smooth skin, seeing the damage she'd obtained from saving us from the Picas had disappeared. We could tell she had a lot of questions, but when she saw the Theos shadow looming beside us, she seemed to forget them all. She got on one knee and glared back at us, upset we didn't join her.

"Looks like we've passed the test," Slate said.

"It appears so…" I was cut off by the Theos. It had no mouth to speak from, but its voice carried into my earpiece.

"You have completed your task." The same phrase as before, in the same voice.

"Are the Picas gone?" Mary asked it.

"It is gone," it said in a solemn voice.

"Is it safe for them to move back home?" I asked, looking at Aquleen, who was getting none of the conversation.

"It is safe."

"Why upset their world?" Mary asked.

"To challenge you. Do you think you should be able to walk right through each stop on the map?"

Since it was a recording, I didn't know if it was going to wait for an answer. We didn't give it one.

"Welcome to your third challenge."

The sand shook, and beneath the box the Theos shadow had come from, the sand caved in, revealing a room lit by more blue light.

"Do we want to just go like this? We don't have any weapons." Slate picked up a spear from beside him and spun it slowly in the water.

They both looked at me, expecting me to give advice. If they wanted to know what I thought, I wouldn't hold back.

"Let's see what's in the room. They gave us masks to breathe underwater. I have to think they'll give us the necessary tools to survive what comes next. They even gave us...whatever that healing stuff was, in case we were harmed. They intended to help if the Picas injured us." I didn't want to stay another minute. Suddenly being a couple hundred yards underwater, breathing through an impossible mask, was all too much. It felt like the weight of the ocean was pushing down on me, and I wanted nothing more than to escape it.

"I'm with Dean. Let's keep going." I'd expected this from Mary. She was gung-ho to solve this missing Theos puzzle. Slate shrugged but kept hold of his spear.

"Okay, Theos, we're ready. What's next?" I asked the wavy black ink-shadow.

It moved slightly before speaking through our earpieces. "Next is darkness."

"Darkness?" Slate leaned closer to it, as if listening for a further clue.

"Bring them light. End the dark. Only then will you move on."

"Bring *who* light?" Mary asked, but it was over. The crude man-shape began to blend together, back into the Theos symbol, before pouring into the clear box.

"That sounds easy. Let's go to the next world, find a light switch, and be done with it." Slate made it sound so simple. We knew it would be anything but.

Aquleen's mouth was wide open, and Mary reached for her arm, helping her to her feet. She shook her head and pointed to the box, to which the black shape had returned.

"You don't need to pray to it." Mary repeated the motions, and Aquleen nodded along, as if understanding.

The woman of the water glanced up, and I followed her gaze. The village already looked more vibrant. I wished we could stay around just to see the Apop people's expressions when they were brought there.

"Dean, bring her back. She's tired and drained of energy. Take her to the beach and return to us so we can keep going," Mary said.

I smiled at her and reached for Aquleen's arm. She pulled away, but when I took out the Relocator, she caught on and let me grab her forearm. She touched Mary's hand briefly, giving a look that we hadn't seen on her before. Joy.

Mary gave her a hug, and Aquleen stood there, hands at her sides, with a blank expression. She eventually copied Mary and gave her a hug back.

"I'll be right back."

Slate smiled, and I tapped the Relocator. The familiar buzz surrounded me, and we appeared on the beach. The sun was much lower, close to setting. My legs almost gave out at the sudden weight pushing on them. It appeared the healing waters didn't take away exhaustion.

Aquleen's two friends were waiting there by our tent, and they reached for their knives the second we arrived. Relief washed over their faces. I had my translator turned on.

"We can go to *Aquadomum*," Aquleen said as her arms reached to the heavens in triumph. They were all talking so fast now that I couldn't make out the words. I reached for the waterproof pack with our meager rations in it. We carried our few possessions inside the pack, and I tucked in two pulse rifles. Three wouldn't fit if I was going to bring our jumpsuits.

It hurt to leave the tent, but I didn't have space for it either. Mary had the cloaking device, and I the Relocator, so we weren't empty-handed, and Slate had a spear. That was something. I laughed, thinking about him running around in the dark on the next world, trying to stab an adversary with it.

I watched the three alien females dance as they rejoiced, ready to head back to their village and tell everyone the good news. Instead of breaking it up, I hit the Relocator one last time, happy to have helped another race find their home.

I was back at the bottom of the ocean in a blink. Without asking, Slate grabbed the pack and headed for the hole in the ground. He dropped the bag, and it sank down. He followed it inside.

"Was she okay?" Mary asked, worry on her face. She was such a kind-hearted woman.

"She's more than okay. She was ecstatic. The Theos seem a little sick, don't you think?"

Mary looked insulted. "We don't know if they set the Picas on her people."

"Come on. It's obvious, and the shadow all but ad-

The Ancients

mitted it. And the holograms? Just some convenient local Picas technology?"

"Maybe you're right, but they need to make sure whoever finds them is worthy."

I didn't love the way Mary's eyes widened as she spoke. "Do you think we're worthy?" I asked, to see what she'd say.

"We'll find out soon enough." She turned from me, ready to head into the room where Slate was silently waiting.

I grabbed her arm, stopping her from going. "Mary, this is serious. They've manipulated lives. They think they can do anything they like. Do you really think we should find them? Maybe we should just try to go home and leave them to stay hidden."

Mary was just angry now. "You know we can't. They told you they needed you. The *True*, remember?"

"Maybe I'm not the True."

"Maybe not, but we won't know unless we finish this and find them. And how about a little plan called the Unwinding? If that doesn't sound like something we need to stop, I don't know what does. Did you save humanity to watch it get taken from us so soon?" Her passion was evident, and I loved her for it. Her behavior did feel uncharacteristic, though, and I worried about her.

"Okay. I trust your gut, Mary, even if mine is telling me to turn around and find a portal back home. Let's stay on the same page." She nodded and smiled, and kicked off the ground, swimming down the hole headfirst. I followed her into the room, which was lit by more blue stones.

"You guys know I can hear everything, right?" Slate asked. He pointed to the four corners of the room, where pillars stood. We were in another portal, more similar to the ones we were used to than the one from the metal tree we'd grown on Atrron.

There was a screen in the middle of the room, only one icon plastered in the center of it. It was the third symbol from the cube map we'd found on the ice world. Slate held a long box in his hands, and it remained unopened.

"From the water into the dark," I said and tapped the screen. White light covered us, then darkness.

FOURTEEN

I fumbled for the pack Slate was carrying. He gave it up to me, setting it on the cold, hard surface. I found the LED switch on one of our jumpsuits, and silently thanked Clare and her team for adding a light to the EVA's undergarments.

It was Mary's suit, and I passed it to her. We were all soaking wet, dripping on the black clay ground. I already had a small pool around me and moved away to slip into my jumpsuit before turning my own LED on. The light was on the right breast pocket, which allowed the beam to follow my body's movement.

"Isn't this quaint," Slate said. He was using his suit's light to scan the room, and he stood nearly naked in the small space we were cramped into.

"Would you mind covering that up?" I asked, getting a laugh from the big man. He didn't reply; instead, he just jumped into the legs and pulled the clothing on, zipping up the front.

"That feels better." He slid his mask off, testing the air.

"Slate! Wait!" Mary called, but it was too late. He'd already breathed in a lungful.

"It's fine. Little thick in here. Musty. But the air is fine."

"You don't know that. Have you heard of airborne viruses?" Mary said.

I decided to slip mine off too. This got me an angry glance from my wife. "We don't have the tools to check the air quality. I don't think the Theos let us get this far to have us die from the air."

She shrugged, letting it go, and removed hers as well. I tucked the three masks into the pack and took out the two pulse rifles, hoping we weren't going to need them.

"Let's see what we have here." Mary stood, and I joined her, getting a good view of our surroundings. We were underground, which seemed to be the most common location for a portal to open into. The Theos wanted the openings to other worlds to be hidden. There was no table in the middle of the room, telling me this was a one-way trip.

We had no way of hopping out of here, at least not from where we currently stood. The room funneled to an opening a few yards away.

"Guess we go that way." I zipped up my own uniform and passed Slate a pulse rifle. Mary took the other, leaving me with pack duty. In this case, I was okay with it.

"Aren't we forgetting something?" Slate asked, eyeing the box sitting on the ground. I still had the underwater gift bestowed upon us from the Theos.

We all stood around it, and since Slate had lugged it here, we waited for him to do the honors.

The Ancients

The box was four feet long, and it opened on nearly invisible hinges with ease. Inside lay a weapon much like a bow. Beside it were two sets of goggles.

"Just two?" I asked, hesitant to touch anything.

Mary reached down, taking the metallic bow. It had a few buttons in the middle of the lower limb. She touched one, and it quietly hummed in the otherwise silent space. A white light shone down from the upper tip, entering the lower. It was a bowstring made of energy.

Mary held it up, grabbing the angled center grip with her left hand, and touched the string-beam. She pulled away as if it burned but quickly went back to it, drawing it with no ill effect. "This is cool," she whispered.

"That's badass. Where are the arrows?" Slate asked, looking inside the box for them.

Mary tapped the next button, and an arrow of light appeared on the bow, nocked and resting with a hum. She looked ready to test it out, and she smiled as she yanked it back with a grunt.

"Maybe we should wait until we're not in a cramped space smaller than my childhood bedroom," I said, but it was too late. Mary spun and loosed the arrow beam. It flew and stuck into the wall several yards away. It flashed and flickered out.

"That was anti-climactic," she said, a look of disappointment in her eyes.

"Let's go. We can play with it later," I said.

"Who gets the goggles?" Slate asked.

I passed them to Slate, who tucked them into his pockets. "We can draw straws later."

The hallway beyond the room was tight, and Slate's wide shoulders covered any vantage point of what was coming ahead. He held the pulse rifle at ready. I now held the other one, with Mary taking the bow. I followed behind, Mary covering the rear. The walls, roof, and ground were all the same hard black clay-like substance. The area had a strange scent to it, and it took me a moment to remember the smell.

When I was a kid at a summer camp back home, we made an outdoor sweat lodge with a fire and stones. We would pour water on the hot stones, and the steam would create the effect of a sauna. The musty, warm rock smell carried into my nose now, and the memory rose to the forefront of my mind.

"Anyone else know that smell?" I asked.

"Not sure. It's familiar." Slate turned sideways, glancing back at me as the passageway narrowed. "If this gets any narrower, I might start to freak out. Being this size, I've never loved cramped spaces, boss."

"I know, Slate. It'll be okay." I couldn't know that, and if he did get stuck, we had no way out. Behind us was the only direction to go, and that was where we'd come from. An empty room. If we tried to blast our way out, the whole place could cave in on us. I didn't like our options, and I could see the sweat beading on Slate's neck as he thought about it too.

It went on for another few minutes before I could tell the walls were getting wider, the ceiling rising higher with each step we took. I saw Slate take a deep breath and relax in turn.

The Ancients

The hall ended abruptly and we all looked up, noticing ladder rungs carved into the wall. Without any preamble, Slate raised his right arm and gripped one of the footholds. He began to work his way up, his rifle slapping his back as the strap ran over his shoulder.

"After you." I waved a hand forward, letting Mary go in front of me. She smiled and began her ascent. With a last look behind us into the darkness, I went after them.

By the time we were near the top, sweat poured off me in droves. I stopped frequently, wiping my brow with my sleeve, hoping it would keep some of the perspiration from blinding me. Our LEDs aimed where our chests did, so looking up only allowed me to see the wall where Mary's and Slate's lights hit. Every time I glanced up, my eyes stung.

It was getting progressively warmer, like we were climbing into hell. The thought startled me, and a shiver ran over my overheated body. There were a lot of places we could visit, but hell wasn't a likely destination on this trek.

"We're at the top," Slate called down to us, and my protesting arms and legs gave it their all to finish the climb.

Slate disappeared at the entrance, and soon Mary did too. When I reached it, Slate's hand was there to steady me, and he made sure I didn't fall backwards. He took the pack and set it down on the ground. I rolled over onto my back, a few yards from the drop, and took a few deep breaths. When was the last time we'd slept? Or eaten?

As if reading my mind, Mary found water in the pack

and passed it around, giving it to me first. I took a liberal amount and handed it back to her. We each ate half an energy bar and stayed put, discussing what we knew so far, which wasn't much. Sleep was becoming a luxury we couldn't afford, and I knew we'd end up making mistakes because of it.

"We must be inside a big cavern here. I can't see walls anywhere," Slate said. His light beam went on for a bit before fading to nothing. The beam spread was wide, and was meant for seeing things up close rather than farther away.

"I don't know. I can't hear an echo." I wanted to test the theory but was hesitant to yell out. It might draw unwanted attention to our position.

"You're right." Mary got up and began to walk away from us.

"Stay close," I said, but she either didn't hear me or chose not to listen to my urging. "Crap. Let's go, Slate."

"Whatever you say, boss." He took the pack without complaint. We trailed the bobbing light coming from Mary.

"Do you smell that?" she asked, her voice rising to carry back to us.

I sniffed, smelling the faint odor of rotten eggs.

"Smells like my brother's socks," Slate said jokingly.

"It gets stronger. And look!" Mary was waiting for us, and when we made it to her side, she was pointing forward, where a dark orange glow shone from beyond a ledge.

We kept moving along, each step taking us closer to

The Ancients

the dim light. The smell got more potent as we neared the ledge, an acrid sulfur smell that threatened to bring tears to my eyes. My throat started to stuff up, and each breath was harder to push through.

"We should stop," I said, but Mary kept going. Slate set a hand on my chest, and I coughed, a burning sensation filling my lungs as I did so.

"It's lava!" she called back. "We're in a volcano. Or on one."

"*On* one?" Slate called.

"Look up!" Mary's words hit us, and we both gazed toward the roof, only there was no roof. We could see that now, under the dim glow of the lava down below. I could make out a few twinkles in the distance.

"We're outside." I was surprised. It was so dark. "What did the Theos say?"

"Stop the dark, I think," Slate said.

Mary was back beside us. "Bring them light. End the dark. Only then will you move on. That's what they said."

"Bring who the light?" I asked, knowing we didn't have that answer.

"That's what we're going to find out, but I have a feeling 'they' aren't beside this volcano. Let's go the opposite way." Mary took the lead.

"Have you ever seen such a black night?" I asked them both.

"Never. I remember being in the middle of the desert in the war. No cities for a hundred miles in any direction. Clouds were so thick, we hadn't seen the sun in days. One night out there was terrible enough to make an atheist a praying man. This is bringing it all back." Slate's eyes were wide as they darted around.

"The goggles," I suggested. "Let's try them on."

I took one of the pairs and slid them over my head. The lenses formed against my face, just like the underwater breathing mask had done.

It took them a moment, but the surroundings became visible. "Turn your lights off," I said, and soon Mary's and Slate's jumpsuit lights flicked off, leaving us blacked out. The goggles activated, illuminating the people around me in a green light, much like night vision. Slate's and Mary's eyes looked dark, their skin a pale green.

"Let me try," Slate said. He put the other pair on, and I visibly saw the relief on his face when he could see.

"Too bad we only have two," Mary said.

The ground was dark, flat, bare. I didn't see anything but rock near us. "You can have my set," I said, about to take them off.

"It's fine. Lead the way, and I'll take a turn later." Mary smiled, and I stretched out my hand, feeling her fingers grab mine. I kissed her lips then, the salty taste of sweat and energy bar still on them. I leaned in and whispered in her ear. She patted my chest with her other hand. "I love you too, Dean Parker. Just don't lead me over a cliff."

"Right about now, I'd like to lead you home." We began walking away from the lava, the overpowering scent dissipating more with every step.

FIFTEEN

"We need to find somewhere to camp." I stopped, looking around the barren wasteland for signs of shelter. We'd been walking for hours, and in my head, I kept expecting a sun to rise, giving us daylight, but it didn't change. The darkness was perpetual on this black world.

My feet were aching, the socked padding of the jumpsuit not enough to keep my arches free from rocks and debris. The other two hadn't complained yet, so I shoved my own grievances down deep.

The lower half of my legs and feet were covered in gray film. It was ash, we'd decided. The few tree-like plants we'd passed were dead, no signs of life left in them. This world was depressing.

Bring them light. The phrase started playing in my mind on a loop, until I was humming a tune to go along with it. I wondered if the other two were hearing it, but I didn't ask. I didn't want to make it real.

"This place is getting to me," Mary said. Her hand was still on the small of my back, letting me lead her, since she couldn't see a thing. She said her sight had acclimated just enough to see us as blobs and the ground as a slightly different shade of black. "It's like being in my grandparents' cellar. My grandma would keep her canned goods and preserves in there and said there couldn't be any light. The door had a seal around it, and there was no window. I remember playing hide and seek with a cousin one day, and I got stuck inside. I couldn't see a thing, even after squinting in the dark for what seemed like forever."

"How old were you?" Slate asked.

"Maybe six. I never went near that room again. Grandpa said the door seals acted like a vacuum or something."

We kept moving, happy to have some stories as a distraction from the monotonous journey. I kept looking for somewhere to stop and began to worry we'd never find what we were looking for on the planet. That we'd run out of our measly food and water before figuring it out. "Anyone else feel that?"

"Feel what?" Slate asked.

I decided to be honest with them. "The despair. The second-guessing every move. I'm losing grip over here and it's only been a couple hours."

"I feel it." This from Mary.

"Me too," Slate said quietly. "Let's stop for a while. There's a place we can shelter." He pointed to a spot a hundred yards to our right, and I saw a rocky outcropping and a few tall dead trees. It was better than being out in the open.

Soon we were laying out our few possessions. Slate found a tarp at the bottom of the pack, and he made a crude shelter. It wasn't raining, but every now and then, we felt ash falling from the sky and preferred to keep it from landing on us while we slept.

We removed our goggles and used the LEDs now, making it easier for Mary. I actually felt some of the cloud over my brain lift as I took the night vision off. Mary and I spent ten minutes dismantling a dried-out dead tree beside us before stacking it and making pieces of it into kindling with a folding knife out of Slate's jumpsuit pocket.

"Good thing someone had the foresight to bring a knife and lighter," I said. "We really need to stop leaving supplies at every world we visit. We'll be naked by the time we end up meeting the Theos."

I expected at least a chuckle at this, but the two just solemnly kept working. With the shelter done, Slate came over and lit the small pieces of wood, and I gave a small cheer as it caught, sending smoke into the air as the rest of the kindling took. It felt so much better to have something as simple as a fire and a shelter. I was starting to think more clearly.

"We may have gone too far."

"Coming to this world or our recent walk?" Mary asked, and both were reasonable guesses.

"The Theos wouldn't likely make us walk for hours and days to accomplish a goal, would they?"

"Atrron wasn't that close, but we had our scooters. They wouldn't have known that we weren't on foot." Slate poked idly at the fire, which was now crackling as the timber burned.

I hadn't thought about that. "But at least on foot, we

still would've seen the ball of orange leaves in the distance. Here, we can't see anything. There has to be a sign. I think we've missed it."

"You could be right, boss. Do we double back?" Slate asked.

Mary shook her head. It was nice to see them again with the light of the fire. Mary looked tired, and I tried to imagine we were back home at New Spero, sitting by our firepit. I almost checked my lap to see if Maggie was in it. I found myself missing my new little dog. She'd given us her love so freely, and all I did was continuously leave her behind. At least she was with her family. With Carey.

Emotions threatened to overwhelm me, and I turned from the other two, wiping my eyes. What was going on? This place was getting to me more than I knew.

"Let's call it a night and figure it out in the morning. Or whatever time of day it'll be," Mary answered.

"You two go ahead. I'll take first watch," Slate said.

"Do you think a watch is necessary?" I asked.

"Strange dark alien world that feeds on your insecurities and makes you a little crazy in the head? Yeah, I'd say we could use someone on watch. Besides, I'm a little wired right now. I'll come wake you in a few hours, boss. Then we can trade off."

I agreed, and Mary and I headed into our tarped-off lean-to.

"I don't like it here," she said after we lay down, our heads resting on the folded pack.

"I know the feeling. We can start with fresh minds tomorrow. Love you." I kissed her quickly and felt her

The Ancients

left arm and leg drape over me in our normal sleeping position. Before I knew it, her breaths were coming slower and deeper, and I let her sounds carry me to sleep.

I bolted upright in alert. Mary rolled off me. "What is it?" she asked, panic thick in her voice.

"I don't know. Shhhh." I strained my ears, trying to hear the noise again. I really hoped it had just been a dream.

A few seconds later, and I could hear Slate moving around by the fire. The only other noise I could make out was the soft cracking of a mature fire.

"I think you were dreaming," Mary said, urging me back down from my sitting position.

"You're probably right..." I didn't finish before a screech rang through the air.

"What the hell was that?" Mary asked, getting up herself. We exited the tarped area and found Slate standing at ready with a pulse rifle tight in his grip. He passed the other one over to me, and Mary reached for the Theos bow, activating the string with the touch of a button.

Firelight danced over us as we stood still as statues, waiting for the sound again, or any signs of movement. The scream carried to us once more, this time sounding like it came from another direction.

"We're surrounded," Slate said matter-of-factly.

A rustling sound was coming toward us, and I felt the

grip of the rifle dig into my palm as I held it up high, ready to fire. Another screech, but much farther away than the noise coming at us. Slate looked poised as he scanned the area, but we were unable to see far with the muted light of our fire. It was like the whole world sucked any light into oblivion.

More noise, like boots on pavement coming at us. "It's coming." The quiet words escaped my lips.

The steps stopped just outside our light's range. "What do you want?" Mary asked, knowing whatever it was, it wouldn't understand her.

Words flowed back to us, clearly in an unknown language of chirps and clicks. The translator back under the shelter relayed it to us. I hadn't even known one of them was still activated. The words were choppy, as if it was deciding what was being said. All I made out was… "light. Turn off light."

"Light?" Slate asked. Another loud scream hit my ears, this time closer than before.

"I don't think whatever is right over there," I pointed beyond the firelight, "is the cause of the wail. I think it's telling us to put out the fire. It's drawing in the creature."

"Crap, you're probably right." Slate and I set to extinguishing the fire, using ash and a few logs to bash it out. We had no liquid to spare, so it took longer than we wanted. I heard a few more sporadic words translate, including *light* and *good*.

Another wail from the watching creature hit my ears, and I cringed with the ferocity of it. I didn't want to meet whatever was making that sound.

The Ancients

When there was nothing but the tiny glow of burning embers left, footsteps approached. I threw on the goggles and held my rifle in my sweating hands. The green vision came into focus, and I nearly fell back when I saw the local in front of me. It was over six feet tall, multiple wide eyes staring back at me from a flat face. There were just holes where our noses would be, and a thin slit for a mouth. It was hairless, and when I looked down, I saw it had six legs.

It quickly brought to mind a man mixed with a spider, much like a centaur was a person's upper half sitting on a horse. It was an uneasy sight, and I explained what I was seeing to Mary and Slate. Soon Mary was standing beside me, with Slate's borrowed goggles on her face. She had the translator with her, and she spoke.

"What is it?" she asked, the translator relaying her words into clicks. The being's eyes widened, and it chirped back.

"Darkness," it said, then, "Come." It turned, and we gathered up all our stuff to follow behind. As we packed, a few more screeches bellowed through the flat landscape, and we were ready in record time. All signs of sleepiness were washed from my previously foggy brain, and I wanted nothing more than to find a portal and hop back to New Spero.

"Boss," Slate said quietly in my ear, so Mary wouldn't hear. His left hand gripped the shoulder of my jumpsuit. "Stay close. I don't like the dark."

"I will."

The alien moved nimbly, and we had to power walk

to keep up with it. Slate stumbled a few times, but I was there for him to hold himself upright.

"Where's it taking us?" Slate asked.

Mary repeated his question with the translator. The response was short and sweet: "Safety."

"Safety from what?" Mary asked.

What we got back was a series of quick clicks that didn't translate.

"So much for knowing what's making those screams out there," Slate said.

"It might be better not knowing," I said, starting to sweat now as we trudged along in the dark, my legs and shoes covered in a thick black stain of ash.

"Why do I feel like we're going to find out before this stop on our Theos chase is over?" Mary asked, likely not expecting an answer. I hoped she was wrong, but I had to admit my gut agreed with her.

I couldn't see too far in the distance, as the night vision range was limited, and ash continued to rain down on us in a constant flow, making the visibility even worse.

Another screech rang out, this time from behind us, and much closer than before. "Boss, I don't like this." I looked back at my wide-eyed friend. He was normally as tough as a rock, and as infallible, and it was unnerving to see him scared. Everyone had a weakness. His was the dark. I was about to take off my goggles and pass them over to him when the six-legged alien stopped in its tracks. It turned to us, chittering lightly.

"Silent," came the translator.

We all stood still, making no sound but our anxious

breathing. The creature turned away again and started walking quickly, not saying a word, just trusting we would tag along.

I looked past him and had a hard time controlling my reaction. On the edge of my green vision were hundreds of insect eyes glowing back at me.

"I hope those are its friends," I said, my voice shaking. I'd never liked spiders. Even as a curious little boy, I was terrified of them. Growing up on an acreage, we had our fair share of large jewel spiders hanging their hats on our sheds and barn in the autumn. My father tried to explain their value to the ecosystem, but all I saw were small fuzzy monsters. Now I was seeing huge fuzzy monsters with faces, and a lot of them. Not only that, it seemed there was an even greater threat coming up behind us. It was either go with the horde of spider aliens or take our chances in the dark with a screaming devil we hadn't seen yet.

"Slate, what do you think?" I whispered and turned my head to hear his response. He wasn't there.

"Slate!" I called out and instantly received a scream from the darkness behind us.

"Where is he?" Mary asked, her bow unslung.

Before I could think of what a bad idea it was, I ran back to where we'd come, my rifle held up, ready to fire at anything that wasn't Slate. "Slate!" I called again, getting no answer.

"Dean, over here," Mary called from my right. I sprinted to her side and saw what she'd found: Slate's pulse rifle. I picked it up, holding it in my left hand. Despair at bringing him there threatened to take over, and I had to isolate the thought from my mind. We would find him.

Our six-legged friend hurried to our side. "Come. Come," its chits translated.

The screaming monster bellowed again, this time from farther away. It had Slate.

SIXTEEN

"Right smack dab in the nest." I sat in the darkness of our hosts' underground tunnels. We'd followed the Raanna, as the translator told us they were called. It could be a bad translation, but it was good to be able to think of their species as something other than "spider-monster."

"We need to get out there and find Slate," Mary said, echoing my thoughts.

"What are they waiting for?" I asked, for the fourth or fifth time. Dozens of the Raanna scurried around through the pitch-black corridors, and we watched them pass by the doorway to the large hall we were in.

Mary held my hand, an act that felt out of place in our current situation, but comforting at the same time. We were both nearly sick to our stomach at the loss of Slate, but the Raanna assured us they could help.

"I'm getting tired of sitting here." I got up and called to the creatures as they passed the doorway. "Excuse me! Excuse me!" My translator spit out their words, and a couple stopped, looked in the room but kept moving. Back against the wall, I slid back down to the ground beside Mary and waited.

It was only a few minutes later that a group of six Raanna entered the room and beckoned us. They must have understood we had goggles on that allowed us to see in the dark. Did they think our eyes really looked like that? Round bulbous goggles? Maybe they thought of us as being insectoid like themselves. Maybe that was why they were helping us. I'd been so preoccupied with the oddness of the whole adventure that I hadn't seen it on their eyes. They were also wearing protection on their faces.

"Your eyes. Do the covers allow you to see?" I asked.

"See in dark. Once live above," one of them said. This one had a large scar across his face that ran down to his chest. I got a good look at them now, trying to understand the biology of the aliens. Their six legs were hairy and thin like a spider's, but their top halves were very much humanoid. Two thicker arms jutted out at their shoulders, and the scarred one was missing his left hand.

"Did *it* do that?" I nodded to his arm.

"Yes. We fight. Never win."

"Do you know where it took our friend?" Mary asked, the complex noises echoing from her translator.

"Yes. Nest. Volcano."

"The volcano is the nest?" I asked. "What if he lives there, causing the eruptions, creating the ash cloud, constantly putting the world, or at least their region, under a dark cover?"

I'd been talking to Mary, but they heard me and chittered away. "Yes. Yes. Once radiant. Now death. Only dark."

The Ancients

"Is that why you live down here?" Mary and I stood, looking up at the slightly taller creatures.

"Hide. It kill. Drawn to light. If light, it find. Kill."

Their language, even translated, seemed fairly stunted, but their point was easy to get across.

"So it creates a dark world, and if anyone here uses light, it finds them and kills them." A plan was starting to formulate in my mind.

"Are you thinking what I'm thinking?" Mary asked me.

"There can only be one way. But we need their help." I turned to the Raanna before us, confident that if Slate was still alive, we could save him. "Will you show us where the nest is?"

It took a moment, and they turned into a circle, their conversation a hushed football huddle. When they stepped back in front of us, Scar spoke for them. "We help."

---

*T*heir tunnels were intricate. Raanna were down there by the thousands, and they looked sad and cramped in the small rooms they occupied. They'd made a life for themselves, and Scar showed us a massive space where they grew rows upon rows of mushroom-like fungi, amongst other bland-looking food sources. It was hard to get a lot out of them, but I saw the wistfulness as he remembered life above the surface. The radiant, as he put it, glowing down on them, crops growing heartily in the lush landscape.

Now it was dead, ash-covered, and poisoned. We were there to help them. What had the Theos said as we were about to jump? *"Bring them light. End the dark. Only then will you move on."*

"Bring them light. End the dark," I whispered as we walked in the pitch-black halls.

"Bring them light," Mary repeated.

Scar – as I had taken to calling him, since they'd given us no names – was leading us, and we came to a small room set apart from the rest of the residences. Something covered the entrance with thin lines, and it was sticky when I reached out to touch it. My goggles showed it a dim green. Scar moved past me, lifting one of his front legs. With a sharp protrusion on his foot, he cut an opening into the barrier.

"It's a web," Mary said, and it was obvious she was right. The wall of web shook as he sliced through it, and he held the flap open with his thin hairy front leg, motioning for us to go inside.

I took a hesitant step into the dark room, covered by a humanoid spider web. It was like all my nightmares were coming true. I still felt a detachment from them, like the whole Theos journey was nothing but a game. I had to remind myself it was real. If I died here or, God forbid, Mary or Slate died, we'd be finished. Game over. No respawning, no returning to a saved spot, just gone.

Once Mary and I were inside, Scar came along, leaving a few Raanna outside in the hall to guard the door. I had the feeling what we were about to see was for certain eyes only.

"*Raan*," his chirp translated. He crossed the space and tapped the wall. "Eyes off."

"Eyes off?" Mary asked, unsure of what he meant. He said it again and took something off his face with his human-like hands, revealing his natural eyes. In his palm sat a mask that accommodated his multiple eyes. They couldn't see in the dark either.

"Goggles. He wants us to take our goggles off." I did so, feeling slight panic rise in my gut, and couldn't even see my own hand in front of my face.

"Done," Mary said to Scar, and he tapped the wall again, using his right front foot. A screen lit up dimly at first, and even that limited amount of light was enough to cause me to squint.

"They have this kind of tech?" I stepped toward it, now seeing a desk built into the wall; keys, controls, and screens all along it. The one screen he turned on showed an icon, much in the shape of a spider's web before sliding to a green screen with black writing on it. The language was images and symbols, and Scar typed quickly on the console, script flowing onto the screens in commands.

Pictures appeared, one after another, of a lush and gorgeous world. The Raanna were dark-skinned, as opposed to the much more pallid tone they had now. They looked happy as they did things you could see our colony world inhabitants on New Spero doing: till the farmland, socialize, swim in a lake. It was strange to see the spider people in water, but they played, swinging from vines near a waterfall in some of the shots. If I wasn't already on edge from seeing Scar with this advanced technology, next was a video taken as the volcano began to spew its venom on their world. A series of videos streamed together as more ash fell. Soon the sun was blocked from view, and we saw countless Raanna bodies strewn about the now ash-covered ground. Families wailed in the darkness, the video taken in night vision.

"Dear God," Mary said, clutching my arm.

When I thought it was going to be over, there was one last video. Multiple fires lined the countryside in the shot. The Raanna filming the scene walked around, capturing the sadness and terror. Sound carried to us from the screen's built-in speakers, and it was a howl, the same terrifying one from the creature that took Slate. We watched in horror as the pandemonium began.

The camera shots were shaky and panicked, but we got the point. Hundreds of Raanna were ripped apart by something, never more than a black shadow on the screen.

Scar tapped the screen as the screaming of the Raanna mixed with the dark beast's howl in the universe's worst orchestral union. It went silent, and I walked toward the still frame. Mary stepped to my side, holding on tight.

"There." I pointed at the large screen. In the corner of the shot, the black being hovered above a victim, wings spread wide. It could fly.

"A bat?" Mary asked.

"Could be. They are nocturnal. Maybe a moth?

Drawn to the flame like a moth," I said, remembering the old adage. Whatever it was, it sent a shiver down my spine. That screech, those wide black wings. It was a thing from a horror movie, brought to life for us to confront, and I wasn't looking forward to it.

"Is our friend alive?" Mary asked, straight-faced.

"Only kill in frenzy. Hunt bring to nest," Scar's string of noises translated.

"When they hunt, picking off the Raanna, it brings them back to its nest. Good to know. Slate might be alive. We have to hurry this up." I turned my attention to Scar. "We're going to need your help."

I saw a glimmer of emotion pass through his multiple eyes as the screen's frozen frame cast a dull glow against his flat face. "We help."

"What do you have to make fire?" Mary asked him. Our plan was contingent on a couple of things, and that was one of them.

Scar looked scared but stood firm. "Fire." The word came out quickly, and even in the robotic tone, I could pick up his hesitation. He turned and spit out a flurry of commands to his people. They started running down halls in preparation. It seemed they'd been in hiding so long, some of them were anxiously ready to help us end their plight. It wasn't just a rescue mission for our friend, it was the salvation of a race of oppressed beings.

The Atrron flickered to my mind, being forced to stand guard for centuries as they waited for someone worthy of the Theos quest. They'd also been oppressed, just not directly. They'd been manipulated by the ancient race to do their bidding.

Aquleen's people, the Apop, were forced to land by the Picas. Now the Raanna were required to live underground, with the constant threat of death if they used any light at all. It was getting worse with each challenge, and even though I was cognizant of the current task at hand, I was trying not to think about the next step.

"Come on, Dean. Let's get Slate back."

SEVENTEEN

The Raanna with us were battle-worn, some missing limbs, others with marks on their bodies like Scar. I wanted to end this monster even more after seeing the video of it tormenting their people, and now meeting those who'd stood up to it and lived to tell the tale.

Mary touched the bow she'd been given. "I know it didn't do much when I tested it earlier, but why else would they give it to us? It has to be our tool to kill the moth."

We'd gotten to calling it "the moth" instead of another name. The name the Raanna had for it didn't translate, though I suspected it would be something along the lines of "the devil," or another variant of the word. We decided to give it less power by naming it after a harmless flittering night insect.

"When the time comes, we'll kill it. We just need Slate first." She wanted to separate from me, staying with the distraction we were using to lure it away from its nest. "It'll be angry when it realizes our trap, and I don't want you there when it goes ballistic."

She nodded, her face a light green, maybe paler than it

had been before we arrived on this ash-covered world. I wondered how far the cloud of ash spread. Was the entire world under ash? If we traveled to another continent, would we find another group of Raanna being hunted by a different giant moth?

We were moving quietly, the volcano visible now in the distance, even through the thick ash falling from the sky. The ten Raanna with us were keeping pace, even though they could move much more quickly than us on our two legs. If they had a hard time escaping the moth, then what chance would humans have?

It was getting hotter as each long minute passed. My jumpsuit was sticking to my chest and back, sweat pouring down my brow. I was thankful for the goggles, as they kept the perspiration from leaking into my eyes.

"What I wouldn't give for a nice cold beer and a hot shower right now," I said to Mary.

"I'd even take a hot beer and a cold shower." Her smile cut through some of my tension, and I grinned back at her.

"At least we're together. Not quite the first year of marriage I expected. If this is the honeymoon phase, what's the rest of it going to be like?" I asked.

"Hopefully, much quieter. We can go back to the Shimmali…remember the falls?"

I remembered vividly. It had been the best, most romantic and relaxing time of my life. "I more than remember. When this is over, we're going back. That's a promise."

"I'm going to hold you to that."

The Ancients

Scar held an arm up and pointed to the left. It would take us around the clearing we'd initially walked through, away from the lava pit. Seeing it now, knowing the moth was nearby, I couldn't believe we'd emerged there and walked in the open with our lights on. How did it not see us? It must have been sleeping, or maybe it was off looking for other prey.

We cut hard left, walking for what felt like eternity in that direction before gradually heading back toward the far side of the volcano. They knew where they were going, but the longer we waited, the less chance Slate would make it.

Zeke Campbell was like a little brother to me. Where Magnus was a tough as nails, boisterous best friend, Slate was a quiet, more contemplative soldier, who had more loyalty than anyone I'd ever met. I wasn't sure I was owed that loyalty from him, but he still gave it.

I'd forgiven him for killing Mae, and even though that had happened almost two years ago, I still saw the image far too often when I closed my eyes. It wasn't Slate that I faulted for it now; it was Mae…or Janine. I knew he was riddled with guilt for killing her, especially when he found out her real connection to me. I needed to get to him and assure him once again that he wasn't to blame.

The ground was slick with ash now, and the smell of sulfur and molten lava was heavy as the air thickened. Scar led us to the side of the volcano, and he stopped at a fissure in the sidewall of the black stone that carried upwards for a hundred feet at a steep incline. He pointed into it. "Here. Nest."

The crack was just wide enough for one of the Raanna to get through, but they didn't look in a hurry to do so.

"Are they going to be ready?" Mary's question translated.

"Yes. Fire soon," Scar replied, and they turned around, gun-like weapons in hand. They were an advanced race, but they didn't have space travel or pulse rifles yet. The guns looked like something from the Civil War, just on a larger scale. They didn't move, which told me they were on guard duty.

"Guess it's just us, babe," I said, taking the first step into the crack in the wall. We were on the opposite end of the volcano from where we'd emerged from the one-way Theos transport, and it wasn't going to be easy winding our way through, trying to find the nest. We'd been shown a crude hand-drawn map by Scar, but it didn't show elevation changes, or much at all, other than lines with directions for the pathways leading to the open spot near the lava where the moth lived.

"Turn here," Mary said, her hand pressing lightly on my left shoulder as we walked the tight halls. The good news was that the moth was far too large to fit into these tunnels, so at least we wouldn't encounter it.

"They should be starting the fire any time." I waited patiently as we walked, expecting to hear the moth's screech any moment as it saw the large flames in the distance. We kept moving, but it didn't sound the alarms. By the time we were almost out of the tunnels, according to our memory of the map we'd seen, we still hadn't heard a peep coming from the moth.

The Ancients

We needed this plan to work, or we'd have to face it here and now, and going off the cuff wasn't ideal. The walls were black and smooth, like the worn lava tubes I'd seen in Hawaii on vacation there years ago. They curved more than bent as we meandered through them, coming to an opening eventually. Still no sign of the moth leaving.

"Maybe it went silently," Mary said in hushed tones, her lips touching my right ear. I stood still, feeling the weight of her body lean against mine. The touch of her hand on my shoulder and her close proximity felt intimate, in juxtaposition to our current predicament. I knew she wasn't intending it to stir feelings in me, but I suddenly felt overprotective of her and wanted to ask her to hand me the bow. I'd risk myself to leave her unharmed. "What is it? Did you see something?"

"No. Nothing." My green night vision showed an open room with bright green at the right edge.

"You went rigid for a second," she said.

"Just worried, that's all. Look over there," I said and flipped off the night vision to get a better look. Most of the room was covered in a dense layer of darkness, but on the right, we could make out the orange glow of flowing lava. Breathing was getting harder, and I wished we had our EVAs on, or at least some masks like the ones Slate, Suma, and I had found on that abandoned planet.

"We're close. Let's hug the wall." Mary went ahead of me as we exited the tunnels and moved along into the darkness. I left my goggles turned off as my eyes acclimated to the dim lava glow nearby.

The room we were in acted as a foyer to a couple of other rooms, and as soon as we found the entrance to the next space, this one alongside the molten lava, we instantly knew we were in the nest. Steam rose from the pits, exiting above to the open maw of the volcano. Gurgling noises emanated from the pit of orange, and gases hissed as lava shot forth, turning to ash as it rained down on the land beyond.

As if on cue, we heard something rustle from within. A horrible howl erupted alongside the volcano, and the moth peeled off from its nesting spot on the wall, where we hadn't even been able to see it. We were lucky it hadn't seen us, or we could have been attacked before we knew it. The open area beside the lava pit was wide and allowed enough room for the moth to spread its expansive wings and flap. It took off, roaring the whole time, and flew up and out of the volcano's mouth.

The sight of the creature turned my blood to ice, even in the hot room. Sweat poured off me now, every inch feeling wet. I wiped my palms on my jumpsuit, trying to get my grip on the pulse rifle dry. Mary looked warm as well, but much more composed than I was. She was focused.

"Slate!" she called, but we saw no sign of him. I ran into the moth's nest, aware there might be more than one moth creature. Scar had sworn there was just one, but after the tricks we'd seen with the Picas, I needed to be sure.

"Slate!" I yelled, searching the room. There were chunks of something on the floor, and after a quick sniff,

The Ancients

it had to be rotting meat. I turned my gaze from it, trying to not identify just where the meat had come from. In the far corner, I spotted some white objects hanging from the wall.

As I ran to them, I noticed they were cocoons. Were they the moth's family? Insects ready to emerge as deadly winged beasts?

"Slate!" Mary continued to call. "Dean, Scar swore he'd still be in this nest."

I glanced back at the carcass on the floor, not ready to admit that part of our friend might be in that pile. Ten yards from me, one of the white hanging cocoons was starting to sway.

"Mary!" I pointed to the swinging, white woven sack. "I think that's Slate!" I called. The air was getting harder to breathe, each intake burning my lungs more.

She ran to it, and I was right behind her. "Slate!" she called once again, and something pressed against the cocoon from the inside. "We're going to get you out!" I had Aquleen's knife strapped to my leg, and I yanked my pants up, slipping it from the restraint.

"Stand back!" I yelled and jabbed the knife into the wall of the webbing. It was sticky and smelled musty as the gunk covered my arm up to the elbow. One of the Raanna scurried into the room, panic evident in its choppy movements. It made a series of noises, and Mary's translator picked up the meaning. The moth was coming back.

As I reached into the cocoon, finding Slate unconscious inside, the angry call of the huge moth raced down the volcano toward us.

"Get him out!" Mary called, already lining up her Theos-gifted bow. Slate was coming to, groggy and covered in slime from the casing. I wiped his face with a bare hand, then slapped him on the cheek lightly – not enough to hurt him, but hard enough to wake him out of his impeded state.

His legs caught as I pulled him out, and we both toppled over onto the hard black ground, his weight smashing on top of me and taking the air from my lungs. He rolled off and grunted an apology.

"I'm just glad you're alive." I took in a deep breath of hot gaseous air, and coughed before getting to my feet.

"Let's keep him alive. And us too." Mary had activated the bow. An energy arrow waited, nocked and ready to let loose.

Slate didn't have a weapon, so I ushered him over to the crevasse we'd come into the room from, where a Raanna helped get him out of the way. "I can help," he said as he stumbled, almost falling down.

"You can save me next time," I said and went back into the room, pulse rifle ready to fire at the beast. I went near Mary but kept far enough back to stay out of her crossfire. It was my job to distract it, since we were mostly sure only her weapon could kill it.

The figure came racing down, and I gave my wet hands one more wipe before placing my finger on the trigger. The screeches were getting closer, each beat of my heart ringing in my ears alongside the high-pitched noise.

The Ancients

It appeared, racing down from above headfirst. Right when I thought it might go straight into the lava, it changed trajectories much more quickly than I'd guessed it could and headed straight for us. In the seconds from it turning, to me firing a series of volleys at it, everything slowed. I saw its face, and it was one from a horror movie. Fangs rose from its lower jaw, which jutted forward like a bat mixed with a bulldog.

Tiny black eyes darted between me, the cocoon, and Mary, as if it was deciding the most important thing to deal with first. It chose Mary.

I fired, feeling the metal of the trigger press hard against my index finger as I held it down, red beams lashing out toward the moth. I needed a new name for it, because this was no flittering dusty-winged insect. It was a monster with a fifteen-foot wingspan and an anger issue.

The beams hit their target, but blue energy crackled around it as they struck.

"Damn you, Theos!" I yelled. It had turned, coming toward me for an instant, and Mary let loose an energy arrow from the bow. I watched with bated breath as the arrow flew at the creature barreling down on me. It carried past the monster's energy shield and clipped a wing, white light blasting the room as it bounced off the appendage.

The moth screamed in anguish and fell to the ground, sliding along the floor with its left wing in front of its face to slow it.

"Shoot it again!" I shouted even as I fired more beams, blowing lava rock to shreds around the moth. It scrambled to its feet, towering over us in the cavern. Each breath felt like my last as my chest heaved, and my legs pumped away from the lumbering moth. Large hands at the end of its wings swung toward me, and I kept moving, running in circles in the open area, trying to distract it long enough for Mary's arrow to find purchase.

The moth's back straightened as a white light boomed behind it. She'd struck it! The howl of pain that erupted from its horrible mouth was one that would haunt me forever. Warm rotten spittle flew from its lips, finding a home on my face, but I just kept firing near it.

Another scream. This time, Mary fired at its head. The arrows hit, dissipating as their energy spread through the moth. I strafed, moving behind the bellowing beast, and fired at the rocks, directing it toward the lava pit.

Mary was beside me now, nocking another arrow of white light. She let it loose as I fired near its feet. The moth stood screeching as it moved its now mostly limp wings in an effort to stay upright. An arrow hit its hairy chest, and that was it. The moth's eyes closed, and it tumbled backward toward the open pit of lava.

It lashed out, clawed digits flying through the air at us, but it was too far away. The swing caused it to go off balance, and its feet slipped over the ledge. Gravity took over. Soon all we saw were its thick-nailed fingers digging into the lava rock, gouging deep cuts as it moved further down the opening.

I walked forward, ready to end this. Mary held her bow up, another light arrow nocked. She took aim for its head, which was now flailing around in anger. Smoke and ash carried up, the heat threatening to overwhelm me. Mary let the arrow loose, and it struck the moth in between its beady eyes. White light coursed through the creature, and its hands went limp. I took one more step, watching as it started to fall.

"Dear, look out!" Mary called, but it was too late. A clawed hand snapped up so quickly, I never had a chance to move away. The ground was no longer under my feet, and I was falling.

EIGHTEEN

There are times where it takes the brain longer to register something than the body does. This was one of those times. My hands reached out, reacting when my mind was still confused. I gripped the rock ledge, looking down as the moth fell fifty feet to the lava pit. It was still glowing with white light, and as soon as it hit, the volcano shook, jostling my already weak handhold. Soon there was nothing but the moth's extended wing sticking out of the lava, then nothing. It was submerged.

Mary was there, trying to grab my arm, but everything was too sweaty, too slippery. The volcano shook again, and I could feel each individual finger slip. Slate was there now, and Scar. But I had already fallen.

I knew the lava would come soon, and I watched my wife's eyes go wide in horror. In those last moments, I tried to tell her I loved her, but the words came out in thick coughs.

I closed my eyes, ready for the inevitable, but it didn't happen. Something wrapped around my waist and snapped firm, holding me twenty yards over the bubbling lava. The volcano was angry now. Some lava splashed and

The Ancients

nearly landed on my jumpsuit. I could feel myself beginning to burn.

Before I knew what had happened, I was being lifted in the air, away from the gurgling pit. For the first time, I looked to my waist, seeing a thick web of material swathed around me. I was face-down as I was pulled up, and could see changes in the lava. It was hardening as the white light from the arrows spread through it.

Strong arms grabbed me and dragged me over the ledge until I was lying on my back, staring up at Scar, Slate, and Mary.

"Oh, Dean. I thought I'd lost you." Tears fell down Mary's ash-covered face, spilling in straight lines.

"What happened?"

"Scar shot some webbing out of his…" Slate stopped short, smiling. "I think you get the point."

"Thank you, Scar," I said, and when it translated, he warned us we must leave.

The volcano was changing, the lava going hard. But the whole area felt volatile, and that meant we needed to make a quick exit. Now that I was on my feet, we made for the crack in the nest's wall and left the way we came. Dust and ash fell on us, and I blinked, seeing the horror of the moth's face as it was dying.

"Wait! Each world had a prize. A seed…" Mary ducked as a chunk of rock fell. Slate and I were on the opposite side of the cave-in from Mary and Scar: them on the outside and us inside.

"It has to be inside the nest," Slate said, already turning back.

"It's too dangerous; this place is falling apart!" Mary called.

"We'll be back. Get outside!" I called as the tunnel shook again. Scar shot webbing out of his body and handed me a line of sinewy rope. I looped it up and swung it around my shoulder.

Slate was running blindly in the dark, and I followed, with a last look back at Mary's worried eyes. "Get outside!" I shouted one last time, and then they were moving. "Slate, get behind me," I said, and he let me pass him, then set a hand on my left shoulder as we went back to the nest. The smell was less invasive now that the lava was drying up. The room actually had some light peeking in from above the volcano's vent, and I removed my goggles.

"Where would it be?" Slate asked, rummaging through the space. There were chunks of bodies under piles of ash, and I wrinkled my nose as I stepped near them.

"Hopefully not under this." My foot kicked out, hitting the mess with a splat. The shaking slowed, and ash no longer floated down on us as more light poured into the room from outside. "The ash cloud must be dissipating."

"Good." Slate was in the corner, looking at the cocoon he'd been stuck inside. He ripped it down, tossing the sticky case onto the ground. Behind it was a smaller cocoon, hanging closer to the ceiling. "We can't reach it."

I pictured getting on Slate's shoulders, like a kid on his father's back at a summer parade. It wasn't a good idea for my wobbly-footed friend to be hauling me around like that.

"The rope," I said, unslinging it from my arm. Slate found a bone on the ground and picked it up with a grimace. I wrapped the rope end around it, tying it tight. Small rocks were still falling from the ceiling and walls. "Let's hope this works."

I felt the Relocator in my pocket and chided myself for not even thinking about it earlier. It was set for the area just outside the volcano, from when we'd first arrived on this world.

Slate took the rope, and with surprising skill, swung it in small circles and let the bone-weighted end loose. It arced for the sac and nearly wrapped around it before slipping off and clattering to the ground. He did this again a few more times, with no success. He was pale, and he needed to lean against the wall in between throws. He'd been in the cocoon too long, and his lack of sleep was dangerously apparent.

"Do you want me to try?" I asked. As if some competitive nature in him took over, his next throw cinched around the top of the white sac, and he gave a light grin as he tugged down. The cocoon broke free from its mount on the rocky ceiling and hit the ground with a thud.

Something wriggled inside it.

"Go ahead, boss," Slate said, motioning me toward it.

"What the hell is inside it? It's too small..." Then it hit me. What went into cocoons? Caterpillars or larvae. I passed Slate my pulse rifle. "Get ready to blast this thing."

I ripped the outer layer back. The same white sticky stuff that had covered Slate was inside, but the smell was far worse, like it had been there for a long time. A three-foot-long, multi-legged larva writhed inside, and there I saw it. This thing was going to become another moth, and a purple light shone from inside its opaque skin.

"Sorry, guy," Slate said as the butt end of the pulse rifle came down. "We can't have more moth baddies hurting our new friends." The sickening noise of the bug dying now over, I found a sharp rock beside me, turned my head, and cut the seed out. It glowed dimly as my hand wrapped around it.

"This may be one of the grossest things we've had to do," I said before thinking about all the dying Kraski on their mother ship as the *Kalentrek* ended their race with efficiency. I added "cutting open a giant larva and pulling out a glowing stone seed" to the list, but it was further down than I would have initially thought.

The seed hummed in my hand, and I didn't know where to put it. Crossing the room to the lava pit, I peered over the ledge, only to see a clawed hand sticking out of the dried lava below. There was no scientific way molten lava could turn so quickly, especially without a large temperature change, unless it was just the surface layer affected. I had a feeling it wasn't.

"There's nothing left for us here. Let's go." I set my hand on Slate's arm, sticking the seed into my pocket. With my free hand, I got the Relocator and tapped the icon.

The Ancients

The system's star shone down, an evident warmth that wasn't there before. The Raanna strolled around happily, finally rid of their multi-eyed night goggles. They were already working at reclaiming their partially destroyed city, and we saw more evidence of an advanced society as their hidden-away vehicles and soldering irons came out of storage. Their city was made up of short buildings, but its expanse was far greater than I would have expected. Agriculture was a huge part of their lives, and it was exciting to learn they had scientists, doctors, and teachers. There was far more to them than their likeness to the small spiders of Earth.

The volcano in the distance was shrinking as the outer walls were crumbling in. Soon there would be nothing but a pile of black rock to mark the area where the moth nest had been, and that chapter would be over and done with for the spider people.

Scar stood beside me, staring at the same thing as I was. He grinned, a strange look on his alien face. "Appreciation," the translation said.

"You're welcome."

Mary approached, looking much more rested after a good night's sleep. The Raanna had taken us in, supplied some fungi and water, and given us places to rest. It was much needed, and I felt like a new man.

"I think we know where to go with the seed. They have a place of shame, the one where they first found this moth. It was in a glowing cocoon, and they kept watch over it, making sure no harm came to the fragile casing." Mary waved over Slate, who was helping a Raanna clear debris from the front entrance of a still-standing building. "There were symbols on the walls of the cave, but none of them have been back since it turned on them, and the volcano started to cover their world with an ash cloud of darkness."

Slate had recovered well, and he looked full of energy once again. "Where is it?"

"They'll show us whenever we like."

I turned around, happy to see the Raanna able to start again. My anger at the Theos was reignited. They'd played with far too many lives, and I didn't think any excuse would make up for that. I wanted to find them, now more than ever. They were going to get a piece of my mind, whether they cared to hear it or not.

"I'd like to learn more about them," I said, and Slate was already off to help move a fallen tree with a couple of Raanna.

It must have taken every ounce of Mary's composure to mask her exasperation. I could see it in her face. She wanted to leave. "We're so close." She kept her voice down and for my ears only. "We only have two more…" She paused, searching for the right word for it. "Challenges." Her phrase was friendlier than mine would have been at that moment.

I could tell I wasn't going to win this one. "Scar, it was a pleasure meeting you." I waited while the strange language passed through the translator and he listened intently. "I'll try to come back if I can."

His mouth tightened, and I wasn't sure if that meant he hoped this was the last he'd see of us or the opposite. "Heroes. Appreciation." He slapped me lightly on the back with his right hand and smiled once again.

"We're ready to see the hatching place," Mary said, and Scar's smile faded in an instant. He barked out a few orders, and then we were ready to go.

A solar-powered vehicle approached, looking worse for wear, and I realized most of their technology relied on the sun. No wonder they were living like cavemen underground. They couldn't power anything. It was a wide unit, with the steering at the rear, and a flat-railed deck like a boat that we all climbed onto.

Massive wheels rolled along the ash-covered ground. I wondered how long it would take for the landscape to change. Maybe with the sun and no ash cloud, normal weather could return, along with rain to wash away the memory of their time in the dark. For the Raanna's sake, I hoped so.

Mary stood at the bow of the deck, the wind blowing her hair in a flurry of brown locks. I walked up behind her, careful to stay on my feet as the vehicle moved at a modest speed. A small mountain range lingered in the distant horizon; our target, Scar had said. She spoke, not turning back to look at me. "I love you, Dean."

"I love you too." I wrapped my arms around her. "Sorry for the smell. I was elbow deep in some larvae, and apparently, it sticks with you."

"That's the least of my concerns." She didn't expand

on her thoughts, and I didn't ask. I just stood with her in my arms, watching as thin white clouds raced across the bright sky.

We rode like that for over half an hour, the mountain range growing larger with each passing minute. Eventually, we came to a rigid stop, and I had to hold on to the rail to keep from upending myself as the Raanna stepped forcefully on the brakes. It had been a while since any of them had driven.

Slate had been lying on a bench, where he was still recovering from his time spent in the grasp of the moth. The three of us exited the flat vehicle by way of the steps down on the aft side of the deck.

"Scar, are you coming?" Mary asked when the Raanna didn't move forward with us.

"Stay. Cursed." He handed me a map scrawled out on a gray piece of paper. "Here." His finger pointed to a large X on the crude map.

"Thank you for all your help," I said, looking up to the alien. His scars seemed even heavier in the bright daylight.

"Appreciate," he said one last time, and the vehicle backed up. The three of us stood and watched as they left us alone on their remote world, at the hatching place of the moth that had nearly destroyed their lives.

"I guess we're on our own." Slate hefted a pack in one hand and his pulse rifle in the other. Mary still carried her bow, and when I offered to take the bag from Slate, he ignored me.

The map took us around a hill and into a valley be-

The Ancients

tween a couple of the mountains. They were still covered in ash, and the desolate landscape was depressing to see. We followed the map into the center of the valley, where the X was marked. An entrance into a cliff face opened on our left as we neared it.

"It's always a cave, or a cavern, or a pit with these guys," I said.

"They do have a style," Mary said. The opening was manufactured, cut in parallel lines with an arch at the top. We entered it, the seed from inside the moth larva in my hand now. It was warm to the touch, and I knew its home was nearby.

We were done with three legs of the hunt; the final stretch was before us. As soon as I stepped into the cave, I felt the familiar presence the Theos left behind. After being visited by the shadow man a few times, my senses were now picking up the Theos essence. I wondered if the others felt it too, but judging by the blank looks on their faces, they didn't. Was I their fabled True? Would I discover them and be able to assist in saving the universe from this mystical Unwinding we knew next to nothing about?

"Over there," Mary said, pointing to a corner where a cocoon-shaped stone sat carved into the rock wall. A divot was cut into the front center of the stone, the perfect indent to place the palm-sized oval seed into.

Without any further delay, I set it into the cocoon rock and waited for the show. Black mist emerged as expected from the stone; their theatrics were getting a little old. Mary still held a look of awe and interest, while Slate just wore a deep frown. I think he was sick of it all, like I was.

The mist took the form of the shadow man after a brief pause as the Theos symbol.

"You have completed your task," the familiar voice said once again. This time, I decided to not bother arguing with a program and waited for it to speak again. "Welcome to your fourth challenge. Put on the suits before proceeding."

"What suits?" Mary asked, looking around the empty, musty cave. There were no hiding spots visible to our eyes.

A rectangular stone drawer opened out of the wall beneath the carved cocoon. Inside were three suits.

"How do they know how many of us there were going to be?" Slate asked, talking to us, not the Theos shadow. He was the one who answered anyway.

"There are three because you are three. If you were one, there would be one."

Apparently, none of us were up to the task of questioning that logic, so we instead grabbed the folded EVAs and pulled them out. They were thin: thinner than the ones we'd started the trek with. Masks, much like what we'd used underwater, were on top of each suit, but these would cover the whole head in the clear, malleable substance.

"Where are we going this time? Space?" I chuckled and didn't get an answer.

"Connect the three. Land below. The Final will be upon you."

The Ancients

"What three?" I asked, hoping to glean any additional information.

We didn't get any. The mist faded, swirling this time into a vortex an armspan wide. Beyond was blackness with pinpricks of light. Stars, maybe.

"No time like the present," Slate said, grabbing one of the suits from the pile before us. It was too big, but it fitted to him by itself, another technology that made knowing your size a thing of the past. Mary began to step into one as well, and I joined them, feeling the legs cinch up before I had the clasps closed.

"Make sure your earpiece and mic are in first," I said, plugging mine into my left ear. Slate fumbled with his, getting it in before he threw the last piece of his suit on: the mask.

It conformed to his face; a layer of a thin clear plastic substance molded itself to fit his head. There were still no signs of oxygen tanks, but I trusted their technology. It worked underwater; I knew these would function in the vacuum of space. The Theos wouldn't bring us this far only to let us die.

Mary finished getting her suit on, and the three of us stood at the gaping hole in the room. Mary's bow was slung over her shoulder, and Slate and I had the pulse rifles on our backs. Slate held the pack with our few remaining objects. My Relocator still sat in my new EVA pocket.

"What do you think he meant by 'Find the three. Land below'?" Mary asked while staring into the opening in space. It felt out of place in a cave, like we were in a dream.

"Same old cryptic Theos. Who knows?" I answered.

"Do we just go? This one feels different," Slate said, his right hand stretching forward toward the vortex before us.

He was right. The other seeds had each acted in some dramatic way. The massive steel tree on Atrron, Aquleen's healing, and now, comparatively, an anticlimactic rift in space.

"It does feel different. The sooner we go, the sooner we go back home." I stepped forward first. I could feel a tugging on my body as I stood a few feet shy of the opening. I turned, giving Mary a quick smile, and lifted a leg, walking into the vortex. It was time for our fourth challenge.

NINETEEN

*T*hey were gone, nowhere to be seen.

"Mary? Slate?" My earpiece returned silence. Where did it send them? They'd been right behind me.

Where was I, for that matter? I'd been so worried about the other two not being there, I'd been blind to my surroundings. I was inside a room. The walls were cold and metallic: silver with a blue line running around the room at waist height. I floated, lightly, two feet from the ground. I was either on a planet without gravity or I was in space.

"Mary?" I asked again, and I swore I heard the slightest feedback before it went silent. I was torn between investigating where I was and staying put, hoping the others would arrive soon. I decided to wait five more minutes and explored the room in the meantime. It was empty, at least twenty feet high and thirty feet wide and long. I waved my arms, moving slightly until I could touch the roof. I ran a gloved hand along the metal and pushed off, down toward the side of the space, to where a door sat nestled into the wall.

When no one arrived, and I was sure there was nothing to be found in the cold room, I searched for the door access. A tablet came to life as I tapped it, and with the touch of a button, the door slid open. I tried to tell myself it was a good guess, considering the text was in an unknown language, but since there'd only been two options, I couldn't give myself too much credit.

Feeling stupid for not thinking of it sooner, I pulled my pulse rifle from my back and held it firmly. The feel of the ridges pressing against my palm calmed me. It made me feel better about being alone on a creepy empty ship, or station, or wherever I'd found myself.

The door made more noise than I expected, sounding like a rushing train on a warm summer morning: the kind that would run behind our home on Sundays before the sun rose, startling the roosters into a cockadoodling frenzy far before their real alarm clock went off.

I pulled myself through the doorway, noticing that the lines of blue continued to run along the walls and down the narrow hallway. I scanned ahead, seeing what appeared to be a window halfway down. I didn't see any doors, which meant less chance of an ambush. I'd just have to watch the end of the hall, not behind me where a room stood empty.

Feeling better, I used my left hand to push off the side of the wall, and my right foot to steady me on the other. The hallway was only four feet wide, and this allowed me to bounce down the corridor without hitting the ground or the ceiling.

The window was coming up on my right, and I stopped pushing off, letting myself float slowly toward

The Ancients

the viewport. It had a lip of a ledge, and I used my fingers to grab at it, stopping completely. The view was overwhelming. Gigantic rocks hung in the distance, while pieces of large space vessels were scattered between them. We were in orbit of a world that looked like nothing but blue-green water from this vantage point. A hazy yellow star hung way back, like a tennis ball about to be served, giving bright light over the whole image. It was beautiful.

I appeared to be in a long corridor, one likely used in a space station in orbit above a planet. A planet with nothing but water. A world like this would be highly valuable. I thought about my bargain with the Bhlat and wondered if I'd be able to find this world's coordinates after it was all done. Water would solve their issues for decades to come, maybe forever.

It would have to go through the Gatekeepers first. We'd have to ensure there was no intelligent life, and that was a sticking point for many of us. To Mary, all life was important. To CR-3 from PPSD1, a world of half-synthetic androids, the term meant a very different thing.

Where were Mary and Slate? I wanted to share this moment with Mary by my side. Determined to get moving and find them, I cast myself off again, floating faster down the way until I found the door at the other end.

I used the tablet beside the door and was greeted with another loud slide of a long-unused metal slab. I found myself on the left side of a huge room, small ships lining the floor in straight lines that would please even the most severe OCD sufferer.

I pushed over to one of the ships and was surprised

by the small size of it. They were made to be personal vessels – that much was clear – but for whom? They were pointed at the front, like leaned-over elongated pyramids. I moved to the back of the ship, seeing inset thrusters there, larger than my head. Four of them sat on the base, one on each corner.

The ships were black, and I could picture the whole fleet out there in space, hiding in the dark backdrop beyond. There were row upon row of them, and with a quick count, I estimated there were two hundred in the room. It was impressive.

I wanted to know what happened. Were they wiped out by a runaway asteroid? Wouldn't it have hit the planet too? Or maybe massive chunks of rock did hit the world below, sending it into a cataclysmic state, which in turn caused it to be overrun with oceans. Mary always knew more about that kind of thing, and I couldn't wait to pick her brain about it.

What had the Theos said? *Connect the three.* If I had to guess, which apparently I did, that meant we each needed to get something. They'd separated us so we could each get something, bring them together, and take them to the world we were currently orbiting. *Land below.*

That had to be it! It comforted me to know they were likely somewhere similar to me, contemplating the same problem at that moment. Mary was probably already solving it, and Slate was, without a doubt, seeing if he could fit into one of those ships. If he could, it would be a funny sight.

It became a challenge now, a race amongst friends. I

would find my piece of…whatever I was supposed to find and be there waiting for the other two.

With newfound energy, I searched the huge hangar. First, I headed for the left front corner, where the walls met at a ninety-degree angle. I walked the perimeter, hoping to see anything out of the ordinary. Unfortunately, it was all out of the ordinary.

The room was well lit: an energy source still powered the orbiting station. If I had to guess, it was solar-powered, since the star in the distance was giving a lot of rays toward the floating debris around the station inside.

My slow methodical paces took me to the far corner of the room now, and I turned, heading toward another large doorway on this end of the hangar. Initially, I thought this must be where the ships exited, but with a crane of my neck, I looked upward, seeing large lines in the ceiling. It would slide or split open, allowing the pyramid ships to rise and depart.

This door would lead somewhere else on the station. Before I opened it, I wanted to scan the rest of this room. I passed the doorway, letting it be. A computer screen sat integrated into the wall as I walked along, and I stopped, turning to it.

With a tap of my finger, it came to life. Strange lettering cascaded onto the screen with some flourish. With the program running, I tried to make some sense of it. I had nothing with me to translate it, but like many alien programs I'd seen, they used small icons beside some of the options.

An image that could only be one of the pyramid ships

was on the bottom left, with lettering beside it. I tapped it, and the room shook lightly with a constant vibration.

"Dean, stop being careless," I chided myself out loud.

A loud noise started from above, and I looked up to see the large ceiling panels slide apart, like massive pocket doors. The darkness of space hung above, and I spotted a flicker of blue energy between the roof and space. At least there was something preventing me and all the contents of this station from being sucked into space.

I tapped it closed and waited with a little anxiety as the doors sealed. The last thing I wanted to do was trust the forcefield of a busted-up alien station. Not wanting to activate anything else, like a self-destruct, I left the comp screen alone and moved back toward the doorway I hadn't explored yet.

With a tap, I had access to the next room, which was much smaller than the one I was coming from. It looked like an office, with four work stations; three doors lined the edges of the area. I set to looking at the desks. Their screens showed various programs, but the one with a 3D map caught my interest. On it, I could see the planet we were orbiting and the two moons around it, as well as a large space station. The same yellow star was further out, with two other planets nearer than this one in various stages of their elliptical orbit. One appeared to be nearing its perihelion and looked closer than I'd want to be to a star.

Most days, I could close my eyes and my memory of floating near Earth's sun, trying to save the suicidal vessels full of humans, would flash in my mind. It wasn't a moment I liked to dwell on, but there it came, flooding back to me like it was happening. I felt the heat of the sun and the tug of the tethered rope. I closed my eyes tightly, and when I opened them, the moment had passed. All I saw was the map once again.

Three things interested me. One, that there were no asteroid chunks on this map. That meant it was being looked at before the damage was done. Two, the planet showed lines and texture, unlike the waterlogged world we currently had nearby. Also, there was no sign of a space station on this map, which I found intriguing.

I sat down at the hard metal bench. Whoever had designed the workspaces was more about function than comfort. There were a few options on the two-foot-wide screen that was built into the desk space. Eventually, after a little trial and error, the map system started loading an updated version. First, lines appeared, dancing across the screen as the sensors identified the objects nearby.

Within a few minutes, the lines were filling in with realistic images, even though some of the color appeared wrong to me. The rocks had been lighter gray when I saw them out the window in the corridor twenty minutes earlier, but these were dark.

I was shocked to see both moons were gone. I'd assumed they were being blocked by the limited view I'd had. That explained more. Something came and destroyed their moons; chunks inevitably would have rained down on the planet below, and a combination of tsunami and tides being altered ended up in a water world.

"Who did this to you?" I asked no one in particular.

Was this another sick game by the Theos, or did they set it up to look like the scene I'd just played out in my head? Was any of this real? Either way, I still had the same objective. Finish the task and get home. That was all I wanted. To be in my house on New Spero, with Maggie licking my face as morning broke. Mary and I had talked about a family, and when this was over, I was going to broach the subject. She'd been so distracted, exploring worlds as a Gatekeeper over the past year, that I wasn't sure she'd mentioned having kids more than once. We'd both been distracted, and now with the Theos conundrum, we were digging ourselves deeper into the universe. The deeper we dug, the harder it would be to get out of the hole.

I zoomed on the map, finding the station I was inside. It looked to be one of the smaller chunks, still intact. Slate and Mary could be in any of the others, maybe even together. Maybe the initial Theos plan had been to send us to three corners of the same station, but now that they were busted up, things had changed.

Connect the three. What did it mean? Connect what? I looked over the map more, zooming in and out of the station debris. Then it made sense. Amongst the waste, three sections of the station were very similar. From an aesthetic point of view, the station would have many parts that made it symmetrical, but I'd originally assumed it was a circle. The design was the most functional for the sake of gravity and for long-term sustainability in space.

The Theos would have no need of that. They were so far advanced, they could choose any shape they wanted.

In this case, they chose the symbol for their homeworld. Now that I saw the three pieces, I couldn't unsee them. Stacked together, they would form the symbol, with three horizontal lines connected in the middle. I was in either the top piece or the bottom, depending on perspective. The other two were close by, and that was where I'd find Mary and Slate.

The question became: how could we connect the three?

TWENTY

With the objective clear in my head, it was time to figure out how to accomplish their challenge. We had three sections of the station; presumably each of us were currently on one of them. Looking at the map, I mentally assigned Mary to the section nearest me, and Slate to the middle piece on the other side of some large hunks of moon.

I needed to get in contact with them. I checked the other workstations and was sure there was a communication link between the sections, but I couldn't figure out how to use them.

"Mary. Slate. Come in." Static. "If you can hear me, I think I know what we have to do. We're each inside a section of a space station. We need to connect them. The end result is a station in the shape of the Theos symbol." There was no reply. I'd have to find another way to get the message through.

I tried the left door first. As expected, it was nothing more than a small room with more computer screens. I already knew the layout of the portion of the station I was in because of the 3D map I'd seen. The hangar was the middle piece of the symbol, with the corridors making up the symmetrical length. It was like a squat letter T. I headed for the hallway door and found a corridor much like the one on the opposite end of the hangar.

I floated through it, pushing myself along the walls as I had before, and made good time down the long stretch. I paused midway as the window approached, this one aiming in the reverse direction of the first. I got a much different view from there, the planet and star no longer in my sight lines. Now I saw the other pieces of the station, and I squinted, looking for a window on one of them.

The closer of the two would act as the middle, and I did see a tiny square window much like the one I was peering out of. Was that someone moving past it? I silently hoped it was Mary. The thought that I might have just seen her float by the viewport filled me with a needed burst of adrenaline.

I willed her to go back, to see me there waving, but she didn't. Around the station sections were more moon-rock pieces. Some were immense; others were small pebble-like stones in clusters. Light radiated from the star beyond, casting shadows on them. I kept moving.

The end of the corridor found me soon, and I tapped the door open. Catching a glimpse of what was beyond had me waving my arms in panic, trying to get clear in a hurry. My heart pounded hard as I saw space on the other side of the room. The wall was ripped clean off. It didn't pull me, and my fear subsided as I realized the same forcefield covered the tear in the station.

Hesitantly, I gripped the doorframe, tugging my body

slowly into the room. It mirrored the room I'd arrived in, except this one was missing the entire wall at the end of it. Ragged edges jutted out of the existing walls, evidence of the destruction the moons had caused when they were demolished. I tried to calm my racing heart, but seeing open space a mere few feet away was terrifying. No matter how much I'd been through, floating around in space still caused me to panic.

There was a tablet on the wall, mounted on a bracket. I floated over to it, and it turned on before I touched it.

"That's interesting," I said to myself, more to fight the feeling of being alone on the derelict station than anything. "If it turns on by itself, that's by design. It wants you to see it." I grabbed it, sliding it from its perch on the wall.

"Dea...wher...stati...theo..." A series of words cut in and out of my earpiece, startling me. I dropped the tablet, but instead of falling to the ground, it floated beside me.

"Mary!" I called back. "We have to join the pieces. We're each in one of the three. We need to drag them together." I prayed she'd hear me, but there was no reply. I kept talking for a few minutes, then waited another five for an answer, but the connection was lost.

Focusing my attention back on the task at hand, I looked at the tablet. The symbol for the Theos appeared on it, glowing blue. If I hadn't found the hint at the map station, this was the failsafe clue.

The image swirled, melting into a finished picture of what the station looked like intact. My guess had to be right. There was only one way to accomplish this, and I was going to test my theory. I held on to the tablet and raced back down the long corridor, casting my glance toward the other section, where either Mary or Slate was trapped right now. It flew by in a blur as I kept pushing myself, floating quickly toward the hangar.

Soon I was back inside the large, open ship-lined storage box, looking for supplies. I hadn't walked in the center of the room, and that was where I spotted what I needed. The mechanics area sat there, right in the middle of the action. From here, a mechanic could get to any corner of the room in a matter of seconds if they hustled. Spare parts lined shelving units and, as I hoped, there was a tow rope coiled up on a hook beside a desk.

I tested the dexterity of the line, unsure of the material, and found it oddly familiar to the ones we'd attached to the Kraski vessels after the Event. It turned out to be three lines, and after unwinding them, I measured them to be about a hundred yards each. They'd have to work. Now the test became attaching them to my station. I didn't relish the idea of going for a space walk, but I knew I needed to. My pulse sped up at the thought, and beads of sweat dripped down my face, fogging the clear mask momentarily before the built-in filtration released some cool oxygen, dissipating the condensation. I could do this.

First, I needed to get off the station. From my point of view, there were two places to do that: from the far room where I'd just found the tablet, and from the hatch above, where the fleet would be able to exit the station. The blue energy field had to be a containment field. It would keep the deadly vacuum of space out but allow an object to travel through it.

The ropes had clamps on them and would let me connect to a hook or handhold outside. Without overthinking it, I strapped one of them around my waist and carried the other two on my shoulder. I wound my way across the room, between dozens of pyramid ships, and made it back to the computer screen, where I knew I could open the hatch to space. With a few taps, the room was vibrating again as the large slabs slid open, revealing open space.

Grabbing a nearby shelf, I pulled myself to the ground so my feet touched down on the metallic floor. For a mechanic's shop, the area was spotless, and I wondered again if this place was ever used, or was just a testing facility for the Theos.

Bending my knees, I lowered myself and pushed with all my strength, floating up toward the ceiling. I stretched my arms out, realizing my aim was off just enough to set my mind into a panic. If I missed my target, I'd fly out of the station, with no way to stop once I crossed the barrier into space.

My arms flailed as I attempted to adjust my trajectory. Even though I was moving slowly enough to see it all coming, it was almost worse because I had more time to think about the outcome if I missed catching the edge. As the barrier neared, I flopped my body, my back now facing the ground and my fingers stretched to their limit.

My grasping hands hit the edge, seeking something to grab on to. The momentum caused my legs to swing out through the energy field, but I had a firm hold, so my

The Ancients

body bent at the waist. My breath came fast and ragged as I struggled to keep a grip; the energy of the containment field sent a constant light jolt over my lower half. My legs twitched as I struggled to pull them back into the station, but after a stressful moment, I was able to calm down.

I moved away from the energy field, looking for a spot to attach my rope. I quickly found a manual handle lever for the bay doors, and I clamped an end to it, tugging it to make sure the connection was solid. After triple-checking it was firmly clasped to my suit, I moved back toward the exit, craning my neck to see the closest station piece, which would play the middle of the station once all three were connected.

I couldn't tell how far away it was, but it seemed much farther than I could reach with these paltry ropes, even if I could get my trajectory right. I was confident I could find a spot to attach one to, but the trick was going to be arranging them so that I could grab them using a pyramid ship.

"Worry about that afterwards," I said to myself.

I ensured my pulse rifle was firmly secured and shook my head back and forth, giving my brain a quick reset. I could do this. I wasn't afraid of being in space. I'd be back home soon, and all of this would be behind us.

Not entirely convinced, I took a deep breath, exhaling through the strange Theos-designed filter mask, and pulled out through the containment field, the energy tingling through my body as I entered it.

I was out of the station. The EVA had a built-in temperature adjuster, and I didn't even notice the cold, nor had I when I'd been inside. I hoped they also had radiation protection. For all I knew, I was being blasted with some serious rads.

Pushing the concern to the back of my mind, I focused. When my foot touched the outer metal wall of the station, it pulled down, sticking to the surface. This was new.

"A built-in magboot. That's cool." I stepped down with the other foot, and it pulled toward the flat veneer. With a little effort, I lifted my left leg up, breaking the tension seal, and stepped forward. I repeated it, like a toddler first learning to walk. Soon I had a system, and I was walking along the outside of the station, a man on a mission.

The hangar went on for a way, and when I made it to the edge, I decided that would be far enough to attach one of the ropes. Before I went any further, I took a moment to look around. From my vantage point, the water planet beyond was staring straight at me. It was mesmerizing to watch as immense soft white clouds swirled in a dance.

With a tilt of my head, I scanned over to the station piece nearest me and swore I could see someone in the window of the closest section's corridor. From this distance, there was no way to see anything more than a dark outline.

"Mary. Slate. Come in." I had to give it a chance.

"Dean?" A feminine reply came through crystal-clear.

"Mary? Oh, thank God." My whole body tensed up in excitement at hearing my wife's voice.

The Ancients

"Where are you?" she asked, her voice choking up instantly. I could picture her eyes welling up and her chin quivering just slightly, like it always did when she was caught off-guard with emotion.

"I'm outside."

"Outside? Are you on the planet?" she asked, the first word a shout.

"No. I'm walking on this hunk of busted-up space station. I'm on the one farthest from the star. Which one are you on?"

A pause. My stomach dropped, thinking I'd lost the connection. Just as I was about to repeat my question, she answered, "I'm in the middle. I think I can see you!" The excitement was back in her voice.

"Do you know what it is we're doing?" I asked, hoping she'd figured it out.

"Making the station whole again?" She asked it like a question that didn't need to be answered. "Just how are you thinking of doing that?"

"You first," I said, curious to hear her plan.

"I was going to wait for Slate to figure it out and do it for us," she said, and I laughed. It felt like a while since I'd smiled like that, and my cheeks hurt.

"Good plan." I could see her now in the corridor window, and she waved at me. I waved back, a tiny stick man waving a stick arm.

"Seriously, though? I was going to get into a ship and try to find you. What was your plan?"

"I'm out here attaching some heavy-duty tow ropes so I can latch on to it with a modified ship, and then I was going to drag it over to your section. From there, we'll have to set it in place. At this angle, I can see how they would fit together."

The corners of the hangar section stuck out in a V shape, and the whole square had a lip a yard tall. I got this view as I leaned forward, looking around the side of the space I was standing on. They couldn't connect where the hangar doors opened. I realized it wouldn't matter who was the top and who was the bottom. Their symbol could be flipped, and it would still look the same.

"I love it. Do you know how to fly one of them yet?" she asked.

I laughed again. "I've been a little too busy to learn. Let me guess, you're self-taught?"

"Best damned pilot in the system. Or maybe the tablet with the clues on it had a training video."

"You have to be kidding me. I didn't get that far." I'd been so preoccupied with getting here, I hadn't taken the time to see if the tablet held any other secrets. Evidently, it did.

"Why can't we talk with Slate?"

"I'm thinking there's a block when two of us are inside, or maybe he's too far away. I really can't tell you for sure," I replied.

"Should I get outside and try to reach him?"

I pondered it for a moment. "I'll set up the ropes, then we can decide." With one rope clamped down, I made the slow walk around the perimeter, making sure to keep one foot magnetically locked onto the metal station's outer shell.

"Dean," Mary said with a lingering question that didn't come.

"Yes?" I attached the clasp at the end of the rope to the other corner. I now had a loop I could catch. It reminded me of the wire on the back of a cheap painting. I just needed to attach the nail to the bottom of the small pyramid ship, if necessary.

"Are we going to get through this okay?" Her energy sounded wilted. The wide-eyed, excited Mary at the start of this quest was giving way to the exhausted, upset Mary. I was right beside her in that feeling.

"I think so. Look how far we've come in...what? Two days?" I honestly had no idea how long we'd been gone from New Spero.

"This place. The isolation...it had me thinking. I couldn't live without you. At first, not being able to contact you..."

"I know, babe. We're in this together. All of it. Not just this crazy mission, but life." I stood still, watching the station Mary was floating inside, wishing I was there with her to hold her, to kiss her neck and smooth her hair while her breath caressed my cheek.

"I'm sorry I dragged you into this. I don't know what came over me. I got so excited, but right now, I just want to be home. At our farmhouse outside Terran One, not Earth. I miss it."

Mary typically wasn't so open about her feelings. I knew she loved me, but no one would ever call her sappy. "I do too. We'll be home soon, then we can relax. I know we keep saying it, but I mean it this time. We can tell Sarlun and the Gatekeepers we need a break."

"What about the Unwinding?"

"What about it? When did that message even come from? A thousand years ago? Longer?" I made my way back toward the containment field.

"Maybe it explains the outer reaches you saw emptied. The world where you and Slate met Suma could have evacuated because of this Unwinding."

"They could have left for any number of reasons. Speculating won't help us get home. I'm heading back inside. Can you help me fly one of these things?" I used my first rope and pulled on it, through the energy field one more time and into the station.

"I can. Then you can pull that hunk of junk over here, and we can get one part done. If I know Slate, he'll either have this solved or he's currently shooting something on his station."

I unclasped my anchor rope and pushed against the ceiling, heading back down to the ground at a medium pace, feet first. It was time to fly out of here.

"I'm getting in," I said, looking for a handle.

"Dean…" Mary's voice trembled slightly.

"What is it?" I quickly asked.

"We're not alone. A ship just arrived."

TWENTY-ONE

*T*he ship that arrived wasn't much more than a dot, and I was surprised Mary could even make it out from her window. But she was right. Mary had explained how the tutorial on the tablet worked, and in ten minutes, I felt confident enough to have a passing ability at maneuvering this small pyramid ship from point A to point B. The tricky part was seeing if the ropes would hold, and lining up the landing gear to snag the floating tether.

"Are we pretending it doesn't exist?" Mary asked. She was concerned with the visitor.

"Like I said, it might be them." I didn't have to say who "they" were. "This could be it. The final countdown. Let's get the task done and move on."

"There are five sections before their homeworld. They said to follow the map. The cube map had five symbols before theirs."

I was hovering in the ship, just about to exit the station, and I bumped the ceiling lightly as I tried to make it to the containment field unscathed. "Damn it!" I said, louder than I planned. With both our hangar doors open, we were still able to communicate. There was still no sign from Slate.

"What?"

"Nothing." I let her conversation slide and lifted out of the station. The inside of the ship was abnormal. I'd flown the landers on New Spero a few times, but this was nothing like them.

I was lying down, totally enclosed in the ship, with no viewports. A large screen was above my face, displaying all angles of the ship outside. The forward view was centered on the viewscreen, the side and rears on the edges. It was confusing at first, but I guessed by the time you were used to it, it was effective. The controls were in a strange spot, and I wondered what the biology of the native users was like.

My hands already wanted to cramp as I adjusted the thrusters and direction, each independently, on opposite sides of the cockpit. I narrowly managed to avoid clipping the hangar roof as I slowly urged the ship closer to the hanging rope loop. I felt the ship tug at the rope as the landing feet passed over it, but it slid free.

"I missed the first run. Why am I doing this again?" I asked, half joking.

"Good question. It seemed to make the most sense, but now that you mention it..." She let the jab go without finishing it.

I spun the ship around and tried again. After missing it for seven straight attempts, I was ready to give up.

"One more time," Mary said calmly. I closed my eyes and took a breath, lowering down from my previous positions. The rope hung in space, like that wire from the back of the painting, and this time, I ran the front of the ship into it, letting it slip underneath. My ship jarred as it pulled tight.

"Got it!" I called, getting prematurely excited. I still didn't know if this little thing had enough juice to get the station moving. If I went out and tried to push the station with my arms, I would just float away. But the thrusters acted as my forward energy, and when I fired them up, the ship pulled on the rope, which carried the station with it. "It's working."

I moved slowly, because stopping it at the other end would be a hell of a task if I raced over there. I inched along, sweating more with each passing second inside the cramped cockpit.

"Steady." Mary repeated the phrase a few times. As I neared, I saw her form on the viewscreen, standing locked onto her station hangar roof, wearing the thin EVA. She was tethered securely in case something went wrong.

Moving along at a turtle's speed, the station followed me, and soon I was cutting the thrusters entirely, letting the inertia carry us forward. I had to line up the sides, where they would fit together. Her end was the plug, and mine the receptacle. We just had to time it perfectly.

"Dean, I don't want to alarm you, but our new friend is moving," Mary said, her voice under control. She didn't want to panic me.

"Is it coming toward us?" I looked at my viewscreen, checking the side and rear views. None of them showed the recently-arrived ship. It was still out of my proximity.

These ships weren't equipped with any long-range sensors, but they did have weapons, which the quick tutorial didn't detail.

"It was, but it looks like it's taking the long way around. It's still far enough away."

"But close enough for you to have a visual. That's closer than I'd like."

"Don't worry about it. Just finish the task. You need to pull down a few degrees. We have to do this by eyeball, so stick to the plan."

Our plan was relying on my brain's spatial mapping skills, which didn't fill me with confidence. But I had no choice. It was either crash this thing and end up stuck here with no food and water while waiting for our friend to destroy us, or I landed the pieces together, and we move on to work with Slate and get out of here.

I tilted the stick while giving the slightest thrust from my left side. This gave the desired effect, and the prongs rubbed against Mary's middle station piece just enough to cause her to cry out.

"Are you okay?" I asked her.

"I'm fine. Just about lost my footing. You're there!" she said, and I could make out her peeking head on the side viewscreen feed.

The large hangar sections merged, magnets taking over when they were feet apart. The force pulled the rope I was attached to taut, and my ship tugged backward with it, sending me and my ship floating into the side of the station.

I didn't care. I'd done it! I'd connected the top piece

of the space station with the middle. Now we needed to focus on Slate's section.

"I don't mean to cut your celebration short, but the bogey is heading for Slate," Mary said, and I found the landing controls, recessing them. The rope fell free from the ship, and I flew toward Mary, making sure to stay well enough away that my ineptitude at controlling it didn't threaten her safety.

"Get into a ship; we need to get over there." She was already moving before the suggestion was out of my mouth.

I flew toward the last piece of station that would complete our puzzle, moving slowly so Mary could catch up.

"Slate!" I called into my mic.

"Dean?" His voice carried as I closed in on his perimeter.

"Slate, are you all right?"

"I'm fine. There's nothing here to harm me, is there? Other than boredom, maybe."

"There's a ship coming toward you – "

"What kind of ship?" he asked, cutting me off.

I zoomed in with my viewscreen, now able to see a pixelated version of the bogey. It was probably smaller than our Kraski ships, with tendrils extending from the rear and front of it, reminding me of an insect. I'd seen its kind before. "This may sound crazy, but I think it's one of the insectoid ships from Leslie and Terrance's planet." There had been a couple that had landed on their world over the course of our visits, but the race behind them hadn't reached out to us. They seemed closed off, and unwilling to converse with humans.

After the rumors, and the harsh treatment of the hybrids, I wasn't sure they ever would. Now, in some remote part of the galaxy, one of their ships was here. My gut wanted to think they were here to help us, but my brain told me otherwise.

"Slate, is your hangar open?" I asked, watching the insectoid ship lower near Slate's hangar doors.

"Yeah. I was about to bust out of here, to look for you two. I figured it out. We need to..."

"Connect the pieces, we know. The other two are already attached."

His laughter passed through my earpiece, and I could picture his goofy grin. "Of course they are. Dean and Mary are at it again. Come help me and let's get out of here."

"Aren't you forgetting something?" I looked at the ship, which was just hovering there quietly. Were they waiting to talk?

"Oh, them? What should we do? I've always been a shoot first kind of guy." Slate's voice was tense now, unsure.

"Let's see if there's a way to communicate with them," I said, but it was too late. "Slate, close the doors!" Two figures were dropping from the ship, thrust packs aiming them directly for his hangar entrance.

"Boss, I'm on it."

"No, Slate, leave it open." I heard Mary's voice at the same time I saw her race by me in her own ship. She didn't hesitate as she flew the pyramid ship at breakneck speeds toward the containment field the two figures had just dropped into. Her ship arced nose up before diving directly down into the station's open hangar doors.

"Be careful, Mary," I called, but she was already gone. I swallowed a dry gulp of air as I chased after her. I slowed the ship, wondering if one of us should stay out and watch their vessel. I also had no idea how to use the weapons on this thing, so I elected to assist on the station. I knew how to fire my pulse rifle.

"They're here," Slate said, and I lowered my ship into the hangar bay, the energy field glimmering around my viewscreens as I passed through. I was moving too fast, so instead of slowly landing, I aimed for the corner of the room, hitting the ground hard between two other parked ships. I'd forgotten the landing gear in my haste.

The landing jarred my head, and shouting carried into my earpiece from both Mary and Slate. As I opened the pyramid ship door, the sound of pulse fire erupted around the room.

"Where are they?" I asked, staying low to the ground. I unslung my rifle, ready to take the invaders down.

"We're by the control panel. Mary split the room when she rushed inside. She nearly clipped one of them with her ship," Slate said, and I peered over the rows of ships, seeing the pulse-damaged walls above their location.

A beam of orange light passed over my head, causing me to roll behind one of the many pyramid ships lining the hangar floor. "Slate, buddy, this is a good time to shoot first," I said, and he gave me some cover fire, allowing me time to rush over to their side of the room.

Slate and Mary were there, and my heart melted at the sight of my wife safely in front of me. I wanted nothing more than to get her the hell out of there, but we had to stop the insectoids from killing us first. She gave me a quick smile before firing her bow toward the far side of the hangar. The arrow stuck in the wall with a flash of light.

For a moment, the room went silent. No talking, no pulse fire, just silence. My ragged breath was all I heard.

Slate lifted his rifle and took off along the wall at a crouched run. Mary went the other way, and I followed behind her. Our boots clanged lightly, and I hoped we weren't giving away our positions. Another orange beam passed above us, but we kept going.

More pulse fire, and a grunt from Slate in my ear. "Boss, I got him. The other one turned away. He's heading for you."

Mary knelt. Half her body was covered by a crate in the corner of the room. We were near the corridor entrance, and when the insectoid entered our line of sight, it stood straight up as it spotted us. Instead of firing, it moved for the doorway.

"Crap, come on," Mary said, running after it.

"Wait!" I called to her, worried it was an ambush. Instead, I arrived to see the creature face-down on the metal grate floor. It was only then I realized there was gravity inside the station. I'd been running on adrenaline. A wave of vertigo coursed over me as Mary stood over her fallen

The Ancients

advisory, bow with nocked arrow raised and ready to go.

"Hold on," I said, kicking its fallen gun out of its reach. I knelt beside the alien, noting how it was the same race as the ones we'd briefly met when we'd first followed the hybrids to Kareem's world.

I pushed it over, revealing a hard-helmeted head, pinchers, and antenna accentuated with painted designs. Through a tinted face mask, a multitude of black eyes looked back at me. It tried to lift an arm but failed. The sound of its hand hitting the floor was jarring in the otherwise quiet corridor.

"What do you want?" I asked, suddenly drained of energy. My voice was a whisper.

"Theos," a tinny voice said, speaking our language.

I grabbed it by the collar, lifting it off the ground a foot. "What about them?"

"Don't..." It was dying, and the words were hardly more than a rasp.

I needed to hear what they'd come here for. "How did you find us? Don't do what?"

"Don't wake..." It coughed, an alien sound like the mash-up of a cricket and human. "...them." For effect, its hand gripped me weakly on the arm.

I set it down carefully. They wanted to warn us? "Don't wake them?"

It twitched, and I let it be.

"It's dead, Dean," Mary said.

Slate walked up behind us, gun tight in his hand. "They might have more coming for us. The ship, remember?"

I hadn't remembered.

"I found a camera system." Slate led the way from the hall, and I glanced back at the body as the door to the corridor slid shut. They'd come to warn us about the Theos. Why did they come with guns firing? If they could speak English, why not talk first? Unless the easiest way to make sure we didn't find the Theos was to kill us and move on. No one would be the wiser as to what happened. They'd just think we were killed during our journey to find the ancient race.

Mary kept an eye on the hangar door as I ran to the controls on the wall. The doors began sliding shut, sealing us off from the insectoid ship.

"Over here." Slate was by the offices. He was changing cameras and looking for the invaders' ship. "It's gone. What in the hell's going on here?"

"They came to warn us. It was a drop-off," Mary said, staring at the screens.

"But why leave them?" I asked, confused by the whole thing.

"I wish we could ask them." Mary was leaving the room, and I followed her to the one Slate had felled. It was clearly dead as well.

"Let's finish this and get out of here. Any fun we were having on this trek is gone for me," Mary said.

"Fun? Yeah, this was loads of fun until now." The sarcasm dripped off my words.

TWENTY-TWO

*I*t turned out Slate's section of the station was indeed the rear, or "bottom" as I thought of it, and the gravity drive was intact, as well as small thrusters on the end. This allowed us to fly it to the other two connected parts of the station. In an hour, we were latching on, completing the puzzle.

"Good work, Mary," Slate said from his seat beside her control desk, where she flew the oversized letter T. The station shook as we attached, and the dim lights brightened as everything became fully operational.

"Now what?" she asked. I think we all expected some big show of success, but we were left sitting in the room in complete silence.

"Land below. That's what it had said. Then the Final will be upon us." I reached for the tablet that was now vibrating on the desk in front of me. A planet appeared on the screen: the water planet we were orbiting. The image zoomed toward the water and kept zooming until I saw a speck of land. Soon the island took most of the screen up, and coordinates scrolled below it.

"I guess that answers our question." Slate stood up

fast, his chair noisily clattering behind him.

"Does it? Are we supposed to take the station down there, or the pyramid ships?" I asked.

Mary tapped a gloved finger on the desk's surface thoughtfully. "That island doesn't look large enough for the station to land on."

She was right. It was deceiving with nothing but water around it, but when you looked closely, it was obvious it wasn't very large. "Then we take the small ships."

I lowered my ship toward the rocky mass, at last recognizing it as I got closer. It was the same island I'd seen when the Theos shadow had first touched me back in Sarlun's room full of artifacts. There was no mistaking it now.

My screens showed Slate and Mary had already landed. They were both better pilots than I was. I bumbled my way down, this time remembering to use the landing gear.

I hit the door release, and it slid open. A breeze blew around me, and I wanted nothing more than to take my mask off and take a deep breath. I couldn't do that quite yet. I was amazed at how familiar it felt, standing the thousand or so feet above the crashing waves below. It had only been a few days since I'd been there, but that time, it was all in my mind. I expected it to feel more solid, more real now, but it didn't. It seemed exactly the

The Ancients

same.

"Dean, is this..." Mary started to ask.

"It's the same island." I cut her off. It was strange to see Mary and Slate in their EVAs in the sunlight like this. The masks glimmered as light and sky reflected off their shiny surfaces. Mary's eyes were wide, and the three of us walked near the edge, casting our gazes toward the horizon. The sea of blue went on forever in all directions, giving me a sense of loneliness on the waterlogged planet.

This must be it. The Final had arrived, just as the Theos shadow had warned, or urged, depending on how you looked at it. I was ready for it to be over. Slate's shoulders slumped, and I knew he was on the same page as me. He'd only come along to protect us.

"It's beautiful," Mary said, and even though being there shot a series of emotions through my mind, she was right. Even from that distance, I noticed something moving in the water and pointed it out to them. A black form raced along the water's surface, longer than any sea creature on Earth. The tail end of it emerged and splashed down, sending a burst of water into the air.

"It's huge," Slate said, stepping forward to get a better view. I grabbed his arm and he looked down, scrambling back when he noticed he was only inches from the edge of the island. To fall from there meant certain death. If you didn't die from the fall, the waves crashing onto the cliff walls below would finish the job.

"What now?" I asked. As if answering me, rock crumbled behind us, directly in the center of the island.

"I hope it stops." Mary's voice had a panicked edge to

it.

Once again, on cue, it ceased the internal cave-in, revealing crudely carved stairs covered by large mossy boulders.

"Ladies first," Slate said, grinning at Mary.

"You wish. What do you think we brought you for, Zeke? Cannon fodder. What's the saying, Dean?" Mary jibed back.

"Youth before beauty? That would fit in this case," I said, getting a light punch on the upper arm from Slate.

"Yeah, yeah. Send the big guy in first. I feel like the canary in the mine shaft." Slate still grinned but turned from us, taking a step onto the carved-out stairs. "There are lights down here."

"Mary, whatever happens, let's stick together and get home."

She looked me in the eyes as water brimmed along the bottoms of her lids. "Dean, I think I'm ready."

"Ready for what?" I asked.

"That family we talked about. All of this has opened something inside me. I don't know why I was so gung-ho to do this adventure. Maybe I just felt like I needed a last hoorah before becoming a mother."

I grabbed her hand, the glove on glove contact not enough to connect us like I wanted. "I get it. We've been through so much. Some painful, and some exciting and rewarding. I'm ready too." My heart leapt in my chest, and I imagined Mary and I blowing bubbles in our backyard with a little baby on a blanket. Maggie would chase the bubbles along with our child, and it would end with

The Ancients

us all rolling on the grass.

"Then let's finish this," she said, taking her first step down into the center of the island.

"You guys really need to remember I can hear everything you say," Slate said, tapping his helmet where the earpiece sat.

I couldn't even bring myself to be embarrassed. "You're family. It comes with the territory."

With a last glance at the sunny sky, I headed down the steps, ready for the final challenge.

The stairs spiraled downwards, and we kept moving along them. There were glowing crystals merged into the walls every few yards, allowing us ample light to see where we were going. We didn't speak as we climbed down, just marched at a solid pace. It must have been five minutes before the staircase ended, opening into a room.

"What the hell is this?" Slate asked, crossing the sterile space toward the far side, where three chairs stood. They reminded me of dentist's office chairs, the kind that leaned back to a full one hundred and eighty degrees. Otherwise, the room was carved out of the island rock, like the spiral stairs had been.

We each stood at the base of one of the chairs, looking at them. The material was strange, silky but stiff at the same time.

"Who wants to go first?" Mary asked.

"Go where?" I asked, still poking the chair with a finger. I watched as the material sank in, then slowly rose back up to its original form.

Mary didn't answer. Instead, she hopped on the chair

and lay back on it. "Kind of comfy. I could use a nap..." She closed her eyes, smiling. They darted open, wide and afraid. She let out a stifled cry, her whole body rigid and taut for an instant before it fell back on the chair like a marionette without its puppeteer.

"Mary!" I ran to her side, grabbing her hand. Our suits were alien enough, I had no idea if they read vitals or not. I noticed a drop of blood on the gray chair, behind her head, and knelt beside her. "Slate, look at this."

He knelt on the other side of her and saw the same thing I did: a wire going into the back of her head. "Damned Theos. What do we do?"

Her chest rose and lowered slowly, a weak but constant breath. "I think she's okay. This must be the last part of our journey. We have to plug in to find out."

"You sure this is a good idea, boss?"

I shook my head. "I'm not sure of anything, but I can't leave Mary to do this herself. You stay here and guard our bodies."

Slate looked frazzled, but he grabbed his pulse rifle, moving to perch himself between the chairs and the stairway. "I don't like the sounds of that either, but I'll do it for you guys. Hurry back."

I gave Mary's hand a last squeeze and stood by the chair beside her, leaving the end one open. I felt the back of my helmet, noticing a small circle on it. They had planned on connecting us here. The suit was made for it. This was it. The final chapter before we got the location of their homeworld. Love or hate the Theos, we were damned close to finding them.

"Finish this thing, boss." Slate nodded toward my wife's still form. "And bring her back with you."

"I will. Hopefully, we'll be back soon." I didn't think the Theos would do anything to harm us while we were linked to the chairs, but I couldn't be certain. The idea of letting something jab me in the back of the head to force me unconscious didn't excite me. My hands trembled as I sat down, and with one last look over at Mary, I leaned back.

I expected the sudden stabbing feeling, but it still caught me off-guard. I let out a loud enough yelp that Slate rushed over. The last thing I saw was his worried face, upside down.

TWENTY-THREE

A radio announcer talked in a low constant buzz, and I opened my eyes, looking for the source. My clock radio alerted me it was seven AM. I'd slept in. Wait. For what? Something was wrong. I jolted up, flushed panic making me far too warm under the blankets. I pushed them off, recognizing my old room the instant I focused.

I found the pull chain on my bedside lamp, turning it on. It was a fake Tiffany lamp. Janine had found it at a garage sale for what she'd dubbed "the bargain price of the year." Memories flooded my brain as I tried to make sense of what I was seeing.

Light poured in lines between my white blinds, casting striped shadows on my wall. Where had I been? I shook my head, trying to free the cobwebs, but it wasn't coming back.

"No one has an explanation for the ships, but we expect the president to make a statement soon. Please do not panic," Rollie Armstrong said with a slight tremor in his voice.

Ships? Images flashed in my mind of large black vessels hanging over New York City; of smaller, sleek silver ships over my hometown. The Kraski! I remembered

The Ancients

them now. An overflow of missing details forced themselves into my confused mind, causing my vision to swim. I leaned back, pushing a pillow over my face to ease the pain.

Eventually, they subsided, and I knew this wasn't real. I'd already lived this day. I was sent here to do something, I just didn't know what. My breath slowed as the anxiety and stress eased from my tight muscles, my headache now just a dull throb.

I rolled off the bed, carefully stepping over the slippers I knew would be there. With eyes mostly closed, I crossed to my en suite bathroom and washed my face. The reflection caught me off-guard as water dripped down my chin. I looked so young. It was me from this day in the past. The real me was a few years older; more gray speckled my hair, deeper lines carved in my face. Mary called them laugh lines, but it felt like a long time since I'd laughed enough to make some.

Mary. Flashes of her beautiful face flipped through my mind like a stack of Polaroids being dropped from the sky. I saw her the first time she'd knocked on the Jeep window, just after the silver ship had nearly scared us to death. I saw her piloting one of those ships as we rescued humanity from its doom near the sun. A picture of her wearing a gorgeous dress for Magnus and Natalia's wedding appeared, making way for an image of her as we sat hiding from the rain on Kareem's world. Her hair was wet, goosebumps rising on her pale skin as a breeze carried through our pitiful shelter. Then our wedding night, resplendent in white. All of these shots came and went.

She was here somewhere. I knew it. That was my mission.

With new energy, I threw on some pants, amused at how accurate the scene was. The jeans fit me just like they had, and the knees had exactly the right amount of fade. Throwing a short-sleeved button-up plaid shirt over my tank top, I headed for the front door. I didn't even close it as I walked barefoot down my driveway. Just as I thought, Susan was there with Carey beside her.

My heart melted at seeing the young pup. He wiggled and came to say hi. I knelt down, petting him far more closely than the old me ever had. Susan studied me with a grin and asked, "What do you think they are, Dean?" I'd known she was going to say those exact words. It felt like a pre-emptive déjà vu.

I didn't say anything at first. I just stood and hugged her. I told her everything was going to be okay. For her, it wasn't, but if I could make her last day on Earth a little better, I wanted to. Carey barked at me as we embraced, and when I let go, Susan looked up at me with weepy eyes. She mouthed the words "Thank you" and turned back to stare at the ship in the sky.

I left her standing there. The weight of what was coming for Earth pushed me down, and my knees felt weak. I didn't want to live this again. I'd barely made it through the first time, and now I had to see it repeated. "Damn you!" I shouted as I entered my house. Theos. That was who'd done this to me. The recent quests came back to me now. How dare the self-righteous bastards do this to us?

The Ancients

If I ever did find them... I slumped down on my couch and ran my fingers through my hair. I didn't have an answer for it. I just wanted to get through this and get back to Mary and Slate, in my real life. The anger evaporated. It wasn't going to help me.

"No time to waste," I said, grabbing my keys. This time, I threw some shoes on and left my house, firing up my old truck. It felt good to be driving it again. Some things you did miss when they were gone. Earth was gone now too, so I vowed to let myself enjoy these aspects of the mission I was on. I counted myself grateful to be able to visit Earth again, Earth before everyone was ripped from it, changing our paths forever.

Of all the worlds I'd been to, none of them compared to being home, and that was where I'd found myself. I just needed to get to Mary and figure out what that meant.

I passed the same church I had all those years ago and slowed as my client Steve waved at me. Today, I kept driving, not making way for small talk. It came to me that I never did find out if Steve survived the Event. There was so much I didn't know. If I made it home to New Spero, I was going to look into it.

I needed to reconnect with my old life to complete my new one. I'd been treating them as separate entities, but they both made me who I was. It didn't have to be broken down into pre-Event and post-Event. It could just be my life.

I took another direction, bypassing the backed-up traffic I knew was on the main drag, leaving James and his fender-bender behind. I silently wished my old friend the best and made for the storage unit. It wasn't long before I had the pendant around my neck. If this really was a replay of that day, I wasn't going to be beamed away with everyone.

What was I going to do? I nearly crashed into a car parked in the middle of the street as an idea came to me. I swerved to the side of the road and parked, seeing a sobbing teenage girl in the stopped car.

I pulled my cell phone from my pocket and dialed information. "Mary Lafontaine in Washington, please."

"There is no Mary Lafontaine listed, sir."

"How about Bob or Robert Lafontaine?"

"Please hold, connecting."

The phone rang, a land line still active. Mary hadn't changed the name on the bill, and I hoped she was still home.

"Hello," a very familiar voice answered.

"Mary, it's me," I said, relief flooding through me.

"Dean?" she asked, and tears came to me in the blink of an eye. I hadn't been sure my real Mary would be there. I'd worried she was stuck in her own version of that day.

"Of course it's Dean."

She laughed; not a calm, funny sound, but the kind when you're so happy, the laughter merges with crying to make the perfect heart-warming sound no one wants to share. "I was so worried and confused. How did they do this?"

"I don't know. But we need to get together. How

quick can we meet up?"

"The roads are looking bad, but nowhere near as backed up as they are this afternoon. I'll start driving now. Let's meet outside Philly." She named a small town I hadn't heard of. It was close enough to a main highway but had access via a less busy road, should the traffic get too congested.

"This is weird, isn't it?" I asked. I could hear her starting a car and noticed the sound change as she switched to hands-free.

"It is. I miss you, and it's only been an hour since I saw you. Being here, in this place, is so odd. As much as we all talk about our old lives, I'm much happier with my new one with you."

I threw my truck in drive and turned it around, leaving my phone on speaker. My truck didn't have Bluetooth, so I cranked the volume up and set the phone upside down in my cup holder. "Mary, just who are we dealing with here? What kind of race could send us back to Earth? Everything we've seen tells me they're literally conducting this from beyond the proverbial grave. How could they send us to this specific time?"

She was silent for a few moments, and just when I was going to make sure the call hadn't dropped, she spoke. "I've got it!" I could sense her enthusiasm from a few hundred miles away. "They didn't know where they were sending us. Their program locked into our minds, and sent us to the most traumatic, life-changing day of our lives."

"To what end?" I asked.

"That I don't know. Maybe they just want to see how we deal with it. I expect a message or hint at some point. They've given us one every other time." I could hear someone honking loudly from the other end of the call.

"Everything okay there?" I asked, raising my voice so she could hear over the racket.

"I forgot what jerks people could be. Some guy just rammed into a parked car, and now there's a full-out melee going on. Was it really like this?" she asked.

It had been much worse in a lot of cases. The horror stories of what happened that day, on Earth and then on the vessels, would linger with me for life. I remembered hearing some of the things that people had done to one another, and it took me a week to get out of the hotel room once we were back. I had seriously regretted saving everyone. Part of me thought the universe might have been better off without us. Mary had talked me down at that point in time, reminding me of all the good stories, of the countless heroic and selfless acts hundreds and thousands of people had done.

"Dean?" Mary asked, and I realized I hadn't replied. My heart was racing again; the repressed trauma from that time was trying to surface. I took a long swallow of water and decided to cork the pain for a little while longer.

"Humans are stronger than ever, and this may be a reminder, but it isn't who we are anymore. Maybe this is our lesson."

"I hope so. Keep me posted on your progress. I'm going to double back and hit the other way out of town. Things are hectic here. You're farther from Philly, but I bet you beat me there."

She was probably right. I would avoid any major cities on my route, but on a good day, she would still beat me by an hour. Today wasn't a good day. "I'll call you in an hour, unless something goes awry."

"I can't wait to see you, babe," Mary said.

"Right back at you." The call ended, and I looked up to the west, catching the sun glimmer off the silver ship above my hometown. Shivers ran down my spine, and I turned to focus on the road. I had an arduous drive ahead of me.

TWENTY-FOUR

The diner's lights were still on, telling me this was the one place in town that was open for business. Mary was beside me, worry lines creasing her forehead as we pulled into the parking lot. I'd beaten her by an hour, as she'd guessed, but the fact was, we were both there, together in the past.

"It's hard to believe we're not really here. That our bodies are inside a rock amidst a water-covered world." Mary smiled at me from the passenger seat of my truck. She'd suggested we ditch her SUV, saying it was originally Bob's, and that she'd rather leave it behind. I agreed.

"Wherever we really are, my body's telling me to eat something." I was surprised at the urgency of my hunger.

There was only one other car parked in front of the diner, where a sign flashed "All Day Breakfast" from behind a smudged window pane. Chimes rang as I pushed the door open, holding it for Mary to enter first. My gut instinct was to have a gun when entering an unknown room. I shoved this feeling down as a smiling elderly couple greeted us.

"Are you guys open?" Mary asked them.

The Ancients

"Seven days a week," the man said, revealing a gap where he was missing a tooth.

"Even today?" I prompted.

"Even today," the man's short wife said. She watched us from behind large rhinestone-lined glasses as we walked inside and took a seat at a booth along the window. Music from the Fifties played through crackling speakers, and the smell of the place reminded me of every diner I'd ever been inside. It was comforting.

"What's on the menu?" I asked, feeling my stomach grumble again. I fidgeted with the condiments, then the salt and pepper shakers, before tapping one of those little jam packets.

The lady was already moving for our table, carrying a pot of black coffee. Mary and I flipped our cups and let her fill them. I read her nametag, which said "Esther" in capital letters. "Since it's just Cleve and me today, we could do up some eggs and hash. Side of bacon?"

Mary answered for us. "That sounds perfect." Cleve had already begun to turn toward the kitchen as she spoke.

"How are they going to communicate with us? I keep expecting a text from the Theos, giving us directions." I sat my dark-screened phone on the old faux wood table top. I took a sip of my coffee and couldn't believe how good it was. New Spero had a lot of amenities, but good, old-school roasted beans were getting harder and harder to find. A lot of smaller backyard growers and then roasters were starting to pop up. There was always a market for coffee, no matter what the circumstances.

Mary finally took a drink from hers and closed her eyes, taking a deep breath of the steaming cup before gulping down more. "That's amazing. But to answer your question, I was thinking the same thing. Cell phone. But who knows with them? They have a mist-man telling us what to do next most of the time. I think their way of communicating may be different than ours."

I laughed at her term for what I'd dubbed the "shadow man" in my head. I liked "mist-man" too. "Hopefully we don't have to wait long. I don't really want to stay here any longer than I have to."

Mary looked contemplative. "What is it, Mary?" I asked.

She started, then paused, instead taking another drink from her cup, this time a sip. "Doesn't Ray live in Pittsburgh?"

Her question nearly took the air from my lungs. Up until now, I hadn't been thinking of the others. Magnus and Natalia were here too. They had a head start on the details, so they were probably already starting their journey to South America.

"He does live there," I said quietly. It started to rain outside, a light patter of drops hitting the window as the breeze carried them toward the building. "Mary, I think I need to go see him."

"I'm not sure..." She was cut off by the approach of Cleve and Esther, carrying plates of food. They set them down with a clatter, and I looked down to see food piled high, with about the worst presentation I'd ever seen, even from a small-town diner.

The Ancients

The two of them lingered longer than I expected, and I looked up to meet Cleve's gaze. I pushed myself back in the booth seat, startled by what I saw. Black mist coalesced through his eyes, pouring out of his sockets and dissipating into the air. Esther's were doing the same.

"What are you?" I asked, raising a hand to Mary, who looked ready to attack them with a butter knife.

"We are Theos," the elderly couple said in unison.

"Why here? Why this time?" I kept the questions coming.

"You chose this place, not us." They still spoke at the same time, though not quite perfectly aligned, so there was a slight echo.

"How did we choose it?"

"We programmed it to bring you to the most significant day of your lives. We didn't expect two beings to choose the same time and place. This is…curious." Mist continued to dance in their eyes.

"What are we supposed to do? How do we pass this event?" I got goosebumps at my own use of the word *event*. There would only be one true event in our lives, and that was the traumatic encounter with the Kraski and Deltra. Even the Bhlat battle and the eventual loss of Earth didn't impact us to the same degree, at least not psychologically. Humans were a hardier breed now, and on the other end of the spectrum, we were also a more nurturing and loving race.

"You must succumb to your biggest fear. Change your actions." Esther and Cleve stood side by side, she a full head shorter than her husband. I briefly wondered if they'd survived the original Event, but chances were they hadn't made it. My heart hurt at the thought.

"What's our biggest fear?" Mary asked them, and they shrugged in a very human way.

"That is for only you to know. Face this fear, and you will pass. Our home will become accessible." They turned, walking away, leaving us with our unappetizing cold food and a lot to think about.

"This is it, Dean. Our last stage." Mary poked at a runny over-easy egg, and after putting some pepper on it, she took a bite. I smiled at her, at how well she was taking all of this. I decided to eat something too.

"Face our fears. On this day of all days. It can only mean one thing." I squirted some ketchup on my hash browns, the squelching sound the only noise in the whole restaurant.

"What?" Mary asked.

"We have to let them beam us up."

Mary spit out her mouthful of coffee as I said it. "We can't do that!" she yelled. "Sorry." She lowered her voice. "I'm not sure *I* can." She twisted a lock of hair between her fingers nimbly, avoiding eye contact.

"None of this is real. What are we afraid of...what *were* we afraid of?"

Mary looked at me doubtfully. "I was afraid of all of it, but brave when I needed to be. We were so busy and frantic, we didn't have much time to worry about what happened if we failed. Failing humanity...I think that's my biggest fear."

She was on the right track. "I believe that's it. We

The Ancients

have to let them beam us up. If we're beamed, do we win? No. We lose."

"What about the others?" she asked, referring to Magnus and Natalia, and even Ray.

"I wonder what would have happened. We haven't really talked about it before. Would they have stopped it? Teelon might have convinced them, though Magnus probably would have just shot everyone and turned the thing off. And Ray…" I left the sentence to linger there. I missed him. I'd only known him for a few days, but he was the kind of guy I could have been great friends with. I felt like I'd failed him too.

"We'll never know."

"Mary, if we're going to do this, I have to find Ray. I have to make things right and warn him."

Mary set down her fork and reached across the table, grabbing my hand in hers. "I agree."

"You do?" I thought she'd have some objection to spending our one afternoon there searching for our old friend.

"Yeah. I know how much it's bothered you." She looked ready to say more, to say that I was the one there wrestling him when his gun went off, killing him. But she didn't.

"Then let's get out of here and track him down." I reached into my wallet and tossed a twenty on the table. Esther and Cleve hadn't come out of the back yet, but it didn't matter. None of this was real.

The door chimes jingled as we passed through the exit, toward my truck. Dark clouds rolled through the sky, heavy over Philadelphia.

"Where did he live?" That I didn't know.

"We'll call information again." I handed Mary my cell phone as rain started to pour down around us.

She dialed the three digits and after a moment said, "Ray Jones. Pittsburgh." She looked at me and mouthed, "There are three Ray Jones."

"He worked at a place called Steel House. Try there?"

Mary asked for Steel House's phone number and was patched through. She clicked the speaker icon and we listened to the automated voice message system. When the option for reaching Ray Jones came through, she hit his three-digit extension.

The phone rang, and a gruff voice answered. "Hello?" he said it in the form of a question, like the idea anyone was calling him on a day where aliens were invading was absurd. He was right.

"Ray?" I asked as my heart began to race in my chest.

"Who is this?" he asked, his voice dripping with impatience.

"You don't know me, not yet, but…" I wasn't sure how to put it. I wished I'd thought of the conversation before calling. "We need to meet you. We have the green stones too. We're friends."

All we could hear was his breathing for a moment before he replied, "How do I know I can trust you?"

"You don't. My name's Dean Parker, and I have Mary Lafontaine" – I said her old last name without thinking about it, but she didn't even seem to notice – "and we lived this day already. We watched the whole world get

The Ancients

lashed into the ships and taken away. We traveled with you to Peru, where we stopped the invasion." I hesitated before saying the next thing; a lump was growing in my throat. "We were like brothers."

"Is this some sort of a prank? I don't know anyone named Dean, or Mary. What makes you think you can call me and make up this crazy story?"

"It may sound insane, but you know it's true. Kate knew about it, didn't she?" I asked.

He was angry now. "Don't you ever say her name again! You hear me? She doesn't get to be spoken about from the likes of you!"

I recoiled at the venom but tried to see the phone call from his perspective. "Kate knew my wife, Ray. She was at my wedding. Janine Parker." I let it sink in, and when he spoke again, his anger was gone.

"I'm sorry for snapping at you." He sounded deflated. "Dean, what's happening?"

"Meet us on seventy-six. You have to leave now. We don't have much time. They take everyone in less than six hours," I said, trying to sound confident.

"I can't just up and meet you, can I?"

"Ray, you have to. Believe me. You'll regret it otherwise. Do it for Kate," I said, hating that I had to use her name as bait.

He paused again. "I'm leaving now. My Jeep is already packed. Just tell me one thing. If you've been through this, do we make it out okay? Do we survive?"

"We do. Humans are survivors, Ray." Mary didn't hesitate. Telling him about his impending death wasn't going to help anything, though in this reality, that same outcome wasn't likely. I'd change that. It was my chance to redeem something I'd been carrying for years now.

"Good. I have your number. We'll keep in touch." Then, before he ended the call: "Dean, Mary, thanks for calling. I've been feeling so alone."

I felt his resolve change already. The scared man who did what he thought he had to do to save his family had adjusted his viewpoint on the situation. He now knew that our race would survive, and now he could focus on helping the right side.

"Maybe that was enough?" Mary said after the call was over.

I shook my head. "I need to see him."

Mary gave a light laugh. "What else do we have to do? We have a few hours until we let the Kraski beam us away."

TWENTY-FIVE

The sky was still black and stormy in this part of the country. We'd avoided listening to the radio, instead relying on our cell phone maps to show us the least densely-trafficked areas of the commuter highways. We'd had some success and arrived at the halfway mark as the clock hit five thirty in the afternoon. It had been seven o'clock when James was torn from my living room, giving us an hour and a half to meet and talk with Ray.

We were at a truck stop along the seventy-six. We'd taken the back route there, and I was glad after seeing the sheer volume of slow-moving traffic sitting on the main highway. Ray had heeded our advice and was traveling by the side roads heading east. His latest text said he was only minutes away.

I got out, seeing the "open" sign was turned off on the gas station. I took a moment to use their unlocked bathroom at the side of the building. The lights were off, and I propped the door open, using the kickdown foot attached to it. Inside, I caught another glimpse of my younger self in the mirror. I was more youthful, but I also felt sad thinking about myself at that point of my life.

I'd been so depressed and lonely. I'd spent my days by myself, sorting through other people's finances and business receipts. I never truly knew what it was to live until this day happened. When I met Ray, then Mary and Magnus and Natalia. Their zest for life and adventurous natures took me so far away from my shell, it was hard to remember a time when I'd constantly worn it as a protective cloak.

I wanted to trade in my reflection for the one I'd earned, with gray-lined hair and experience wrinkles. That was me, and I loved who I'd been forced to become. I used to hide my fears with jokes; now I made them because I was light-hearted.

"Dean, he's here," Mary called from the parking lot.

I dried my hands with paper towel and walked outside to see a Jeep pull up beside my truck. Ray looked over to us with skepticism, and tears filled my eyes at the sight of him. The last time I'd seen him, he was telling me what a good friend I was as blood spilled out of his body. Careless of what he thought, I ran over and hugged his wide chest.

He must have believed I was nuts as I embraced him tightly. "Whoa, buddy. I didn't know we were that kind of friends." He hugged me back, even though he didn't know me. It made me even more upset. I let him go, stepping back and wiping tears from my eyes. Mary went in and hugged him next.

"What are we supposed to do now?" he asked. He was wearing a black Steelers hoodie, and I nearly laughed at how classically *Ray* he was at that moment.

The Ancients

"We talk." The gas station had a rest area with picnic tables, and we headed over there, sitting down at one. Ray took one side, with Mary and I on the other. "Ray. Things are complicated. We aren't here for long. We aren't even sure if this is real or just a figment of a long-dead race's imagination. Either way, I needed to see you."

"What exactly happens to us?"

I looked at my phone and saw we had over an hour before the vessels took us. I was still wearing my pendant, but I removed it then, setting it on the table in front of me. Ray raised an eyebrow at that but didn't say anything. Mary took her chain off, with the ring, and placed it beside my pendant. She gave a nervous smile in my direction.

"It's a long story and not an easy one to talk about," I said. He waved his hand in the air in the universal get-on-with-it gesture.

I told him everything. About him being approached to make sure it was turned off, at any cost, and how he was bribed with his family's safety. His eyes broke from my gaze, and I wondered if he'd already been approached. My guess was yes. By the end of it, rain was drizzling on us, and when the sun peeked through the clouds to the west, it caused the tall, thin trees to cast long shadows over the gas station parking lot.

"That's a lot to take in. What do I do with this new knowledge? Are you coming with me? Am I even real? I mean, this version of me, is *he* real?" Ray was taking it well. Better than I would have expected him to.

"We don't know," Mary said. She'd been fairly quiet

while I told our story, only pitching in to explain her side of things on occasion. Ray and Mary had been together for the last part of our trip to Machu, a leg of the journey I wasn't around for. I'd met Magnus and Natalia after trying to distract the ship from seeing the others.

"You're going to let them beam you up?" His chin motioned toward the green-stoned jewelry on the table before us.

"We're supposed to face our biggest fear on this monumental day in our lives. We think that by doing this, the Kraski will have invaded and won. We don't have another choice." Deep down, I knew we were lying on horizontal chairs far away from here, but the idea of being taken alongside the rest of Earth's billions made my stomach ache.

Ray nodded along. "Seems right. I'm going to keep going. If any of this is real for a version of me, I'll stop them from invading. I promise you. I'm sorry for the way it all went down." He averted his eyes again, and I wanted to tell him it was all right, because at the end of the day, we'd won. He was a sacrifice among many during the Event, one that I'd missed dearly every day since.

"It's time." Mary stood as dusk took hold of the cloudy day. The air changed; electricity coursed through it, sending shivers throughout my body.

"Ray, I had to get this off my chest. I've really missed you. I know we could have been fast friends for life. If this is real, I know you can stop the invasion. Remember everything I told you. Now you know who and what you can trust." I stood too, my palms sweating at the idea of being pulled up in the green beam that was inevitably coming for me.

The first time, I'd watched it take James from my house, and it repelled me as I fought to grab hold of his floating legs. This time I'd be with Mary, the love of my life. She gave me a sad smile and hugged Ray. I went in and gave him one too, getting a firm back pat to end it.

"You seem like a good dude, Dean. Catch you on the flip side." He stepped back from us, rain soaking all of us now, but no one seemed to care or notice. It was time.

Lightning struck nearby, sending a boom of thunder across the highway. Cars honked as they struggled to move in the crowded traffic. It wouldn't matter soon.

Ray kept walking backwards, watching us while waiting for the big show. He wasn't going to be disappointed. Beams dropped to the ground just as another flash of lightning arced over the darkening sky. My heart pounded in my chest as I reached for Mary, holding her against me. We were both soaked, and she was trembling. From the cold or fear, I wasn't sure.

Our faces pressed against each other. "We're almost to them. The Theos." She said their name with a reverent tone, and I wanted to curse them for making us relive this day. Instead, I just smiled and kissed her as the beams found us, ripping us from the ground. I broke apart from Mary to see everyone from the cars being lifted, thousands of pinpricks of light cascading along the road and countryside. The higher we rose, the more beams we could see. We were pulled at a heavy angle eventually, our trajectory changing to pull our bodies to a transport vessel. It was sick and beautiful at the same time. Mary held on tightly, and my fear was gone. I looked up and saw one of the black square vessels over us. From this vantage point, they were even more intimidating.

I could hear the screaming and shouting of the thousands of others being pulled toward the vessel ship. The terror was palpable.

We started for the bottom of the vessel, but before our heads emerged inside it, the green light gave way to a white brilliance. I was expecting to find myself back on the chair inside the small island. Instead, I was greeted with pandemonium.

"Dean!" Mary shouted, as hundreds of people suddenly found themselves cramped in a room with us. She was being forced away from me, and I shoved my way through to her, grabbing her reaching fingers and pulling her in.

There I held her, while strangers screamed and panicked. This was why we were here, to see the other side of the Event. We hadn't been on the ships when everyone had been taken by the Kraski, so now we were being forced to witness it. I tried to detach myself from the terror I was seeing, but even though I knew we weren't really there, I couldn't. My heart raced as more people appeared through the room's floor, walls, and ceiling. With each drop, there was a green light, then a flash of white, and there they were.

"What's going on?" a man beside me asked. He was naked, soap suds still clinging to his damp head.

A baby cried, and I was grateful to find it was being

The Ancients

held in its father's arms. There had been countless tales of babies being beamed up by themselves, totally separated from their parents. This was one of the lucky ones. I briefly wondered if that was truly the child's parent.

"You're going to be okay," I said in a calm voice. I wasn't sure the man even heard me among the cacophony of fear being thrown around the room.

I pulled off my jacket and handed it to the man. He accepted it without thanks and wrapped it around his waist.

I'd read about those first few moments when all of our population had been beamed up. I'd seen the made-for-TV movies and television interviews, but nothing had prepared me for the feeling. The air was thick, making it hard to breathe. It was as if everyone's fear was pulsing through their sweat, clogging the room with it.

I led Mary through throngs of people. By the time we made it to the wall near the doorway, I was wet with water, tears, and God knows what else. We stood there, silent observers of Earth's darkest moment.

We'd all been through so much, and now I appreciated what the survivors had really conquered.

"Get away from me! Sally! Sally!" a woman cried, shoving a man beside her.

"Why don't you screw off, lady?" A portly man was grabbing at an older woman's water bottle. She looked at him through her glasses like a teacher considering a misbehaving child.

"Let go of that and mind your manners." She shoved him, and I pushed through a hugging couple to assist.

I laid a palm on the man's sweaty chest, and his unbelieving eyes shot me death stares.

"What do you think you're doing? I need that more than she does. I have a heart condition!" He spat while he talked, and I wiped it off my face with a quick flick of my hand.

"Calm down!" I yelled. A few people stopped what they were doing and listened. The room quieted, some sobs still cutting through the otherwise silent space.

I spun around, seeing countless eyes on me, all red-lined and scared. "Everyone's going to be okay." Mary was at my side now. She took over, calmly speaking.

"We don't know what happens now, but we're together in this. We're now a community, and we won't let our humanity crumble because of *them*." She pointed upward, as if indicating the invading aliens. "Gather anything you have that can be useful. Water, food, medication" – she looked to the man holding the baby – "milk, and get an inventory. We're going to name a few of you to go pass word to the other rooms. Any volunteers?"

A rail-thin girl stuck her hand up. She had on cropped denim shorts and a rock t-shirt. "What other rooms?"

Mary didn't want them to know we had more information than them. That would be dangerous. "Did you see the size of the vessels we were just beamed into?" A few nods, and shouts of affirmation. "Then there will be countless rooms like this one."

Questions began flying at us from around the room. At least they were focused now, working together, not as individuals. *What are they going to do with us? Are we dead?*

What can we do? And finally, *how can I help?* This was from a little boy, no more than twelve. He was wearing 76ers pajamas.

"We need to identify doctors, nurses, EMTs, anyone who can help the sick or injured. We need to work as a team now," I said. A short woman wearing scrubs came forward, letting me know she was a nurse at a retirement home.

The space was dimly lit, and it had the exact same layout as the one Magnus and I had first beamed through as we'd raced toward the sun all those years ago. People were already organizing themselves and heading into the halls, relaying what we'd suggested to them.

We'd only been there a short while, but the musty fear smell was nearly gone. The people were now distracted, with a goal in mind.

I wondered how many of these people lived at New Spero now. Had I ever crossed paths with any of them?

I was proud of Mary; she was leading this distraught group better than I could have. She turned and smiled at me. Before I could wonder how long we'd be there, an energy rushed through my veins. An image of the shadow character shimmered in my mind before I transported.

My eyes blinked open. I quickly squinted to protect them from the bright light, only there wasn't any; just a dim room with a blurry figure coming for me. I held my hands up in defense and blinked, seeing the man come into focus.

"Slate?" I asked. I was still lying down, and I screamed as the wire connecting me to the chair recessed from the back of my head, letting me sit up. My hand flew to the puncture, where a sharp pain emanated. Slate held a hand on my back, saying calming words that I didn't quite hear. "Mary."

I turned to her rigid form on the chair beside me. With wobbly legs, I stumbled over to her just as her eyes widened.

"Mary, it's okay. We're back. The wire is about to come…" I was cut off by her shouting. I leaned over, seeing the small three-eighths-inch cord disappear into the head of the chair.

She stayed down, but her hand darted out like a striking cobra and grabbed me by the wrist. "I saw it."

"Saw what? The vessel? Is that what you mean?" I asked as I pried her firm grip from my arm.

She shook her head and sat up, swinging her legs over the side of the chair. "I saw their homeworld. I know how to get there."

I hadn't seen anything but the briefest glance of the Theos.

"Wait, what the hell's going on here? You guys were gone for like five minutes," Slate said.

"Where is it?" I asked, ignoring Slate's demands for answers.

"We have to use the stones to get to the edge of the universe, or as close as we can. From there we fly. There's an empty world with a ship waiting for us."

"How do you know all this?" I asked, worried about the look in her eyes. It was unsettling.

"They showed me before I came to. Their world

looks amazing. Blue gemstones line the landscape, and we'll find them inside a mountain of crystals. I know how to get there." Mary tapped the side of her head lightly. "It's all up here."

"Will someone tell me what happened?" Slate's voice was a low growl.

We explained it to him quickly, and he listened with rapt attention. Describing the terror on the Kraski vessel brought back instant trauma.

"That's some heavy stuff." His face was long as he mopped a glove over his mask. "How do we get out of here?"

The stone wall on the opposite end of the room slid apart. A portal room was set inside: four pillars with a large stone in the center. A clear table floated above it through magnetic technology. We all stepped inside, our boots clanging against the hard metallic floor.

"Which one do we go to?" I asked, but Mary was already using the table, scrolling through the icons, looking for the one she was shown while still under the Theos' influence. She stopped at one, pointing to it.

"This one," she said.

"Hold on," I said, setting a hand over the icon. "Why don't we travel back home first? Get some food, rest, a hot shower…"

"We have to go now," Mary said. I looked over at Slate, who was frowning at my wife.

"I don't know about you, but I'm with Dean. Why not get some rest first and do this with fresh faces?" Slate was going to bat on my side, but Mary didn't look to be having any of it.

The scary zombie Mary was gone when she looked up at me from the table. Her eyes were damp, and she gave me a sweet smile. "We've been through so much, Dean. We're almost there. The trip will take a week or so in the ship. We can rest on that part of the journey."

"What are we going to eat?" Slate asked, stealing the question from my lips.

"The world we're going to has abundant vegetation. I know what we can and can't eat."

I looked at her skeptically. "They sure gave you a lot of details for you being out thirty seconds more than me."

She nodded. "Dean, I'm going one way or another. We have to find them. You know we have to stop the Unwinding."

"Just what is this damned Unwinding? We don't know anything about it. Maybe the threat's already over with. The Theos could have been gone for thousands of years, making us worry about nothing."

She shook her head this time. "It's real. I've seen it."

"Of course you have." Slate took a step forward. He was about to speak again when she tapped the icon. I didn't have a chance to stop her. Light enveloped the room, and once again, I had no idea where I'd open my eyes.

TWENTY-SIX

*W*e followed Mary's hurried steps out of the portal room and down a series of alien-built corridors. She led the way, seemingly knowing where she was going. It wasn't long before we were heading through a colorful hangar with a few ships inside. Mary ran a hand along the side of one ship near the building's exit.

"This is ours," she said, stopping briefly to appraise it with a smile.

"This one?" I asked, nodding my approval. It was sleek and green, with large thrusters on the rear, one on top of the other instead of side-by-side. Judging by its diminutive stature, it was made for a very small crew, which was exactly what we were. I shoved the doubts and fears of the last section of our expedition down and decided to take some of Mary's excitement and roll with it.

If everything went as planned, we'd be waking up the Theos in just over a week. Even Slate was grinning while looking at the ship. "You're sure this world is empty? Where'd they go?"

"They didn't tell me. They only said it would be waiting for us." Mary spun on a heel and pushed the exit door open. Heat blasted us, and I instantly began to sweat inside my EVA. The built-in temperature modifiers kicked in, and I felt my skin cooling.

I stepped outside the hangar and onto thick green grass. Plants grew out of everything in the area. The erected buildings nearby were covered in green moss, and a few had been ripped apart by massive trees growing through them. I thought about the world Slate and I had met Suma on and wondered how many developed worlds sat empty. Where had their people gone? Disease? War?

I had to do a light jog to catch up to Mary's quick strides. The sky was bright blue, with two large stars hanging in it. I looked in the other direction, and a pale crescent moon held its place in the horizon.

"Over here," she said. She turned at a twenty-foot-tall statue that was still half standing along the street. It was made in the likeness of a multi-limbed creature, with short legs and a head half the size of its torso. The left side of it sat in a crumbled pile on the ground. Mary called for me, and I broke my gaze with the strange statue.

We passed over a road, with three-story metal buildings lining it, before entering a copse of trees. A dark, heavy fruit weighed the branches down, and Mary reached for some of them.

"We don't know if this is edible." Slate poked at one, and it fell to the ground with a splat. Some were quite ripe.

"They told me it's fine." Mary reached for her mask and pulled it off. She took a deep breath and smiled at

The Ancients

me. "Don't worry. The air is fine too."

"Damn it, Mary, be careful. You don't know what their motives are. This place could have been fine a thousand years ago, but a lot can change on a planet, especially an unoccupied one." I hated seeing her jump to conclusions without thinking. It wasn't like her at all.

"The worlds left to the plants are the best-off ones. Take off your mask and have something to eat. It's been a long time." Mary plucked a fist-sized fruit from the tree, smelling it before taking a bite. It had a dark outer skin, which she spat out before eating the meat. I wasn't even going to try to talk her out of it. I rubbed my belly, remembering that the bad diner food I'd eaten wasn't real.

My mask slipped off easily after I killed the power switch to it, and I took a long inhale of the planet's air. It was amazing. Lush tropical smells created a euphoric feeling through my brain, and I reached for one of the fruits. Slate was right behind me. Mary laughed as she grabbed another one, and soon the three of us were sitting among the trees, savoring the planet's delicacies.

Mary knew which ones to stay away from and which were eatable. It was as if they'd downloaded information into her mind with the connection. I wondered what else they'd put in there. She still seemed like Mary, but something was off. I'd have to keep a close eye on her.

"Something wrong, Dean?" She'd caught me staring at her. Juices ran down her chin, but instead of engaging, I just wiped the remnants of the last thing she'd eaten away from her face.

"Nothing at all. Slate, what do you think? Are you

full?" I asked. He leaned back on the grass and stared at the sky.

"This is nice," was his reply.

"What is?" Mary asked him.

"Lying back, watching the clouds. I don't even know how many days or nights we've been gone. We're running on fumes. Having food and just relaxing is nice."

"We don't have a lot of time. Enjoy it while you can." Mary was already getting to her feet.

"Wait. Can't we take a break?" I asked. "Are the Theos going somewhere?" If I was the True, I doubted they'd care if we made it there a day late.

Mary looked at me with a hard stare, but it broke and melted after a moment. "You're right. We have food and a ship with cots. Let's take some of this stuff and see if we can't get the thing fired up."

"Sounds good to me," Slate said from his horizontal position. He'd found a piece of grass to chew on.

I rolled onto my feet and stood up, wiping the remains of my dinner off my EVA. Mary came over and kissed me on the cheek before glancing over to Slate, who was doing his best to ignore us.

I led her a few yards away and put a tree between us and our third wheel. I kissed her on the lips, which were warm, sweet, and slightly sticky.

"What was that for?" she asked, kissing me again, this time deeper and longer.

When she broke it, I gathered my wits and answered her. "That's for picking your battles. That's for getting us this far, and for being an amazing person. Without your energy and focus, we never would have made it here."

Her eyes watered, something I wasn't expecting. "Dean, you're the best. I can't wait for us to find these Theos and to affirm you're their True. You can save the universe from this threat."

Her words brought it all back to me, reminding me it was real. For most of this quest, it had felt like a game, but if the galaxy really was under duress, and it was up to me to help save it, I wasn't sure I wanted the weight on my shoulders. I'd do what I had to but wasn't relishing the idea.

"Boss, are you two done playing kissy face?" Slate was starting to come out of his shell a little more each day, but he still liked to call me "boss." It wasn't a habit I expected him to stop any time soon.

"Zeke Campbell, one day you'll be a strapping groom, and you'll have your very own best friend to kiss." Mary ripped a bright pink berry from a bush beside her and threw it toward Slate. He easily evaded it.

"Get me home first. Then I can see about that date with Denise, if she hasn't given up on me yet." He kicked at a rock, giving him an overgrown child's silhouette.

"How could she resist a big lug like you?" Mary asked him.

"Yeah, yeah. Let's get some food and check out our new home for the next few days," Slate said, changing the subject.

I opened my eyes with protest. Mary was shaking my shoulder lightly, and I groaned and rolled onto my side. "Can't we sleep just a little longer?"

"We've already slept for nine hours. It's time."

The room was tight for space. Two bunks were on either side of the cramped quarters, making just enough room for Mary and me to have an uncomfortable sleep. Slate was snoring away, face-down on his cot, his bare feet hanging over the end. Whatever alien race lived here, they weren't very tall, judging by the ship. Slate had hit his head twice the night before on low doorways and walked around after that in a perpetual hunch. He wasn't going to enjoy his week onboard.

"You're sure you can fly this thing?" I asked her again. She'd told me "yes" the night before, but I wanted her to reiterate the fact.

"Dean." She placed her hand on my chest. "We'll be fine. They're close now."

"If you say so. Want to get going, then?"

"No time like the present." She stood up, wearing the jumpsuit we'd started the trip with. I pulled mine off the floor beside us and slid it on before waking Slate. He swiped at me like a hibernating bear, but I could hear him getting out of bed as I entered the hall.

Everything was miniaturized on board. The ceilings were just high enough for my hair to brush against, and the walls were only a couple of feet apart, forcing me to walk at a slight angle instead of straight forward.

Mary had adjusted the air levels to accommodate us,

and after finally understanding the complicated bathroom area, we were set. Other than the sleeping quarters and the bathroom, there were just a corridor and the bridge. No real room for storage. We did find a cooling compartment near the rear of the ship, and that was where we stored the berries and nuts we'd found on the lush world we were about to leave behind.

"We should come back here for a vacation at some point. The small amount we've seen looks amazing. I bet Nat and the kids would like to run around the hills here," I said, wondering how close Nat was to giving birth. I was glad Magnus was able to sit this one out. He'd grill me about every detail when we got back. He was living vicariously through my adventures now, he said.

I hoped one day I could live through someone else's.

"Engines are on." A humming vibration shook the entire ship. The hangar was open from above. We didn't know if the ceiling was always recessed, or if it had never had one. The look of the place told me they'd left in a hurry.

The bridge was small, like everything else. A molded white plastic bench was bolted to the floor in front of the pilot controls, which were on a screen on the console. Mary keyed things into them like an old pro.

"How much did they dump into your mind?" I asked.

She shrugged as I stood behind her. "Just what I needed to know, I suppose." She slid a finger along the screen; yellow bars of light followed the movement. We lifted up slowly.

She tapped the console again, and a viewscreen

popped on. It was no larger than my old flatscreen TV at home, but it let us see outside of the ship. There were no real windows or portholes on the vessel, just cameras to allow us to see our surroundings. Mary claimed those weren't even necessary. I took her word for it.

Slate lumbered to the bridge, coming to a stop directly beside me. He chewed on a nut before holding out his hand, which held more. I shook my head, watching as we rose into the sky. The green landscape went for miles and miles. Hills rose and fell like the waves of a large ocean.

"Ready?" Mary asked as we broke the atmosphere. The ship shook as we emerged into the darkness of space.

"Ready." The Theos were waiting.

TWENTY-SEVEN

The trip was as expected: uneventful. By my standards, that was a good thing.

"There it is." A quiver in Mary's voice told me she was nervous. We all were. We'd had nothing but time over the last week to speculate on what we'd find when we arrived. As much as we tried not to, we always came back to the subject.

Mary wasn't told anything about their home: just an image of a crystal mountain, seared into her brain to direct us there.

She clicked off the FTL drive; the stretching stars became dots in space again as we slowed to in-system speed. A planet hung there, beckoning us to come see it.

From our vantage point, it had the look of the ice planet where we'd first seen the symbol for their homeworld. The closer we got, the more we saw it was nothing of the sort. A small gray moon orbited the planet in a stark contrast of dullness and beauty.

"Hold on," Mary said as we eased into the atmosphere. Gravity tugged at us, but the ship's built-in inertia dampers made it nothing more than a light shake.

"Wow," Slate said from beside me. I had to agree. The land was colorful, like the showcase at a rock and gem store on Madison Avenue. Janine had taken me there a couple times, and I could still see her face as she'd longingly looked at the expensive specimens. We'd left empty-handed each time.

Mary took us lower, toward a section of land covered by orange gemstones. As we got closer, I could make out the independent mountains of glorious stones. A wide river of water flowed between a valley of gemstone hills, and it wasn't until we were right above them that we fully understood how large they were.

"This is amazing." Mary slowed and flew us lower, careful to stay far enough away from the jutting peaks and terminations.

"I feel like we shrank, and I'm looking at a crystal showpiece," I said.

"Should we land and check it out?" Slate asked.

Mary shook her head from the pilot bench. "This isn't it. The image I was shown was blue. Light blue. We just need to find that region."

"That shouldn't be too difficult. We can see the colors from ten thousand feet up." I rested my hand on Mary's shoulder, and she looked behind to see me. Her smile was wide.

"We made it, Dean." She turned back and increased our altitude, heading over the huge orange ranges.

We kept climbing into the sky. From our current angle, the system's star was casting brilliant white light toward the world, and the lime green crystals on the ground

The Ancients

just before us danced with light and color. We soared through the atmosphere, passing various landscapes. Each colored region brought a slightly different type of crystal and layout. Some were close to the ground, the formations lower and stout. Others, like the white crystals, reached high for the sky, each termination thin and stretched out like tree branches in the autumn. We were covering a lot of distance, but we could only see so much at a time.

An hour passed, and then two, with no sign of the blue region Mary had us looking for.

"What if it's not here?" she asked, her shoulders slumping just enough to let me know the earlier wind was billowing out of her sails.

I watched a blood-red mountain pass underneath us as we raced through the dusk-colored sky. A tingle coursed through me, from the back of my head down to my toes. We were close. I closed my eyes and saw the Theos shadow from the first time it spoke to me alone, on the virtual version of the island we'd just left.

I was the True. I would help the Theos stop the Unwinding. My back straightened, and all the doubt and worry from the past few days sloughed away from my mind, like a snake shedding its skin. I was too big for the previous version of myself. That version was weak, always concerned with what the future brought, never living in the present where life was really happening.

As I watched, the red crystals flowed into a deep purple, then light purple. The shapes and tones made me think of cubes of Jell-O.

I reminisced about the past few years. All that we'd done; all that I'd done. Why did I still have a block around my mind? I could and would save the universe, if that was what was needed. Mary seemed to sense a change in me, and her posture improved too.

"It's here," I said after a long silence. My words were a little too loud, and Slate's head lifted, like I'd startled him out of a daze. "It's here." The words repeated out of my mouth without my intending them to.

"What do you think they look like?" Slate asked.

"That's a good question. I really have no idea," Mary said.

"They must be some iteration of the shadow form they portrayed themselves as," I said.

After a brief pause, Slate said, "Not necessarily. Maybe they were using a form we would understand and recognize to put us at ease."

A shiver ran through me again, but not a good one. A presence I'd noticed the first time I saw the shadow pour out of the cube we'd brought Sarlun; it gave way so fast that I hadn't given it another thought until now. I pushed it away. It was just me being overly concerned with every detail.

"You could be right," Mary said. "When they showed me the ship and the planet's location, it was the same misty black figure speaking for them."

"Either way, we'll find out soon enough," I said, feeling my heart begin to race in my chest.

Mary was looking back at us and followed my pointing finger to peer at the viewscreen. She and Slate saw what I'd noticed moments before them: a light blue crystal paradise.

Mary's hands darted to the console, slowing the thrusters so we could coast toward our destination. "That's it." Her voice was nothing more than a tight breath.

I walked in front of the white bench and stood enough to the side to give the others a view. It was like nothing I'd ever seen before. Blue crystals merged together to form a pyramid-shaped mountain. It was so high, clouds lingered over the top of it. A massive lake sat on the ground to the left of it, reflecting spectacular colors as the star's last beams of light coursed over the landscape.

"What is that?" I asked, once again pointing to the screen.

"Where?" Mary asked.

"There, just before the mountain."

She tapped the controls, and the image zoomed.

"Right over there." I jabbed a thumb in the air.

The screenshot moved at Mary's control, and the shape I thought I'd spotted appeared to us.

"Holy crap," Slate whispered. "That's their symbol."

It was the same shape we'd seen on the ice planet. The same shape from the end of the cube map we'd found there. It was the same shape of the space station we'd recently put together for one of the challenges. It was the symbol of the Theos. It looked to be carved out of the crystal ground, water sitting in pools to form the mark.

"Taking us down." Mary zoomed back out and lowered us toward a flat spot close to the range, but not right at it. We didn't know where we were supposed to go from there, but investigating the symbol first was probably a good start.

"You're sure we can breathe the air?" I asked, even though Mary had assured me we'd be able to, countless times during the week-long trip.

She nodded, too distracted to waste words. The ship lurched slightly as it hit the ground. "Sorry about that. I'm just excited to get out there."

Slate was already reaching for his pulse rifle. "Good call, Slate," I said. We all slipped into our Theos-gifted EVAs, leaving the helmets off. The fabric felt tight against my skin after being in the flexible jumpsuit for the last week. It would keep us warm and protected out there.

Mary picked up her bow, and I took the other pulse rifle before we headed to the ship's exit. Mary went first, her quick steps leading to Slate's more tentative ones down the metallic grate steps. I followed them down and out, gingerly jumping down the last one to land on the hard blue crystalline ground.

The air was fresh. Considering I hadn't seen any vegetation, I found it surprising.

"How deep down do you think the crystals go?" I asked.

"All the way to the core," Mary said, standing apart from us, her gaze watching the gargantuan crystal protrusion a mile or so away.

"Where there's water, there's life." Slate's use of the old adage was an apt one. But was that life the Theos?

The Ancients

"Let's go. It's getting dark, and we don't know what's out there." Mary passed us each puck-shaped lights that clipped on to our collars. She'd found them on the ship as we'd explored it during the week traveling on board. Mine flickered on as soon as I attached it, sending a widespread beam forward. Slate clipped his on and turned the front dial, adjusting the spread of his beam to a narrow one, giving him more focused lumens.

"All set." Slate unslung his pulse rifle, and we looked down to the symbol and toward the mountain from atop a cliff. The ledge forced us in a single direction, and we let the slope funnel us lower. The crystal ground was solid and far less slippery than I imagined it would be. If it rained here, it would be a nightmare to walk on.

"Watch your steps," Slate warned. "There are little pieces of the rock sticking out everywhere."

It was going to get harder to see them all as night took hold over the dusky sky. I tried to keep myself from looking at the surroundings and focused on the ground before me.

Mary was the first to take a spill, but Slate was there to catch her before she hit the ground. He grunted as his large arm darted out to prevent her from smashing down.

"Thanks, Zeke." Mary brushed herself off.

The declining slope tapered out, and soon we were at the bottom of the crystal mound.

"We should be able to get to the symbol in a few minutes." Slate rested his hand on a gemstone wall. Something moved on the other side of it, showing up as a shadow through the thick light-blue substance. He pulled his hand back, and we aimed our light beams on it.

A dozen eyes looked back at us, all wide, each the size of a teacup saucer.

TWENTY-EIGHT

Slate and I scrambled back, our rifles in our hands and ready to fire in a split second. Mary walked past us, around the three-foot-wide crystalline cluster. As she moved behind it, we could see her take up the entire surface of the wall. It acted as a magnifying glass and a circus mirror at the same time.

"It's so cute," she said.

I kept the rifle up and followed Slate to where Mary was cooing over a palm-sized creature. Its wide eyes were only the size of dimes, and it resembled a mix between a gecko and a kitten. The multi-faceted crystals had refracted the small animal in multiple directions on the other side.

"I don't think you'll need a weapon." Mary gestured toward my rifle, which was pointing at the small animal.

"I'll be the judge of that," I said, not lowering it.

"You think it's here to hurt us?" Mary asked. She crouched down and talked quietly to the creature, who regarded her with confusion. It didn't have the common sense to be afraid.

"Maybe it's a Theos," Slate said, chuckling to himself.

"As much as I doubt that, how do we know?" I leaned down to it. "Are you a Theos?" I asked it in the same baby-talk voice Mary was using.

Mary gave me a light elbow to the gut that sent the creature scattering away from us.

"Look, you scared it away," Slate said.

"Let's follow it." Mary was already chasing after the little thing, which walked on four nimble legs. It didn't seem to have fur or scales. Its skin reminded me more of an armadillo's gray hide.

"Mary, wait. Why are we wasting our time chasing this thing?" I asked, running after her.

"Because it might lead us to them. I saw the spark of intelligence in the little guy's eyes."

It was heading in the same direction as we were, regardless, so I kept my opinion to myself. It was hard running and keeping firm footing on the sloping and uneven crystal ground. We stopped just before the Theos symbol, which was much larger than I'd originally thought. The small creature was also perched at the water's edge. It looked down at its own reflection, then back to us, before scurrying around the linear ledge and toward the blue crystal mountain beyond.

I knelt at the water, rubbing a gloved hand along the clean-cut border of the Theos symbol. It was smooth, and I was curious how deep the water went.

"I don't think this is where we need to go," I said. With a nod of my head, I gestured at the crystal peaks a mile or so away. "That is." The whole thing reminded me of my favorite childhood superhero's fortress. Before I could reference it to the other two, they were already running, once again chasing after the small animal toward our new destination.

While I was thankful for staying in good shape over the last year or two, a few minutes in, I was feeling the burn in my thighs. Maneuvering over the undulating hard surface took more strength and skill than I'd needed while running laps back on the acreage with Mary in the mornings. Maggie would follow along, chasing us, barking at clouds in the sky.

Slate was moving with ease, but Mary was slowing down. I caught up with her just as the landscape began to change. It was dark now, our small lights not giving us enough brightness to safely keep running. As if it sensed this, our pint-sized new friend slowed too. It peered over its shoulder from twenty yards ahead.

Slate's focused light beam reflected off the animal's eyes, which glowed green in return. "Look," he said, moving his beam upward. We were at the foothills of the natural crystal pyramid. Clusters of the gemstone grew from the ground like a forest of flawed stone trees. Our lights cast strange shadows all around the landscape, making me uneasy the thicker the clusters got, and the closer we came to the mountainous wall.

"Do we have to find a way inside?" Slate asked, knowing we wouldn't have the answer.

"It's waiting for us," Mary said, a tinge of awe in her voice. She was right. The creature stood on all fours, its wide eyes beckoning us to follow it. We obliged, and in a couple of minutes, we were at the wall of the pyramid. I leaned against it, noticing the intricate cuts and faces of the humongous crystal stones rising upward from the ground symmetrically. When one terminated, another grew closer to the center, taking its place, ever upward, creating an angled mountainside too sloped to climb with ease.

The air changed in an instant. I noticed for the first time that the whole world had a sort of hum to it, like the stones were alive, moving molecules in a rhythmic internal dance. My body hummed along with it as clouds rolled in above, so quickly I couldn't imagine it being a natural occurrence.

"Anyone else feel that?" I asked. We were all staring up at the sky, our light beams falling well short of showing us anything but a dark blanket of night and clouds.

"They know we're here," Mary whispered.

Wind blew in, a chill against my cheek. At first, I thought it would slow again, but it picked up, sending water droplets down with it.

"It's raining. Great." Slate mopped his face with a glove. "We should get inside."

"They're forcing us to keep moving. We're wasting time out here," I said, sure of my words. Mary was still looking up, rain hitting her face, dripping down her neck and onto her EVA.

"Mary." I touched her arm softly, and she broke her stand-off with the sky, looking me in the eyes with excitement.

"Dean, we're here. It's real." She squealed and raced ahead of us, toward the animal patiently waiting for us to

The Ancients

follow it along the pyramid walls.

A brilliant flash of lightning erupted from the sky above us, illuminating the whole valley for a split second. Moments later, it was followed by a colossal boom of thunder. I covered my ears with my palms, and Slate did the same.

"That was close. Let's go," I said, rushing toward Mary as her form vanished from my puck-light beam.

"After you, boss," Slate said, holding his rifle up and spinning around for one last look as another shot of lightning forked down from the sky. This time, I spotted something above us.

"A ship!" I called over the lightning.

Mary looked up and saw it too. "It's the same kind from the space station challenge. What do they want, and how did they find us?" she asked. She was right. It was small, hornet-shaped, with tendrils identifying it as belonging to the insectoid race.

"It's too late. We have to keep going," I said. Slate looked anxious to shoot them down, but he wouldn't be able to hit them from this distance. Even if he could, I doubted his pulse rifle would do any damage.

We ran along the base of the mountain for a minute or two before the rain really started coming down, causing each footstep on the smooth surface to become a rolled ankle threat, or worse. I looked up from watching my feet to see Mary standing to the side, looking toward the wall. I slid on the ground, splashing water, and narrowly avoided knocking her over.

"It went in there," she said, pointing to a hole just

large enough for a human to squeeze through.

I opened my mouth to reply, and a gust of wind shot a torrent of rain at my face. I spit out acrid water and moved to the entrance. "We should be able to fit. I'll go first." I didn't know what I was about to find, but the way Mary was going forward with reckless abandon, I didn't want her getting inside first. She didn't argue with me as I stuck my left leg into the opening, which was a square hole three feet off the ground. I twisted my body, ducking into it and bringing my right leg through as my other was planted.

Once inside, I held my pulse rifle up, moving it along with my light to see if there was a threat nearby. I was in a crystal corridor, my beam reflecting and bouncing down the hall, igniting a path of light. "Come in," I said to the others. It was dry inside, and water pooled off me onto the otherwise spotless floor.

Mary's lithe figure slid into the opening, followed by Slate, who struggled to fit. He stuck a hand out, and I helped pull him through.

"Good thing I'm wet. I might not have made it through if it wasn't raining." Slate wiped his face again and took a look around, checking both of the corridor's directions before letting his rifle relax beside him.

"Where's our leader?" Mary asked, scanning for the animal we'd followed inside.

"It went that way." I pointed to our left, the direction I'd seen it running when I first entered. Slate shone his light down there, and we saw the animal's green eyes looking back at us. Inside, our lights gave us better visibil-

The Ancients

ity than they had in the night sky, and we easily followed the trail of the small-legged creature, who was either guiding us somewhere or running away from us.

Change the universe. Kareem's dying words looped through my mind as we wound our way through the crystal caverns. Energy vibrated throughout my body, over my soul. I'd had the feeling I was being placed in certain situations a few times since the Event had transpired, and this was no different. I was meant to be here, now.

The crystal clusters were smaller inside, beneath the pieces of solid stone layering over one another to create the pyramid. Here they acted as walls, some rising from the ground, others lowering from above; sparkling stalagmites and stalactites. As we went deeper, moving into the heart of the mountain, we had to be careful not to hit them or get jabbed by any sharp edges. Everything was a brilliant blue, like the color of a Midwestern summer's afternoon sky.

"Are we going to ignore the fact that the insectoids are here?" I asked Mary, who was slowing as the animal changed from a flurry of motion to a walk.

"They want to find the Theos first. I don't know how they got the intel to find this world, but they can't be the ones. We don't know them and can't trust them. Sarlun told us he didn't know much about them, other than the fact that they're extremely religious." Mary was right. We didn't know much. They had attacked us only a couple of days ago, and we'd been forced to kill some of them. I didn't think they'd be forgiving of that fact.

"They won't find the Theos first," Slate said, his voice

somber, the last two words echoing a few times.

"What makes you say that?" I asked. He didn't reply.

He was ahead of us, and when we caught up to him, the corridor gave way to a wide room with a vaulted crystal ceiling. The blue stone glowed softly; every square inch of the hall was lit up.

Mary reached her hand out, taking my arm. I felt her weight push on me, and I held her up firmly. We were in the presence of an ancient race. My knees weakened as well, the whole floor vibrating enough here to be noticeable to all of us.

"It's them," Mary said, releasing her grip on my arm. The floor in the center of the room recessed; long thin stairs were cut into the crystal, leading us down. On closer inspection, it appeared the steps had been formed that way. I wondered if any of this world was natural, or if it was created with the interference of a powerful race of beings.

"Where are they?" I asked. I stepped onto the floor level of what I immediately thought of as the throne room. A seat grew out of the crystal twenty yards away, but it was empty. The whole place was empty.

The little wide-eyed animal stood still before darting away, past our legs and back the way we'd come. It appeared its job was fulfilled.

Mary walked away from me and stood directly in the center of the room, in the space the animal had just occupied. She spun around, looking for a sign of something, anything.

"It's empty. Son of a bitch! It's *empty*!" she screamed.

She thrust clenched fists in the air above her head in frustration. "We've come so far! Too far!"

I was oddly calm, and somewhat relieved by their absence. I wanted nothing more than to go home, without any more talk of the Theos. I didn't want to think about another challenge, or the Event, or the damned portals. I was ready to toss my Gatekeeper title into the trash and start a family with Mary. It was time. We were owed at least that much.

Slate looked exhausted, his face stoic and unreadable.

I moved to be with Mary, and as I reached her, she slid to the ground, tears streaming down her pink cheeks. "They're not here."

I knelt on the ground beside her and kissed the top of her head, which was wet from the rain. "It's okay. We knew there was a chance that their messages were too old, that they might be gone for good."

"I didn't believe that. I really thought they'd be here," Mary said, sounding more composed with each passing second.

"Boss," Slate said, running toward us, "what is that?" His voice was strained, and I looked up just in time to see a black mist rising from beneath the crystal floor as it poured into Mary's mouth, then my own.

TWENTY-NINE

Ohio was dull. I longed for school to start again as the dog days of summer slowed life down to a crawl. My friends were all gone on vacations, leaving me alone with nothing to do but help my dad around the house and weed the garden with my mom. She hated the way I pulled weeds, always trying to pluck them from the tops instead of digging them out from the roots.

I didn't care either way. I just wanted to finish the chore so I could go sit behind the barn under the elm tree and finish my book. I was nose-deep into a classic science fiction. Honestly, I couldn't even remember the name of it, but it had robots, and aliens, and an intergalactic strife of some sort. There was even a tinge of romance, which, for a fourteen-year-old boy, was foreign and exhilarating at the same time.

My mother smiled at me, asking if I'd like something to drink. Sweat beaded on my acne-covered forehead, and I forced a smile back, saying I would. Lemonade would hit the spot. She got up, her knees creaking, and left me to bask in the heat alone, hundreds of weeds still mocking me from the vegetable garden plot. I loved my mother. I saw how hard she always worked, and it made me strive to keep up, even though I didn't want to help. I did it without complaint, for her.

When her form was nothing but a dot against our house, I stood up and took a break. There would be plenty of time for weeding when she got back. My back was aching, and it was hot something fierce.

I closed my eyes, black dots racing in front of my eyelids. When I opened them, someone was there. Fear instantly crept into my mind, sharp daggers ran down my spine, and I nearly screamed for my mother.

Something held me back, and the black figure solidified into something from one of my books. It was shaped like me, and when I lifted my right hand, its left hand followed like a mirror.

"What are you?" I asked it.

For a moment, I expected it to copy my voice, my words, but it spoke in a deep tone. "What I am is life. Or death."

I was still scared, but part of me knew this wasn't real. This was a hallucination from being out in the heat too long. My father called it heatstroke, and he always warned me to stay hydrated. I looked back to see if my mother was coming, but she was still inside the house.

I looked again at the form, which moved its head in time with mine. "What do you want?"

"Are you the True?" it asked.

What an odd question. I didn't know how to answer it. The name felt familiar. The True. I tried the name out aloud, and my tongue felt fat as I said it three times in a row. "The True."

"Are you the True?" it asked again.

I shook my head. "I don't know what that is. I might be, though." My books sometimes had riddles in them, and I didn't want to discount the possibility of adventure, even if it was just in my head. "What does the True need to do?"

"The True is all and nothing. The True will bring darkness where there is light."

I shivered in the afternoon sun. Darkness. I saw myself in the figure mimicking my movements and felt sick. I wasn't the True. This figure was tainted. Bad. Terrible.

Evil.

The word rolled over my mind, and I said it quietly.

"There is no evil. Just balance. You are not the True. You are too weak. Be gone."

I fell backwards, feeling a lush tomato plant soften my fall. My vision was blurry as I lay there, the smell of dirt heavy in my nostrils. I tried to rise up, to tell the figure to leave, but it was already gone. My mother was there above me, leaning over me with concern etched across her forehead.

"Dean?" a man's voice called, shaking me by the shoulders.

"Mom, I'm okay. It's just heatstroke," I said, still lying down.

"Dean, what the hell are you talking about?" Slate asked.

I blinked away my blurry eyesight and saw my big friend huddled over me.

The Ancients

"What happened?" I asked him, trying to remember what I'd just seen. My mother was there, and weeds. The smell of soil still lingered in my nose.

Mary was on the ground beside us, and I scrambled off my back and over to her. Her eyes were closed, but she was breathing normally.

"How long was I gone?" I asked, wondering why Slate was unaffected. "Were you gone too?"

"Gone? No. The black stuff shot into you two, and you were down for just a minute before you woke," Slate answered.

Mary's eyes shot open and she took a deep breath, like a drowning victim fighting to get air into their lungs.

"Mary! Are you okay?" I asked.

She didn't reply at first. She looked at me and set a warm palm to my stubbled cheek. Her eyes were watery and she gave me a sad smile before her look changed and she roughly pushed my touch aside, getting to her feet. Her movements were rigid, uncertain. The Mary that had gazed into my eyes moments ago wasn't there.

"Mary, what is it?" I asked, stepping toward her. I walked into an invisible energy shield around her and jumped back at the jolt.

"Mary…" a voice said from her mouth. It wasn't hers.

"Mary! Come back!" I yelled, making for her another time, but again, I was painfully reminded I couldn't get near her. The memory of the figure standing beside me in my mom's garden came back. *Evil*.

I started for her again, but Slate was there, grabbing

hold of my arm. I shoved him, but he held firmly. "Boss, this isn't her. Something stayed inside her. Let's talk to it. Rationalize. Maybe they don't mean any harm."

But they did. I could feel it in the pit of my stomach. They meant much harm.

"What do you want with Mary?" I yelled at it.

The Mary-thing stood only a few feet away, and I noticed the black speckles of mist floating around her whole body. "I owe you nothing."

"You put us through hell and back, and now you've taken my wife? I'd say you owe me something. The Theos were supposed to be good."

Mary's eyes narrowed when I said the ancient race's name. "The Theos were weak. They could have been powerful. Instead, they turned on us."

This wasn't a Theos. I looked around the crystal throne room, realizing we'd been duped this whole time. "It can't be. The symbol. The ice planet. The challenges. The Theos shadow…"

It laughed, a deep throaty noise Mary had never made before. "Would anyone have played along if they knew it was for the Iskios?"

I'd never heard the name and wondered if telling it that would help or hurt my cause. I ignored the bait. "Why? To what end?"

"We've been here for countless cycles of this world. Hundreds of your lifetimes. But it was worth it."

Slate stood beside me, his rifle raised. Seeing him point the weapon at Mary made me want to punch him. Instead, I set a hand on the barrel and pushed it down.

The Ancients

He nodded to me and relaxed his grip on the weapon.

"Worth it? How?" I was piecing together information, but also trying to stall. There had to be a way out of this.

"Mary. The challenges weren't for the weak of heart. Only a True vessel would have made it this far. Dean," it started, before taking a brief pause. Mary's head tilted to the side like a curious puppy's. "You intrigue us. Had it been you, we would have taken you. You could have been the True."

Without hesitation, I shouted the words. "Then take me instead!"

Mary's head went side to side slowly. "It's too late. She is us. We are her. She is the True. Her heart beats twice."

"To hell with that. You said I'd make a good vessel. Take me. I'm the Hero of Earth. I'm a world saver. I'm a Gatekeeper." I was yelling, tears racing down my face. More quietly I said, "I'm the Kraski killer and barterer of planets." Only after I spoke did I catch its phrasing. *Her heart beats twice.*

"Yes. We know all of this. But where you hesitate, Mary accepts and reacts. She is stronger than you. She is the True. She also holds a spawn. This is a pleasant surprise."

Everything went numb. She was pregnant. We were going to have a family. It all came crashing in on my thoughts when I looked at her, knowing she wasn't in control. "You lie. She's not."

"I need not explain anything to you. I know truths. Be gone."

Slate stepped between us. "Boss, I don't think this is going the way you want it to. We need to pivot." He turned to it. "Where are the Theos?"

Mary's lips curled back in disgust. "They lie waiting as well. In order to seal us away, they sacrificed much. The universe has two sides to it. Opposing forces. We are those forces."

My hand was shaking, seeing Mary speaking those words in a stranger's voice. "The yin and yang. The black and white," I whispered. Mary was pregnant. I wanted to fall to my knees and beg it to take me instead.

It laughed again, louder than last time. "Yes, indeed. We do not have time for you anymore. There is much to do. The Unwinding is upon us."

"What's the Unwinding?" I asked, feeling like the end was near. I needed to know, either way.

"You won't find out." Mary had turned her back to us. I walked forward, feeling the energy field against my outstretched hand.

"Mary, don't do this. You can fight them. It's right. You *are* strong. We can have our family now. You're stronger than I'd ever be," I pleaded.

Slate looked at me with grim determination. He was ready to fight but knew it would do no good. I wanted to tell him to run, to save himself, but he wouldn't leave my side.

Mary lifted a hand. Black energy flickered at her fingertips like dark lightning. She was turned away, straight-backed and still. Slate stepped in between us, resolved to protect me even now.

The Ancients

A pulse blast echoed through the room, and a crystal shard the size of a person fell from the ceiling, shattering right beside Mary. She stumbled out of the way and fell to the ground. I looked back to the entrance we'd come in, and two insectoid aliens stood there, guns raised.

"The Iskios cannot be freed!" one of them said through a translator and fired a volley of shots at the ceiling again.

Mary, from her seated position, waved her hand toward them. Black mist shot like a bullet across the open room, striking each of them in the chest. Dark webs slowly covered their bodies, and with a pop, they were both gone. No sign of them remained.

Crystal chunks fell from the ceiling, breaching the barrier of energy set by the Iskios. The crystals. Of course. They held power, much like the green ones we'd used to avoid being pulled from Earth by the Kraski beams.

As the rocks continued to fall from above, Mary was being covered in them. I ran to her, expecting the shield to stop me, but it didn't. I tossed large shards of broken gemstones to the side, trying to find my wife under the rubble. Slate came to help; eventually, we worked through the pile and found her chest, then face. It was red with blood, and her eyes blinked open to see me.

"Dean?" she asked.

"Mary! We're going to get you out!" Her body was still covered in crystals, battered and broken by the fallen rocks.

"Dean, I can't fight them. I love you."

I touched her face, seeing her eyes start to mist up with black speckles. "I love you too."

Her hand shot up from beneath the broken blue stones. "I send you home!" she screamed in defiance to the Iskios, and I felt a tugging at my being. I was being pulled away from her, Slate beside me.

"Mary!" I yelled, but it was too late. I saw the crystals flowing away from her body and saw her stand, her broken body mending itself. She looked at us with cold, calculating eyes as we flew away, up and into the ceiling. We weren't solid. I tried to talk to Slate, to yell for him, but nothing came out.

Everything turned to darkness.

THIRTY

"Dean, you need to eat something," someone said. I didn't know who it was anymore. The voices of concern were jumbling through my head after I'd holed up in my bedroom for over a day. Or was it two now? I didn't know. Slate and I had appeared on New Spero, on my front lawn, with no recollection of how we got there. At first, I'd only intended to isolate myself in order to come up with a plan, but the longer I lay there, the harder I found it to move.

"Boss, if you don't come out, I'm going to break the door down and drag you out here. It's been two days, and we need to focus," Slate said. I thought about calling his bluff, but he was right.

But the pain of it all was too much to bear. Mary was gone, with our child inside her. I rolled over, pulling the blankets off my head. I was on Mary's pillow, and I could still smell her honey and lemon shampoo on the pillowcase.

The room was musty and dark, and the first thing I did was pull back the black curtains to see what time it was. The sun was high and bright. Mid-morning on New

Spero. Seeing the lush green grass and foliage out back was enough to get me to open the door. It was high time to stop hiding from the fact that Mary had been taken by some evil Iskios bastards, and time to do something about it.

The door opened. Magnus, Natalia, Slate, my sister Isabelle, and her husband James were all there. Worried looks spread over them all, and Isabelle ran to me, wrapping her arms around me, giving me comfort the way only family could. Slate was cleaned up, shaved, and wearing casual clothing. It looked strange on him after our last week of EVAs and adventures.

A dog barked, then another, and Carey was rubbing his head into my shins before making way for Maggie and the others to jump up on me and bark their hellos. I choked back a response and knelt to the ground, petting the dogs, feeling grateful for their love and affection as they licked and played with me.

"I'm so sorry, Dean," Isabelle said.

"Buddy, we'll figure this out. Mark my word. We'll find her, and we'll bring her back home." Magnus' hand squeezed my left shoulder.

I wiped my hand over my face, feeling a week or so's worth of stubble growing out. I needed a shower, and food. I needed Mary.

"Damn right we will." I smelled food from the kitchen and saw a cooling pile of pancakes on the table. Dirty plates lingered around the space.

"Eat something," Natalia said. For the first time, I noticed she wasn't pregnant any longer.

The Ancients

"Is everyone okay?" I asked her.

She nodded and smiled, despite the somber mood of the room. With loss, there was life, only Mary wasn't lost yet. She was far from it.

"Patrice. Her name is Patty," Natalia said, tears forming in her eyes.

"It's perfect. I can't wait to meet her." I slunk to the table, grabbed a plate, and set to eating a couple of cold syrup-drenched pancakes while the others discussed our next course of action.

"We don't know where the planet is, but we know who does," Slate said.

"Who?" Magnus asked.

"The insectoids. They surprised us twice and were hell-bent on stopping us from releasing the Iskios. They're the key to this," Slate said, cracking his knuckles.

"How do we find them?" James asked, and I gave my old friend a weak grin. It felt like two worlds colliding, having him sitting around discussing our insane adventures and current predicament.

"James, imagine if our twenty-five-year-old selves could see us now," I cut in. "Slate's right. We find them on the hybrids' world. We've seen their kind there twice. Leslie and Terrance will be able to help us."

"Will they, though?" Nat asked.

I thought about it and decided I wasn't sure. But I had to put on a strong face. "They will." One way or another. Nothing was going to come between me and finding my wife. Nothing.

"When do we go?" Magnus asked.

I shoved the last bite of pancake in my mouth and chewed slowly. "We go tomorrow. First, I need to see someone." The period alone in my room had been good for me. I'd had a lot of time to soak in my new reality and to decide my course of action.

"Who?" Slate asked.

"Sarlun. He has to know more than he was letting on. The Gatekeepers have been keeping secrets."

Mary stood atop the crystal pyramid. It wasn't a throne, like Dean had suggested; it was a graveyard. The whole world marked the Iskios' burial grounds. Those arrogant Theos thought they could sacrifice themselves and save the universe. Little did they know the Iskios would never let that happen. They'd set a plan in motion to find a physical vessel, like the ones stripped from them by their enemies.

Millions of bodies were buried on Lainna, the crystal world; only then, it was a near-dead world, with little atmosphere or gravity. The energy of the Iskios had created what was here now, the stones emerging from the fallen Iskios. Mary was impressed and proud of the outcome. Lainna was where their journey had begun millennia ago, and the Theos had thought it was where their legacy would end. But they were so wrong.

Mary watched as the star rose beyond the distant crystal peaks, each housing thousands of her brethren. Now they would rise up to do their final bidding. Their fate had been sealed countless ages ago, and each knew their purpose. The Unwinding was upon them.

Mary knew all of this, as she was now Iskios, one of the Ancients. As the first rays of light cast themselves over her, she raised her hands toward the heavens. Power crackled throughout her. She smiled as useless human tears spilled down her cheeks. Black mist rose from the ground, from the crystals. Each buried Iskios was released from their resting place and combined together, forming a swirling vortex of energy and supremacy.

Different colors from the crystals merged with the immense cloud of swirling black mist, the pigment of the stones adding to the influence of the Iskios vortex.

Mary felt the entire world in her body. Her family was with her once again. Black energy coursed through her, mist clinging to her hair and clothing as she floated off the crystal pyramid and into the air. Higher she flew. A bubble of atmosphere circled her as she entered the blackness of space. The vessel needed oxygen to live, and the Iskios wouldn't let the vessel come to any harm.

Mary could feel the life inside her for the first time. The spawn she and her mate had created was strong. It added to her own strength, and Mary understood the importance of this. She was the True. She and her child together were the True.

She floated on, higher and higher, Lainna becoming smaller with each passing minute. The vortex of mist followed her, swirling ever larger, until every inch of the world below became colorless. Each crystal was now tint-free. Where they were once a kaleidoscope of color, they were now clear.

The vortex spun powerfully, and as it passed Lianna's closest moon, Mary watched the huge chunk of rock pull off its axis, breaking free from the confines of gravity. The rock broke apart, devastated and consumed by the vortex before it. It was frightening and glorious.

Mary smiled widely. Yes. She was the True. The wielder of the Unwinding.

ABOUT THE AUTHOR

Nathan Hystad is an author from Sherwood Park, Alberta, Canada. When he isn't writing novels, he's running a small publishing company, Woodbridge Press.

Keep up to date with his new releases by signing up for his newsletter at www.nathanhystad.com

Sign up at www.scifiexplorations.com as well for amazing deals and new releases from today's best indie science fiction authors.

CPSIA information can be obtained
at www.ICGtesting.com
Printed in the USA
LVHW022347120821
695154LV00003B/451